Escape
to the
Rome
Apartment

BOOKS BY KERRY FISHER

Escape
to the
Rome
Apartment
Kerry Fisher

bookouture

Published by Bookouture in 2024

An imprint of Storyfire Ltd.
Carmelite House
50 Victoria Embankment
London EC4Y oDZ

www.bookouture.com

ISBN: 978-1-83525-056-3
eBook ISBN: 978-1-83525-055-6

To every mother who's looked at her adult child and tried not to say out loud: 'Are you going to be warm enough without a coat?'

PROLOGUE

Lainey's last letter was a gift and a guilt trip rolled into one. A gift on many levels, including written confirmation that I was her best friend. Even in these circumstances, I was delighted to note that her university friend Angela hadn't beaten me to first place, with the hand-tied posies from her garden and her 'tone' with the hospice nurses, as though she alone knew what Lainey needed.

Petty considerations aside, I hadn't known what to expect when the solicitor had told me Lainey had left me a letter. I'd been surprised that my chaotic, spontaneous friend had been so organised and pragmatic about her last wishes. I could hear her voice, her words as my eyes flicked over her sentences.

For the most part, her letter was the glorious summary of everything we'd done together, the recollections of one of those rare people who'd lived my history alongside me. The memories particular to someone I'd known long enough for her to have come on holiday with me and my parents. Who'd loved my guinea pig, Geronimo, who knew cheese was a sure-fire way to entice my old Labrador inside, who had the knack of the sharp kick to close our front door that swelled up in winter. The only person who could remind me about my misadventure on the fairground waltzers after too much candyfloss, our crush on the bingo teller at Butlin's, Lainey's ill-advised experiment at her eighteenth birthday party with Galliano. Galliano! Who even drank that any more?

I scanned her reminiscences, acutely aware that there were so many more days when we'd laughed and danced and *lived*. They were lost in time now, days that we didn't know to treasure. We didn't understand the recklessness of allowing life to fly past without pausing to commit those golden times to memory. We squandered joyful moments, letting them flutter away like fireflies, glittering against a night sky. Instances when we should have noted the heat of the summers that seemed to last forever, the euphoria of laughter that reached peak hysteria whenever my mum told us to go to sleep. Loss obscured the warmth of the occasions she listed.

When Lainey had died, people had often told me to take solace in my memories. What they forgot to tell me was that the good times smile innocently, presenting a veneer of comfort, but get too close, try to hug them too tightly and they explode in your heart. It had taken me several attempts to read all the way through, the sight of her sloping writing transporting me to school, when she'd practised her 'married' name to a variety of different boys on her exercise books. My eyes skimmed over the funny stuff until I reached the purpose of her letter.

> So it's up to you now to recreate the summer of '84. Not the concert at Wembley, obviously, though I'm always up for a burst of Nik Kershaw's 'I Won't Let the Sun Go Down on Me'.

I breathed out, feeling the phantom weight of Lainey swaying on my shoulders, arms high above her head in the afternoon sun. Eighteen years old, just finished school, the whole summer ahead of us. We thought we'd live forever.

It's all on you now. I want you to take me to Italy. I know this might be a big ask, but I'm hoping that enough time has elapsed that you won't hate me for forcing you back there. Who knows, you might even lay to rest some ghosts of your own (while releasing mine – win, win!). I'm not going to suggest you return to Rome... that might be a stretch even for someone as loyal as you, but I've become quite taken with the idea of ending up in the sunshine on the Italian coast. Going in a box wasn't quite what I had in mind, but it feels like a fitting tribute to the best summer of my life. Do you remember sitting by the harbour in Portofino listening to that guy play Lionel Richie's 'Hello' on his guitar? Then his cousin invited us onto the yacht where he was a chef while the owners had gone ashore for the day?

That day was one of those experiences that encouraged us to shed a bit of who we were, to let go of the rules that had defined us until then and to glimpse who we might be now we were free to choose. We'd eaten lobster, smoked Lucky Strikes, flirted and felt as though we were destined for something big. I'd never felt so cool or bohemian before. Or since, probably.

We promised ourselves we would come back in the next century – it seemed soooo long until the year 2000 when we'd be thirty-four. Thirty-four! Ancient to us then. And then we never made time for it. Should have told everyone – my work, your family – they'd have to manage without us for a month. So here it is. Twenty thousand pounds. I'm buying you your freedom, my love. You don't need to ask for Declan's blessing. You just have to give yourself permission to put yourself first for once. The twins can wash their own pants for a few weeks.

Get me to Portofino and let me loose into the sea. I kind of like the prospect of wafting about in the waves, travelling to the far corners of the earth ad infinitum. I think the afternoon we ended up on that yacht was one of the standout events of that century. Lainey and Sara living it large! I'm not sure I'd ever drunk champagne before. And that beach at San Fruttuoso with the monastery built right on the sand – no one there, just us, the chef and his cousin and a motorboat that wouldn't start... Great memories, my friend. We had no idea what life held for us then, did we? Or how flaming short it would be!

You go and live for me, my darling. Have an adventure for both of us before it's too late. But don't simply take me back to Italy. Use the opportunity to go where the music takes you, to live freely for a while and let your heart breathe. Con amore, see you on the other side, my friend. My lifelong friend. (Such a bummer that lifelong was nowhere near as long as we'd envisaged!) Lx

A gift of a letter. A homage to our friendship. A written record of the love that existed between us.

And a guilt trip because I kept putting off the day when I'd gather my courage to go on a journey with Lainey for one last time.

I'd never really bought into the idea of ordinary days, weeks, months because we rarely get much warning when life is going to change forever. As anyone who's had an unplanned pregnancy, the first inkling of a serious illness, a chance meeting that leads to a love affair, a sudden windfall, would know. I was willing to bet that plenty of those days started with a cup of tea and a rush to put the washing on before dashing out the door to work. Unexpected life-changing events rarely have a man with a trumpet walking in front of them like an inappropriate funeral director leading a cortège.

But as far as Wednesdays went, there weren't any signs that today would be different from any other day. I hadn't even had a swig of tea before my husband, Declan, launched into a rant about our twenty-one-year-old son, Callum, finishing off the last of 'his' – rather than 'the' – porridge and leaving a scattering of oats and an empty box to clear up into the bargain.

'Who does he think is going to tidy up after him?'

I didn't say 'the same person that you think will clear up after you', though the words hovered around my mouth like a cloud of summer midges.

I frowned at the mountain of dirty dishes piled on the work surface while Declan harrumphed over his yoghurt and granola. My twin sons' very important jobs in London meant that only I, with my piddling career as lifestyle editor at a prestigious women's magazine, had the headspace for pedestrian chores like emptying the dishwasher and stacking crockery. It made a mockery of my frequent announcements, when I was pregnant in 2002, that 'as soon as my kids are old enough, I'm going to get them cooking and hoovering'. What a roaring success that had turned out to be. Callum's fry-ups after a boozy night out regularly set off the smoke alarm at one in the morning. Finn had never grown out of his aversion to anything green and could still barely grill a sausage.

Instead of having breakfast, I headed up for a shower before Declan read me any more doom-laden headlines about rising inflation and everything else that meant there was no money for joyful things. Unless, of course, he needed a new mountain bike, iPhone or posh shoes – 'I can't turn up to meetings in a pair of M&S loafers'. The sight of the bare loo roll holder in the bathroom made me want to ring my sons at work to demand who the culprit was. Sometimes I'd launch into a spectacular shout about how they'd all be up a gum tree if I collapsed with the exhaustion of doing it all. Declan would then bellow at the boys for being so lazy, while continuing to step over his own shoes.

Most days, I focused on all that was positive, which allowed me to rumble along, glossing over things. My sons who made me laugh, who'd turned out to be decent men, whom the years – or a feisty girlfriend – would teach to be more considerate where I'd failed. Today, though, the negatives were claiming centre stage – mainly to do with Declan, the husband I'd separated from in the pandemic but, three years later, hadn't quite got around to leaving. After the initial shock of his 'I think our marriage might have run its course', I'd grown used to the idea remarkably easily. I'd even felt excited by the prospect of a new chapter rather than more of the same on rinse and repeat for the next thirty years. He'd jolted me into realising that it wasn't healthy to be thrilled when he was out for the evening so that I didn't have to pretend to be interested in what he was saying. We'd moved into separate rooms and agreed to live amicably but independently in the same house until the pandemic was over. That arrangement had drifted to 'until the boys finished university', then 'until they were settled in a job'. Now, we'd got so used to it that there never seemed a good moment to call time, to put the house on the market and go our separate ways. Not much had changed really, except that I could read in bed without Declan complaining. For the first few weeks, Declan had martyred about, grilling his own sad salmon – 'I don't expect you to prepare dinner for me any more' – while visibly salivating over whatever I'd cooked. In the end, I couldn't bear the big eyes following every forkful of chicken curry into my mouth. Then it seemed stupid to switch on the washing machine half full. And I couldn't deal with the smell of damp towels every time I walked past the bathroom.

So Declan shouting through the bathroom door with instructions wasn't as rare as people might have imagined. 'I'm just off. You'll be back from work by six-thirty, won't you? The mechanic's coming to pick up the lawnmower – something wrong with the starter motor.'

'I'm going for a drink with Hayley after work,' I said, coming back out onto the landing.

'I've got a meeting with Matt, the financial adviser. Can't you reschedule?'

I shook my head, registering the shock that if Declan was meeting with the financial adviser, our divorce was no longer a nebulous thing that might happen one day. There was, it seemed, a gulf between embracing the idea in principle and confronting the reality of what it might mean. 'No. I'm not letting her down at the last minute. You can't just assume that I'll be here.'

Declan frowned as though me having any social engagements was an affront. 'I'll have to cancel him then. It'll be weeks before it gets fixed now.'

My mind curled around what excuse I could give Hayley that wouldn't be as lame as ditching her for the lawnmower man. Then, suddenly, sharp and unexpected as a paper cut, Lainey's voice popped into my head. '*I reckon there's a lot to be said for getting divorced. As far as I can see, men and women start off as equals, but as soon as you have kids, the woman is suddenly in charge of filling up the salt in the dishwasher, changing the hand towels – basically all the boring shite – while the man's world carries on as normal.*'

Back then, I'd defended Declan, pointed out that I only worked four days a week so had a bit more time to pick up the slack. She'd done that eyeballing thing she'd perfected as a teenager. '*But his working day stops when he arrives home. Yours carries on till bedtime.*' She'd died a year ago, and now and again, I remembered to honour her memory with small rebellions. She'd never understood why I hadn't moved out as soon as the pandemic restrictions were lifted. '*You've made the decision. That's the hard part.*' I kept brushing her off every time she asked about it, then once she was ill, her focus shifted to getting her affairs in order. Apart from an occasional hurtful dig: '*There's you living a half-life and me with no life!*', it fell into the category of subjects we skirted around in order not to spend however long she had left in a merry-go-round of accusation/justification.

So today I stood firm while Declan shook his head at my selfishness. He turned to go. 'So you're okay with me telling Matt that Lainey's money is part of the marital pot?'

'Absolutely not. I haven't agreed to that. And she didn't leave it to *us*, she left it to *me*.'

Declan waved his hand as though I was splitting hairs. 'But it is money that has come into the fold while we've been married, Sara. I didn't ring-fence my inheritance when Mum and Dad died.'

'Nor did I when my parents died, if we want to play that game. The money from Lainey was different. She left it to me for the sole purpose of scattering her ashes in Portofino.' I didn't add that she wanted me to make an adventure of it. That instruction seemed so far out of my reach now, so removed from how we were in that heady summer of 1984, when all the avenues at every crossroad were enticing paths to a thrilling future. Unlike now, when every crossroad felt like a multiple choice, and regardless of which box I ticked, the outcome would be fraught with responsibility and self-doubt. It felt foolish to long for that carefree sense of washing up somewhere new where a random event might push me in an unexpected direction. Yet a tiny kernel of hope persisted that I might still pull it off, if only I could muster the courage to go on my own in the first place.

'But that money – an extra ten grand each – could make a difference to what we can both afford, Sara.' Declan was tapping into my weak spot. He knew that half the reason I hadn't pushed to sell the house before was because I wouldn't be able to afford anywhere with a garden without moving out of the area.

I stayed true to Lainey's instructions. 'But she didn't leave it so we could buy houses. She left it to me so I could fulfil her wishes to release her into the Italian sea.' My voice caught. I'd had nearly a year to become used to life without her. A long time and no time. 'This was money she'd earmarked for travel, later on, when she finally retired. And now she wants me to do it on her behalf because she didn't get the chance.'

Declan patted his hand in the air, as though he was trying to quieten down a classroom of raucous kids. 'I'm not saying you shouldn't take Lainey's ashes to wherever it is she wanted to be scattered. But that's not going to cost twenty bloody grand. An EasyJet flight to Italy is a few hundred quid, plus trains and hotel – a thousand pounds should easily take care of it. Anyway, let's talk some more tonight. I'm going to miss my train.' He hurried downstairs and slammed the door.

I huffed out a sigh of relief, then slipped into the box room we grandly called the office. I picked my way past Declan's exercise bike and Callum's pull-up bar that never made it out of the packaging and put my hand on the turquoise urn sitting on top of the filing cabinet. I still struggled to comprehend that the force of nature that was Lainey could reside within such a tiny space. 'I haven't forgotten you, darling. I'll take you soon.'

Somehow, adventures seemed so much more daunting on my own.

2

I ran into the office at ten past nine, late after getting stuck at the level crossing and missing my train to Waterloo. My mate Linda on reception tipped me the wink that she'd overheard my boss, Amber, asking the production editor whether she thought my freelance contacts were as good at bringing in stories as they used to be. 'She was pretending to act all concerned, but she had it in for you.'

'Had it in for you' had been a bit of a recurring theme over the ten years I'd been working there as editors came under pressure to increase circulation and reduce budget. It was far cheaper to hire young journalists eager to make their mark than pay someone with years of experience. But Amber was by far the worst editor I'd worked for. She operated the office on a divide-and-rule basis, encouraging 'group bonding' on 'team-building' nights out by pushing everyone to get absolutely hammered, then goading the office to take part in a weird sort of gladiatorial teasing that fell far short of anything that could be considered amusing. She often singled me out as someone who didn't like her photo being splashed about on social media after work evenings out – 'Come on, it's just a bit of fun.' I prided

myself on being a serious journalist. I'd excelled at sourcing
celebrities' stories but also at gaining the trust of ordinary
people, who shared what their homes meant to them. I loved
writing about the history of their houses – who'd lived there, the
things that had inspired them, traumatised them, revitalised
them. I'd represent these accounts carefully, resisting the temptation to sensationalise or skew the angle for a catchy headline.
So the last thing I wanted was anyone who'd recounted how
they'd cared for loved ones or rebuilt their lives in the sanctuary
of their house to stumble across photos of me off my face on
cheap wine. I never wanted to look as though their trauma was
just another pay day for me.

I refused to go along with Amber, telling myself that at fifty-
seven I had earned the right to choose whether or not to be
photographed. Nonetheless, I still had to steel myself to ignore
the dread of confrontation sitting in the pit of my stomach. Or
perhaps it was the fear that I might actually blurt out how much
I disliked her.

I pushed open the double doors, struggling against the self-
loathing that I allowed someone twenty years younger to bully
me. I was the oldest woman in the office and she had a way of
making me feel as though I was out of touch, slow to pick up
new things. Maybe I wasn't quite as ferocious at chasing down
interviews with D-list celebrities as the graduates that were
hungry to prove themselves. But that was partly because I really
didn't want to spend another day interviewing someone who
took half an hour to order a drink at our chosen venue: 'I'm
sorry but do you have oat milk? Oh, okay, just peppermint tea
then, is it real leaves? Oh, okay, just water then... oh, but not
that brand because it's got too much sodium and that makes me
bloated,' while their PR was reminding us that I only had
twenty minutes left. Plus, as I'd got older, my facial muscles
were no longer so compliant, refusing to arrange themselves into
a sympathetic formation for a twenty-five-year-old whose catch-

phrase was 'It was literally the worst thing that could happen', when, without taxing my brain at all, I could immediately list fifty things worse than being photographed with the outline of a nipple showing. Nope. I was far more interested in ordinary women, people who often experienced terrible things – illness, bereavement, abandonment – and had dragged themselves up from the rubble.

I wanted a hassle-free life now until I could retire. I'd had enough of the deluded and the dickheads. I didn't care who Amber selected as her pet project, earmarking them for the glamorous industry events that should have been mine. My focus was on knowing I'd done justice to a daughter describing the reality of losing a parent to dementia, expressing the grief but not diminishing the love.

And since Lainey had died, my commitment to work had waned even more. We'd had plans for travelling when we retired. She hadn't even lived long enough for a weekend trip to Paris. My heart ached at the injustice of it all, yet no one seemed to think losing a friend, someone who'd been part of my life for far longer than my husband, was a big deal. There was an assumption that once her funeral was over, I should be up and running as normal. But I'd found it hard to focus on work, craving time in my garden, where I could ignore other people's views on how quickly I should 'move on'.

But today wasn't my lucky day. Amber was standing at the first desk. 'Good afternoon, Sara. We haven't introduced flexitime as far as I'm aware. When you dropped to four days a week, I didn't realise you were shortening the ones when you were actually at work as well. As soon as you're up to speed, I need to talk to you about that double-page spread for the women who've found new careers in their fifties. How can I put it? Not the most visually appealing bunch. Let's hope we can do something with that last one that we're waiting on photos for.'

I attempted to dredge up a contrite tone. 'Sorry I'm late.

Level crossing seemed to stay down forever and I missed my train.'

Amber threw her arms out in a gesture of astonishment. 'Level crossing, eh? You'd think after ten years you'd have realised it was there and made allowances for it.'

I forced myself to square my shoulders and stride, not slink, to the one remaining unpopular desk, within earshot of Amber when she had her office door open. As I sat down, the thought reverberated around my head that I was way too old for this shit. I opened up my emails and discovered that the last woman I'd been pinning my hopes on as passing Amber's bar of aspirational appearance had decided to pull out of the feature altogether, saying her family had advised her against talking about her abusive husband. Amber was going to love that. She'd never believe that I'd spent hours explaining the possible repercussions and making sure she was totally committed to telling her story.

I swivelled around in my chair, wondering whether I had time to carry out a rearguard action before I had to tell Amber. But no such luck. She was heading over.

'So can we lead with this last one? Please tell me she's not another of these grey-haired mumsy types? We need a bit of glamour.'

I hated the way my throat had gone all tight. I was having to fight to keep my voice steady as I explained that she'd pulled out.

Amber looked at me incredulously, as though she'd never ever had a case study go sour on her. 'Do you think this job is getting too much for you?' 'At your age' hung in the air.

And there it was. That flimsy little straw. Snap. Snap. Snap. 'No, Amber. I don't think it's the job at all. I think it's the toxic working environment you've created that is getting too much for me.'

Amber's mouth opened to respond, but her desire to retort

was no match for my desire to heave flammable material onto my bonfire of grievances.

'You could double the productivity in this office just by resigning yourself. Most of us divert more energy into trying to read what sort of mood you're in and how to stay out of your way than we do to sourcing good stories for the magazine and getting on with our jobs.'

In the periphery of my vision, I could see shocked faces, wide eyes turning towards me, and a couple of the younger lads in the art department stifling giggles.

Amber started to say, 'Sara, are you having some sort of a breakdown? I know your mental health has been rather fragile since...' She groped about, desperately trying to remember what issue had caused me to take leave last year.

I couldn't be bothered to explain. 'There's nothing wrong with my mental health that couldn't be fixed by a decent working environment. Some days, I hate coming in here so much that I actually fantasise about having a car crash. I don't want to die or be disfigured, but sometimes I long to be laid up with a broken leg or something that would give me some respite from having to work with you.'

Amber glanced around the room as everyone hurriedly pretended to be engrossed in their computer screens. 'Shall we finish this conversation in my office?' She didn't wait for an answer, used as she was to everyone falling in with her orders.

She turned on her heel and I took a few paces to follow her. Then I thought better of it. As she stalked away, not bothering to see if I was trailing behind her, I grabbed my handbag, my laptop and notebook and marched out in the opposite direction.

At the door, I piled up my belongings and did a deep theatrical bow, flinging my arms far out to the side like a ballet's leading lady. For a reason I was unable to fathom, I adopted what I imagined to be a Dolly Parton accent and said, 'Bye, y'all, it's been a pleasure. I'll be seeing ya!'

My last view was of Amber standing at the far end of our bank of rabbit hutches, hands on her hips, the shock that anyone would stand up to her flashing across her face.

I clung onto the rush of adrenaline, the dizzying high of 'Am I really doing this?', feeling like the school swot who'd suddenly started throwing chairs before flinging exercise books out of the window, pages of algorithms and equations a-fluttering, while swearing at the teacher.

I waved to Linda and burst out into the fresh air. I waited to feel fear, regret, shock as I sat on the train home, shame that I hadn't been robust enough to cope with Amber's endless sniping. But I didn't. Not at all. I felt a rush of strength and liberation that I hadn't experienced in years, the absolute conviction that life was way too short to put up with this nonsense. I looked up to the sunny September sky and smiled. Lainey had indeed bought me my freedom. Her money would act as a cushion while I worked out what came next.

I hopped off the train, threw the remnants of my working life into the car and drew up outside my end-of-terrace house. Strictly speaking, Declan's house. He'd already made great strides on the property ladder when we met at twenty-nine, whereas I was still renting with Lainey. Ten years ago, we'd built an extension out the back, giving both boys a decent-sized bedroom, us an en suite and a kitchen big enough to sit in. Even so, we'd still be hard-pressed to buy a decent house each from the proceeds. And now I'd further decimated my finances by chucking in my job. Declan wouldn't see that as making a stand. He'd no doubt misconstrue it as a cunning plan to make myself so impecunious that I'd get a bigger chunk of the house in our divorce settlement.

But underneath all the uncertainty that was fighting to over-whelm me was a giddy high derived from calling out a bully. There was something fantastic about having a conversation right there on the spot, without weeks of lying awake wondering how to approach it.

I reversed into our drive, manoeuvring carefully into the car port where Callum had left a pile of dumbbells he'd bought from a friend about three months ago – 'Bargain, Mum, bargain.' Another casualty of his delusion that simply owning gym equipment made you fit.

I squeezed past the dumbbell graveyard and opened the front door, picking up two pairs of trainers the size of small canoes and flinging them into the empty shoe basket right within reach. My mobile rang. Amber. I doubted very much she was calling to apologise. In that moment, I knew I was never going to set foot in that office again. I cut the call off. Seconds later, a text message beeped through. I put the phone face down on the hall table.

Forget climbing any further up the ladder, putting myself forward for more senior positions. What had previously felt like an admission of failure suddenly felt like a release. All that writing up copy over a weekend, working bank holiday Mondays, felt like something younger, hungrier people could do. I didn't care about having a career if I had to kowtow to people I didn't respect. I wanted time. When I'd dropped to four days a week, Declan had pretended to be supportive, but, in reality, he'd made me feel way too guilty to spend more time in the garden, explore the bits of London I didn't know, volunteer to help primary schoolkids read. Instead, there was a sense of 'Well, you don't work Fridays. Can't you go and fetch the dry cleaning, sort out our passport applications, deal with the broken fence panel?'

I opened the fridge to get the milk out for tea and there, at eye level, was a pack of cheddar with a bite out of it. Teeth-marks like a dental cast. For a moment, I frowned at the semicircle, trying to work out who the culprit was. Then, slowly, like someone who's had their head down in a blizzard, putting one foot in front of the other against the onslaught, I went upstairs and stared up at the attic hatch on the landing.

Ordinary Wednesdays didn't involve the attic hatch. In fact, it was the one area of the house reserved solely for high days and holidays, the territory of Christmas decorations and suitcases. I'd have probably stuffed a lot more family detritus up there if it hadn't been a two-man job to wrestle the ladder down, when Declan would shout at me for never quite pulling/pushing/putting my back into it in the way he desired.

But today, an ordinary Wednesday, had turned into an extraordinary day. I glanced at my phone. Eleven o'clock. I had about eight hours before anyone came home. Today, I would make them count. Today, reliable old Sara was taking a sabbatical from normal service. Not before I'd cancelled Hayley and got a beef bourguignon out of the freezer for everyone else's dinner, though. I wasn't yet that unreliable.

3

I had to suppress the desire to giggle on the train to Gatwick Airport, light-headed with daring that I'd booked a plane leaving for Italy at two that afternoon. Despite cutting it quite fine timewise, I only had hand luggage so I'd decided to risk it before I lost my nerve. My plan was to arrive in Milan, take a train to Genoa on the Ligurian coast and make my way to Portofino from there.

I looked down at the rucksack I'd brought with me. I'd fully intended to travel with a suitcase until I'd struggled up into the attic and seen my ancient blue rucksack, barely bigger than a day pack. Lainey and I had bought them together from a market stall in Camden, the owner giving us a tenner discount for the double purchase. It seemed fitting that it came with me on this journey.

I checked that Lainey was sitting comfortably, her urn tucked in an upright position, wedged in a walking boot. I'd taped the top down. I patted the lid and whispered, 'I've had to leave my hair straighteners behind to fit you in, so don't you go spilling yourself everywhere.'

I leant back in the seat. Ten past twelve. Seven hours before my escape stopped being a secret. I'd have landed in Milan by the time my family realised that Lainey and I were off on one last adventure. I'd left a note because I wasn't sure anyone would realise I'd gone until rats gathered around an overflowing kitchen bin. Nor did I want them calling the police and having officers turn up at my place of work – the idea of wasting police resources was too much to bear. And there was no way I was going to let Amber have the satisfaction of rewriting my departure as some kind of breakdown rather than the direct consequence of her bullying. I hadn't bothered to explain that I'd walked out on my job. There was only so much rebellion Declan would be able to process in one go.

At the airport, I leapt off the train, eager to get beyond passport control before anyone discovered I'd gone. With no luggage to check in and a boarding pass on my phone, I was through security and celebrating my escape with a glass of champagne in record time.

Champagne on a Wednesday afternoon when I should have been at work. I raised my glass to Lainey, wondering if I'd be able to live with the vim and vigour that she'd harnessed so easily. She'd been genetically programmed not to care much what people thought, whereas I had overthinking woven into my DNA. But for the next few days at least, I could be a much feistier version of myself. No one needed to know that I snatched the shower curtain back when I went into the bathroom at night or jumped when the timer went off on my phone when I was cooking.

By the time I boarded the plane, I was more excited than nervous. I took my seat next to a woman about my age, who'd absolutely nailed the going grey with style look, her thick hair almost white, with dark streaks. She wore a bright pink top and wide-legged trousers teamed with statement jewellery in the manner of an Egyptian queen. She smiled at me and I couldn't help thinking that she would have been perfect to feature in the magazine as the epitome of a stylish woman in her late fifties. Even Amber wouldn't have been able to find fault.

I brushed away all thoughts of work and dutifully watched the flight attendant's safety demonstration, secretly in awe of people who were rude enough to carry on reading their books without feeling the slightest bit embarrassed.

We'd only been in the air a few minutes when Boo, as she introduced herself – 'Belinda really, but it doesn't suit me' – asked me what I would be doing in Italy. She was the sort of woman who would have had Declan sending out a skunk-like mist of disapproval. He would have dismissed her as overfamiliar, intrusive with her way of firing off questions like a speed dater with no time to waste on a duffer. She rattled through, as though she needed to get the facts out of the way – Purpose of visit? Length of stay? Reason for travelling alone? Final destination? Number of previous visits to Italy? – so she could pincer down onto what I could only describe as the essence of me. By the time the cabin crew brought the drinks trolley round – 'You'll join me in a glass of wine?' – she'd already cracked open the floodgates to Lainey's death. Maybe it was the booze. Perhaps it was the intoxication of being able to respond honestly without Declan pouting in my peripheral vision as I told 'our business to all and sundry'. By the time we started our descent towards Milan, we were sharing secrets like a couple of eight-year-olds at a midnight feast. She knew more about me and my family than the colleagues I'd worked with for a decade. Over the years, I'd learnt to keep my anecdotes short – Declan liked the bare bones, preferably factual and feelingless. Boo was the exact opposite, digging for detail and reminding me that there'd been a time in my life when I'd added colour and drama to stories to make them into a vehicle of fun.

Shortly before we landed, with no more fuss than as if she was inviting me for coffee, Boo said, 'Why don't you come with me to Florence tonight and set off for Portofino in a few days' time? It's only an hour and a half by train. I'm staying with an old schoolfriend. He's a silversmith, got a flat near Santo Spirito. Inherited it from a rich girlfriend.' Boo dropped out that information as though flats in Italian cities inherited from wealthy partners were two a penny.

I laughed. 'I can't just turn up with you and demand a bed.' I couldn't deny that the prospect of going with Boo rather than finding my way into Milan on my own and working out where to stay for the night was rather appealing.

'You won't be demanding a bed. I will. He's got a huge apartment, he won't mind. He has people in and out all the time. Carlo's one of those arty-farty types, the sort that parties half the night and then somehow manages to persuade everyone to drive to the beach at Viareggio for a dawn dip.'

I wasn't sure that my desire to be in bed by ten thirty made me a natural match for this Carlo person. The thought of letting Boo down by being 'that dullard you picked up on the plane' terrified me. 'No, really. I'm probably going to stay in Milan tonight, head to Portofino tomorrow and then make my way back to England. I shouldn't stay away too long. They'll think I've abandoned them.'

Boo stretched and lifted all her hair off her neck. 'Lainey didn't leave you that money so you could live a tiny life. She left you that money – correct me if I'm wrong – so you could have an adventure. I mean, not to put too fine a point on it, you don't have a proper husband or a job to go back to.'

I felt a warm glow at the memory of Boo's raucous approval of me telling Amber to shove her job up her jumper. But, of course, I'd sold myself to her under false pretences. Going forwards I'd doubtlessly be the one patrolling the coastline at one of Carlo's skinny dips, making sure no one drowned after too much limoncello. Boo, I was pretty sure, would be whipping off her top with gay abandon and steaming into the waves, not caring what anyone thought of her middle-aged breasts.

No, I'd split while she thought I was her soul sister, a go-getter, eschewing the trappings of a bourgeois existence.

Once the plane had landed, I switched my phone on and saw seven missed calls from Declan. It rang immediately. I scrabbled to answer, afraid that it was against the rules to have a conversation before disembarking. I murmured a hello.

Declan didn't bother with a greeting. 'I came home from work early to sort out the lawnmower bloke and see that you've gone jaunting off to Italy.'

He rattled on, without letting me speak, accusing me of losing the plot and marvelling at how I'd got time off work at such short notice.

My natural inclination was to apologise, to say that grief had muddled my thinking. But I felt more clear-headed than I had done in months, maybe even years. I was doing what I wanted to do, with no timetable, no concrete plan ahead of me.

I humoured him. 'I'd finished a couple of big projects and there was a bit of a gap until the next one lands, so I took my opportunity.' All absolutely true apart from the 'bit of a gap' being a dread that I might never work as a journalist again when word got out about my departure. I tried to remember all the women I'd interviewed who'd had total career changes in later life, ditching corporate jobs to become café owners, counsellors, glassblowers. But perhaps not just as they were about to get divorced and have to fund a mortgage on their own.

I was conscious of Boo unbuckling her belt and gathering up her bag next to me.

Declan grunted. 'Seriously though, Sara, it's not normal to disappear like that.'

'I know. I suddenly became overwhelmed with guilt that I'd had Lainey's ashes for a year and still hadn't carried out her wishes.'

As I waited for the words to land, the embarrassment of having such an intimate conversation in such a confined space made me curl up in my seat, desperately trying to stop the other passengers hearing Declan's voice blaring out of the earpiece.

'Jeez, Sara, but taking off like that on your own? I mean, it's a bit selfish, leaving us all worrying about you.'

'Why are you worrying? You know where I am and what I'm doing.' I kept my voice low and light but had a mental image of jiggling a pin in a grenade, deciding whether or not to plunge straight into an argument of 'We've actually decided to live separate lives. Or does that only apply to you when you fancy vanishing for the weekend without offering up the details of where you're going?' I pushed the pin back in. I didn't want the whole of the plane gawking round.

Declan's knee would be bouncing up and down with frustration. 'You're deliberately misunderstanding me. I could have come to Italy to support you. Where are you even staying?'

I didn't answer – mainly because I didn't actually know – and told him I was just about to get off the plane, that I'd call him later.

I stood up so that Boo could lift her case down from the overhead locker. She waited until we'd made our way into the line for passport control before asking, 'The husband has discovered the empty chicken coop, huh?'

I nodded, feeling my enthusiasm for my impromptu trip dwindling.

We walked together to the railway station, Boo chattering about how she loved train travel and had given up owning a car years ago. We were halfway into the hour-long journey to Milan city centre when Declan rang again. I turned away from Boo, but her face, a picture of concentration on my every word, was reflected in the window.

'How long are you going to be away?' Declan asked in his 'I need some answers' voice.

'Four or five nights. I should be home by Monday. I did think I might have a couple of nights somewhere on the coast while I was here,' I said lightly. Even though I'd already done the difficult part of leaving without discussing it, I could hear the apologetic tone of my voice, offering up the idea as though I was holding out a frightened bird on my hand.

'By yourself?'

Declan made it sound as though I was intending to go scaling sheer rockfaces in the Dolomites rather than stroll along a promenade and eat a few ice creams. He obviously hadn't yet understood that the 'I think our marriage has reached the end of the road' that he delivered as I was puzzling over how to revive my sourdough starter back in 2020 meant he didn't get a say. 'Yes. I'll be fine.'

'Where will you stay?'

'I'm not sure yet. Milan tonight, but perhaps Rapallo or Santa Margherita after that.' A burst of relief flooded through me that he wasn't there, that I could see what suited me at the time, instead of having to commit to a definite plan. He would have hurried me along, focused on 'getting the job done'. He'd have trampled the delicate web of memories that would slip out, beckoned into the light by places revisited. I longed for my brain to flash up forgotten images that captured Lainey's mischief, the way her nose wrinkled when she said something she shouldn't. I was greedy for reminders of her, desperate for Portofino to jolt my mind and deliver bonus moments of Lainey, like scenes that had fallen onto the cutting room floor, discovered grainy and faded years later and restored to former glory.

Declan sighed, his disapproval automatic. There was no right answer to anything that hadn't been okayed with him weeks earlier. The ballet of our union was totally familiar, even now, in this stage of inching towards non-marriage. I'd talk about something I'd really like to do, and Declan would somehow put me off it, either by filling my head with doubts about whether I'd cope or making me feel so guilty about taking time or money for myself that I'd end up deciding that it was just plain selfish.

'It's a shame you didn't plan it in advance. I know the boys would like to go to Italy at some point,' he said.

That was a low blow. I was a sucker for putting life on hold on the off-chance that the twins would want to be part of my plans. But between London and Milan, something had hardened in me. At twenty-one, they could find their own way to Italy. I'd spent enough Saturday evenings sitting in because they'd airily said something about going to the cinema with me, only to find that when the weekend rolled around, they'd casually mention they'd had a better offer.

'They'd like to go anywhere we pay for. For once, I'm going to do what I want to do.'

I pulled the rucksack to me, cupping my hand around the outline of the urn, astonished at how resolute I sounded and catching Boo's eye as I did so. She gave me a cross between a thumbs up and an air punch, totally unabashed about her eavesdropping. I smiled back.

'Are you staying in a hotel?' he asked.

'Where were you expecting me to stay?' I could feel a thread of cockiness entering my voice now I knew I had an approving audience.

There was a silence. I knew that he was doing a quick calculation of how much of Lainey's money I might chew through on this little jaunt.

'I just want to make sure you don't get ripped off.'

I felt the burn of insult. 'I know it's a long time ago, but I managed perfectly well to get from A to B without losing my shirt before we were married.' But the old habit of giving Declan the illusion of control hadn't yet died. 'I'll check out everything online beforehand. Anyway, we're coming into Milan shortly, so I'd better go. I'll be in touch tomorrow to let you know where I am. Give my love to the boys. Don't forget the beef bourguignon in the fridge.'

The train pulled into Milan Central and we stood up to leave. My phone beeped. I braced myself for a pompous message from Declan. But it was Callum.

Dad says you're not home until Monday. Can you order a Tesco shop for tomorrow evening (after 7 p.m. would be great!) because Dad's finished all the Cheddar and I don't like Double Gloucester?

I slung my rucksack over my shoulder. 'Boo, are you sure your friend won't mind if I come with you for a few days?'

As she whooped and shouted, 'That's my girl!' at a volume that made the whole carriage turn to stare, I scrolled through the settings on my phone and switched off my location. For a few days at least, I was going to ignore the cheese wars at home and gallop freely.

4

Then

It was astonishing how many people had a view on love, which, by its very nature, was just between two people. No opinions required. Nobody else's business. But still people judged, and not only when things looked serious, when you were making noises about settling down together. Nope. Those judgements came hard and fast, right from the beginning, with everyone sizing up the relative attractiveness of the pair – assessing who was punching and who was settling.

It didn't stop there. Whether or not your nearest and dearest acknowledged it to themselves, those people – who 'only had your best interests at heart' – were running through their own mental checklist. More often that not, it reflected their own insecurities: education, job, background, dress. And that was just for starters, a little appetiser before getting onto age difference, baggage from previous relationships, ability to contribute to a mortgage. An hors d'oeuvres sweep of who was likely to bring the brains, the property, the earning power – or the problems. With a follow-up main course of how easy it was going to be to assimilate the newcomer if they became a permanent fixture. A deep dive into how well they fitted into the familial or friendship framework. If you challenged those close to you, they'd say it was all about you, of course it was, they 'just wanted you to be happy'. And all those qualities that had drawn you to your partner in the first place would be waved away as mere bagatelle against the ballast required for a long-term relationship.

My parents were the worst offenders. They were against Alessio from the start. We were too young to be so serious. A foreign bartender was a long way from the astoundingly ambitious boyfriend they had imagined for me. Of course, initially, they nodded along when I spoke about him, confident that time and distance would solve all. But then, they didn't understand about love. They thought love was watching the news together and commenting on how the blue tits had nested in the kitchen eaves and Dad pouring Mum a gin and tonic. They didn't understand that proper love scorched through every waking hour, making me vulnerable but also invincible. The ferocity of the emotion was so intense that all decisions had a single purpose: to make it easier for Alessio and me to have a life together.

Because having a life together, however difficult, was the only option.

5

In the ten minutes we had between arriving at Milan Central and dashing for our train to Florence, Boo managed to gather up a bottle of wine and focaccia for us to share. Everything about her was abundant and forcefully generous, as though it never occurred to her that people might not want to join in. I admired her total insouciance of what anyone else might think, while simultaneously cringing at how annoying Boo's voice booming away in the carriage might be.

Two hours later, we emerged a little tipsy onto the platform at Santa Maria Novella in Florence. I followed behind Boo, vacillating between nerves and defiance.

I'd messaged the family chat that I often felt I should separate from, given that we were no longer technically a family.

Change of plan. Taken the opportunity to visit Florence while I'm in Italy, might be a bit longer than five days, will keep you posted.

I stuck an emoji of a smiley face with sunglasses on it for good measure.

It was surprising how quickly the constants that kept me tethered to family life had dissolved – the planning of meals, the overseeing of the minutiae that kept the house from descending into piggy chaos, the responsibility I'd accepted for making sure my sons were going to work with ironed shirts. I wondered how long it would take before someone – anyone – looked down and thought, crikey, where does the mop live?

In the meantime, I trotted along with Boo, my mind a bit disconcerted after over two decades of putting the boys first. I kept feeling as though I'd left something on the train, my brain searching restlessly for something to chivvy, corral, facilitate. My heart, though, was all anticipation at the prospect of plunging into a world where I could reinvent myself, or rather, re-be myself. The woman who slept on beaches under the stars with no thought for the damp of dawn, first and last on the dance floor, gravitating to new experiences with greedy energy rather than ceding to the 'better not, better get an early night, work tomorrow'. A stay among strangers in Florence was within my capability. If all else failed, I could move to a hotel, catch a train to Portofino, fly home. I could buy myself out of trouble in a way I couldn't when I was young, when, contrarily, despite my lack of financial resources, I had much more of what my grandmother would have called 'gumption'.

Even at nine o'clock, the station was still heaving with people. Through the melee of tourists and taxis, Boo suddenly rushed forward. 'Carlo!' She threw her arms around a tall, broad man with a mop of dark curls, his face carrying a five o'clock shadow that suggested careful sculpting rather than a shortage of razors. They did a proper unrestrained jig of delight, unconcerned by the protests of disapproval from the passers-by who were having to swerve around them. He was wearing a white linen shirt with a jacket and jeans, stylishly curated in a way that eluded the vast majority of British men with their hoodies emblazoned with sports brand logos.

I hung back, awkwardly. Boo waved me over. 'Sara, meet Carlo. Well, actually, he's called Charlie – originally from Croydon – but he's gone all affected arty Italian now, so we call him Carlo.'

I didn't know whether she was joking or not. I did that half-laugh that people do when they don't want to appear gullible but also don't want to inadvertently cause offence if the story is true.

'Boo's full of BS. My parents were both Italian and I am called Carlo, but, you know, it was the 1970s and I wanted to fit in, so I decided to opt for the English version of my name – Charlie. Still got teased, though, because my mother kept correcting my friends when they came to my house – "No Charlie, Carrrrlo!" Not helped either by that stupid "Shaddap You Face" song that haunted my sixth-form years. But I live in Italy now, so Carlo it is.' He put out his hand, his palm cool against my clammy little travel-worn mitt. 'Delighted to meet you,' he said.

I glanced at Boo, unsure whether she'd been one hundred per cent clear that I was expecting to stay with him as well.

But Carlo said, 'Right, we'd better hurry before the car gets towed away. I left it with its hazards on round the corner.'

He swung my bag onto his shoulder, and snatched up Boo's case. I had no choice but to scuttle after them, picking my way through the throngs of people.

He bundled us into a navy Fiat Panda and roared off without much attention to his rearview mirror, responding to the klaxon protests with a robust hand gesture that wasn't quite 'the finger' but a much more expressive 'What's your problem?' I clutched the seat as though I was pinned back by G-force and tried not to squeal as we flew round the streets and across the bridge over the Arno. He nearly collided with a *motorino* at the traffic lights – before an astonishing bit of parking that involved reversing into a minuscule space I would have discounted immediately. I was waiting for the motorbike behind us to topple over, but Carlo hopped out, lifted it onto its back wheel and shoved it along a foot or so. Boo's face didn't flicker, but my Englishness about not touching other people's property was firmly welded on mine.

'Right, I'm just a few minutes' walk away,' Carlo said, grabbing my rucksack.

I scooted along, already feeling as though I was living the life Lainey had wished for me. I'd got off to a good start – a chance meeting with a new friend (I sent up a quick promise that no one would ever replace her, but as she wasn't available, I had to do with sloppy seconds) – and the icing on the cake of going home with a total stranger. Look who's getting out of her comfort zone now, Lainey!

We threaded our way through the streets, stepping off the narrow pavements to let the groups of tourists pass, with Boo exclaiming at the top of her voice about the amount of dog shit everywhere. I was far more concerned about the taxis squeezing past the racks of bicycles and not getting smacked in the face by a wing mirror on the little electric bus that seemed way too big for the roads.

Finally, we arrived in front of a glorious building, its yellow façade lit by the lamps in the piazza, grey shutters closed against what lay within. Carlo opened the huge front door and beckoned us into a cool hallway. 'Up you come. You two take the lift, I'll meet you at the top.'

Before I could protest, he shot off up the stairs, with my rucksack, leaving Boo and I to creak our way up to the fifth floor in an ancient lift. I tried hard to remember what you were supposed to do to give yourself the best chance of survival if a lift cable snapped. I was still deciding whether the received wisdom was to jump up and down or lie on the floor when everything shuddered to a halt and Boo released us onto the landing.

'You'll love his flat. It's got the most amazing terrace.'

Carlo appeared and let us in. Unexpectedly, tears sprang to my eyes as he flung open the door to the sitting room, which was vaulted with frescoes of angels and cherubs bursting through clouds on the ceiling. I missed Lainey so much in that moment, the sheer joy of clutching each other and pointing at it all, and wowing about the waist-high ceramic urns embossed with poppies and the painting of the woman's face in neon-pink and turquoise and orange over the fireplace.

I brushed at my eyes and tried to articulate words of appreciation, but they stuck in my throat with the pure lack of Lainey, the absence of her and all the energy she infused into every ordinary day, let alone this extraordinary one.

Carlo bent his head. 'You okay, Sara?'

I did the most mortifying splutter of grief, a proper jet of tears, at the precise moment that I wanted to look like the most glitteringly entertaining guest who would bring so much to the party. Despite my blustering that 'I'll be all right in a minute, sorry, sorry, I bet you're regretting inviting such a cheery stranger to stay,' he simply put a hand on my arm and said, 'Boo told me you'd had a tough time. We need a sit down on the roof terrace with a drink. Boo, show Sara onto the *terrazza*.'

I was so hot and bothered, desperately trying to suck down my sobs, that it took me a moment to register the magnificence of Carlo's view. A huge pillared terrace with ornate swirly masonry, terracotta tiles, sculptures, plants. Everything, in fact, that would make you refuse to contemplate an existence that included anything as pedestrian as sitting in the back garden with the neighbour's bonfire blowing smoke over you or hearing the kids two doors down on their trampoline. No. After this, I was going to be a woman whose only destiny was to sit on stylish chairs sipping a cold beer and watching Florentine life unfold. The priest locking up the church at the end of the square, little dogs peeing up every lamp post, the waiters whirling about with pizzas, the lights glittering on the hills in the distance.

Boo seemed oblivious to my upset and gestured to an intricate metal sculpture on one of the walls. 'Carlo made this. He's really gifted. All the metal arty bits and pieces in the apartment are his.'

I murmured admiring comments before apologising for my outburst, reassuring her that I wouldn't stay more than a night, that I promised to get myself together and not be a misery.

She shrugged. 'It's fine. You feel how you feel' but her words weren't filled with warmth. I'd disappointed her. She was probably downgrading her first impressions of me as a go-getting woman who ditched her job and hopped on a plane on a whim to someone who dragged the mood down.

Carlo appeared with a tray of drinks and had obviously overheard me. 'Don't worry at all. People come here and blub about stuff all the time. You won't be the first person who's cried all over Casa Argento, or the last. I'm surrounded by creative types and we all wear our emotions close to the surface. Especially after a few bottles of Chianti. This apartment has seen plenty of tears.' And in that last sentence, I felt the shadow, the absence of his partner clouding his words. He paused and said, 'I get it. It's not only on the bad days that we miss people we love, but also the good days we wish we could share.' And with a practised air of focusing on the happy times he could affect rather than the sad times that were out of his hands, he put the tray down and said, 'Who's for a little drink? Then I thought we could go and see what's on the menu downstairs at Dante's?'

I felt Lainey give me a metaphorical kick up the backside, the deep timbre of her voice urging me to stop being such a bloody wet weekend. *You're in Florence, for goodness' sake. Save all the drippy moping about for a rainy Wednesday in November. You can fill your boots then.* I gave myself a firm shake and forced a smile. 'That sounds great,' I said, trying to remember the last time I'd gone out for dinner at 10 p.m.

Carlo passed me an Aperol spritz, clinking with ice in a ridged balloon of a glass.

Boo raised her drink to us both. 'Cheers! Here's to good times ahead. And, Carlo, thank you for having us.'

I echoed her words, adding, 'And thank you so much, Boo, for pushing me to be daring, and Carlo, for being so generous to a complete stranger.'

'Got to live in the moment, right, Carlo?' Boo said and I wondered again if I was imagining a chilly edge to her tone. Lainey had always accused me of overthinking everything whenever we'd met new people. I was always the one in the cab, saying, 'Did you think so-and-so was a bit off/touchy about...?' Inevitably, she'd frown and say, 'No. I didn't notice anything.' So I ignored my tendency to assume I was in people's bad books and concentrated on the prospect of sitting outside for dinner on a warm September night.

My attention drifted in and out of the conversation, Carlo's efforts to include me by asking questions about my family made me self-conscious when Boo clearly had so much news to exchange.

Boo waggled her fingers in my direction. 'Sara's in one of those funny places at the moment. Split up with her husband three years ago but still living in the same house. Can you imagine?' She clapped her hands as though it was the most outrageous thing. When I'd told her earlier, I'd felt like she'd really understood the complexities of how hard it was to make that final decision to go, to find the right moment in the boys' lives to uproot them from the family home, even though they were adults. I supposed it was pretty pathetic, but I still didn't want it rolled out as a 'hilarious story' to entertain someone I'd just met.

Carlo offered a soft landing by saying, 'Well, I had a girl-friend for ten years whom I never quite managed to marry or move in with – so I'm the last one to judge anyone else's arrangements.'

I was tempted to slam my drink down and throw my arms around him for his kindness, while wanting to lean back in my chair and say, 'That is really odd!'

Carlo changed the direction of the conversation by getting to his feet. 'Right, we'd better get a move on if we want to eat. But, first, bedrooms. Boo, are you taking your usual one?'

She nodded and I thought how cool it was to have a 'usual room' in a friend's apartment in Florence.

He turned to me. 'You can have a choice, let me show you.'

I followed him down a corridor, lined with eclectic paintings and drawings – naked women hanging next to abstract starbursts of colour, a mosaic of the Florence Duomo positioned next to a stained-glass penis – or if it was meant to be a green and blue stained-glass Leaning Tower of Pisa, rather than a penis, the artist needed to go back to the drawing board. Carlo showed me into a room, dark and opulent, dominated by a four-poster bed and heavy navy brocade drapes. It had the tiniest window in the raw brickwork and I couldn't chase away the thought that there was something of the dungeon about it. I made all the right 'what a stunning room' noises, while knowing immediately that I'd be checking behind those drapes before I got into bed, like Finn had insisted I checked under the bed for clowns when he was little.

Carlo looked down at me. 'I can see that this room might not be your cup of tea.'

I did the whole British thing of 'Oh no, I'm really grateful for...' but he cut me off.

'Come on, have a look in here.' He flung the door open to a bright room with a wrought-iron bed and pale blue organza at the windows. Carlo opened the window and pushed back the shutters. The view was of an internal courtyard, an ornate porticoed affair that resembled a cloister with a fountain in the centre. It made my view back home over next-door's compost heap seem distinctly lacklustre.

This time, I didn't have to dig deep to find enthusiasm. 'I don't know what to say, this is so beautiful.'

Carlo looked at me, amusement marbling his face. 'There are those guests who adore the other room, find it sexy and sensuous, and then there are others who see it as claustrophobic.'

I narrowly avoided clapping my hands to my face with the embarrassment of a man I'd only just met describing a bedroom that screamed 'come in here and have wanton sex' as sexy and sensuous. The colour rushed to my face and I turned away with a sudden urgency to place my rucksack on a chair. 'Is there a bathroom I could use?'

Carlo's face was a picture of mischief. He had that sharp humour, that teasing way about him that meant I was destined to be on my guard in case he came out with a bit of banter that called for a swift response. 'Down the hallway.' He paused. 'Boo can be a bit, you know, acerbic. She doesn't mean anything by it.'

I felt the rush of relief that I hadn't been imagining things, quickly followed by a wave of weariness that I was getting a bit old for tiptoeing around people whose issues I wasn't actually interested in a) understanding, or b) accommodating. I told myself I'd stay a couple of days so I didn't appear ungrateful, make the most of a great location in Florence, then slip away to Portofino and back to my original plan. 'Oh, she's been lovely. I hope you didn't mind her inviting me along, I don't know why she did really.'

'Because you're fun? Because you're intellectually curious and a good challenge for her? Boo's got a really smart brain and it's not very often she meets her match.'

I blushed again, suddenly aware of standing in a bedroom with a man showering me with compliments.

Carlo moved towards the door. 'This way.'

I followed, glad to be behind him to give my face a chance to cool down. He threw open the door to a bathroom that looked like something out of a French boudoir, with a claw-foot bath, the sort you see in films with a woman reclining in bubbles up to her neck, a slender ankle propped on the side. It was all gilded mirrors and cherub plinths, a far cry from my minimalist grey and chrome bathroom in England. I had a sudden image of Lainey parading about in a too small towel singing 'Beauty School Dropout' from *Grease* into a can of deodorant. That woman had a song for every occasion and this bathroom would definitely have been an occasion.

Carlo watched my face. 'My girlfriend loved a bit of kitsch. I haven't been able to bring myself to change it.' He shrugged, regretfully, although I couldn't make out whether he was apologising for not being far enough along in his grief to be able to make changes without insulting her memory or whether he was a bit mortified by his over-the-top bathroom.

Ten minutes later, we walked into Piazza Santo Spirito and were swept onto Dante's terrace by the owner, who was delighted to see Boo and warm with his welcome of me. Within minutes, almost like the crows that stormed the garden when I threw down leftover pasta, a whole crowd of Carlo's friends materialised as though they'd been hovering at the windows round the square ready to swoop down to an impromptu dinner so late at night. The owner, who was actually called Dante – very circle of hell – knitted tables together, shuffling other customers to different corners of the terrace in a move that made me dread a scathing review on Tripadvisor.

Our posse of three morphed into a gaggle of ten, all hugs and throaty laughs and gestures so extravagant I was reminded of police directing traffic at a busy London junction when the lights had failed. I could feel myself edging out of the group, closing in on myself, despite – to my surprise – managing to follow the gist of what they were talking about. Like so many other things from 'that time', the rudiments of the Italian language had obviously embedded themselves deep into my psyche.

Lainey would have been right in the thick of it, complimenting the women on their outfits, asking where she could have her hair cut in Florence, finding common ground with ease. I, on the other hand, felt like a brown sparrow intruding on a gathering of parakeets.

Carlo appeared at the side of my chair and tapped the woman next to me. She'd intimidated me just by sitting there, with her smoky eye make-up, hair tumbling in chaotic but cool corkscrews and a dramatic ruffled blouse that wouldn't have looked out of place on a Tudor courtier. The thought of trying out my rusty Italian made me tongue-tied and shy. She made no effort to engage with me. Carlo indicated that she needed to move along one.

As he plonked down next to me, relief trumped my discomfort. 'We're a bit overwhelming en masse, aren't we?'

Underneath Carlo's extrovert exterior, I sensed something gentle, a vulnerability.

'I'm entirely envious that you can conjure up a great big group of mates on a Wednesday evening and, even better, that we can sit outside in September. I'd never tire of that,' I said.

As enormous bistecca alla Fiorentina arrived, slabs of rare steak on wooden boards garnished only by quarters of lemon, a sprinkling of rocket and a sprig of rosemary, I wondered how easy it was to be a vegetarian in Italy. Trays of garlicky roast potatoes were passed up and down the table, along with carafes of Chianti.

Amid interjecting into the conversation and the ensuing gales of laughter, Carlo explained the food and the history of Florence and mentioned off-the-beaten-track places. The temptation to write them all down loomed large, but I surrendered to what I knew Lainey would have said: *That's what Google is for. Just enjoy the moment.*

'What's your thing?' Carlo asked.

'It might seem sacrilege to say this in a city with so much architecture and art, but since my friend died, I really love outdoor spaces, nature, peaceful places.'

'That's not sacrilege, that's nourishment for the soul. You should check out the Bardini Garden, the Rose Garden near Piazzale Michelangelo, the cemetery by San Miniato al Monte.'

'I wasn't actually supposed to come to Florence, so I can't linger too long.' I filled him in on Lainey's desire to have her ashes cast into the sea in Portofino, although I reiterated that I was grateful to Boo for encouraging me on this lovely diversion.

At the mention of her name, Boo's head swivelled round. 'You bad-mouthing me again, Carlo? Don't forget I know all your secrets and I'm not afraid to share them.' Although she was laughing, there was something territorial and intimate in her voice, as though she was reminding me that she knew him best.

I wondered if they'd ever been lovers. Then shocked myself by considering how nice being Carlo's lover might be. I quickly brushed that idea away. I had learnt some self-protection in the last thirty years.

Boo leant over the table and clinked her glass against Carlo's. 'Love you.' She resumed her conversation with her neighbour, who had closely cropped salt-and-pepper hair and looked as though he'd stepped out of an advert for amaretto.

Carlo tapped my arm. 'You were saying you need to get home. Really? What's burning back there that can't wait a few weeks? You don't have a job. Why rush to be part of the daily sausage machine again?'

I hesitated, aware that fretting about what they'd all be eating in my absence and what state the house would be in sounded pretty lame on the 'great urgency to get home' stakes. 'I said I'd only be gone for a few days.'

Carlo ran his fingers through his dark hair. 'So surprise them.' He grinned. 'Surprise yourself.'

I refrained from pointing out that being here at all was already astonishing to me. Without me even noticing, my horizons had become increasingly narrow over the last few years, reducing down to little more than work, home and Lainey. Sitting in this square seemed to have reawakened my senses – everything around me felt vibrant and intense. My attention was captured by bursts of laughter, the scent of herbs and garlic wafting from the restaurant kitchen, the notes of a saxophone drifting across from another bar. There was something rather intoxicating about this group of people – bohemian, spontaneous and, as far as I could make out from the way they bantered with each other, long-standing and tight-knit. The sort of people I didn't usually mix with – the men in their colourful shirts and raffish hair, the women with their extravagant sleeves, satins, statement earrings. And under that starry Florentine sky, with the clink of the glasses of amaro and shouts of '*salute!*', I knew I wanted to be part of their theatre for a bit longer.

We left the restaurant just after midnight and, mentally, I was already removing my make-up and getting into my pyjamas when Carlo invited everyone back to his apartment. I was shocked at the idea of staying up so late in the middle of the week. Surely some of these people had jobs to go to? But I arranged my face into a party-ready expression and clattered up to the fifth floor with the rest of them.

Carlo put Bob Marley on, Boo threw open the doors onto the terrace and, very soon, wine, whisky and jugs of a cocktail I would steer clear of appeared on the table. 'No Woman No Cry' belted out into the night sky and in between wondering whether the neighbours downstairs would soon be banging on the door, some of the men started dancing with the women in such a sensual way that I worried that my eyes were boggling out of my head.

Carlo came over with a tumbler of whisky in his hand. 'You dancing?'

It was all I could do not to scream and run away. The thought of trying to blend in with all that hip grinding and wiggling without looking like Baby at the beginning of *Dirty Dancing* made me shrink back into my chair.

'I'm not really much of a dancer.'

As I said the words, I wondered when that had become the case. Lainey and I had always been stalwarts of the dance floor – no Scout hut Friday night, no rugby club Saturday evening passed without us flinging ourselves about to Wham! and Michael Jackson and Boy George.

Carlo cajoled and I became more resolute that I would not be unsticking my backside from the armchair. Boo's attention seemed very focused on us, despite her enthusiastic bump and grind with the man she'd been sitting next to at dinner.

'Boo's a good dancer, she's got natural rhythm,' I said.

Carlo nodded. 'She was always the one leading the dances at school. No Saturday was complete without sitting on a beer-soaked dance floor for "Oops Upside Your Head".'

I smiled with recognition. Lainey and I had pulled that one out at every birthday booze-up since time immemorial.

He nudged me. 'Bet you could still do it.'

And before I knew it, Carlo, Boo and I were rowing away to the Gap Band, tapping our hands on the floor and leaning backwards and forwards, to a mixture of bemusement and enjoyment from the Florentine contingent.

Some of the most extrovert Italians joined us, picking up the rhythm with ease. I could feel the echoes of my adolescent self, when a couple of bars of familiar music would lure me to the dance floor like a tribal cry to action. For the glorious minutes of those songs, I'd belonged, part of an energetic group of young people who hadn't yet made any decisions that would determine the rest of their lives.

Being back in Italy was tugging at all sorts of threads, unveiling sharp bursts of memories that the passing years had cushioned but which could still catch me off guard. But there was no denying that distance from home was providing some clarity. As our voices rang out with words that echoed in my heart the way songs from teenage years do, I felt a stirring of optimism. Perhaps a possibility I had not yet defined lay within my reach.

As the song came to an end and cheers greeted our performance, Carlo instructed Alexa to play Bad Manners and 'Can Can' – 'A classic!' he shouted. I caught a glimpse of the boisterous and exuberant seventeen-year-old who knew how to charm his way out of trouble and into girls' hearts.

There was a flurry of pushing back chairs and sofas before nearly everyone joined in and I had to work hard not to say, 'Should we be making so much noise this late? What about the people in the apartment below?'

Eventually, after several more teen classics, including a bout of 'Come On Eileen' for good measure, his friends clomped off down the stairs, making no discernible attempt to leave quietly.

I started carrying glasses through to the kitchen, but Carlo waved me away. 'That's for tomorrow. Sleep well.'

I said goodnight to Boo and thanked her again for bringing me. She threw her arms around me. 'You were brilliant fun tonight. See you in the morning.' I left as she was pouring herself another glass of wine and wandering out onto the terrace. I deliberately avoided looking to see if Carlo was following and headed down the corridor, ignoring the twinge of disappointment that he hadn't shown me to my room.

As I got ready for bed, not so tipsy I couldn't appreciate the total madness of that bathroom, I reminded myself of the mantra I regularly trotted out to my boys. 'It doesn't matter that you make mistakes. It matters that you learn from them.' I'd do well to heed my own advice.

Over the next week, I got up every morning telling myself it was my last day in Florence before going to Portofino then home. Every time I voiced that thought, Carlo acted all mock-offended. 'Come on, you're just getting started here. Go after the weekend.'

And I needed no persuading, despite the barrage of calls from Declan demanding news of my return timetable. I'd hoped to calm him down by explaining that I'd got free accommodation with a woman I'd met – conveniently omitting any mention of Carlo – and that I wasn't actually spending money on hotels.

'Boo? What kind of a name is that?'

The name of a really interesting woman. Of someone who's stayed curious. Whose face lights up with understanding when I explain how I've almost talked myself into slipping uncomplainingly into old age, when really I'm still so young, with so many possibilities ahead of me. Instead, I said, 'It's short for Belinda. Anyway, she's good company.' And she was, although there was an edge to her, a snappiness that prevented me relaxing completely.

'But you're leaving for Portofino in the next day or so?'

'That's the plan.' But it wasn't the plan. I was barefaced lying for a reason I couldn't quite understand. Now I was away, I realised that nothing had changed in the three years since we'd agreed to split up. After the initial shock, the fear of being on my own, responsible for every decision, I'd felt relieved, admiring Declan's courage to want more than a wife who'd done what was expected of her but often didn't listen and, worse, didn't really care. He'd been right to call time, to allow us both the possibility of creating a more fulfilling future for ourselves, whatever shape that took.

When we'd first announced the end of our marriage, I'd been smug about how amicably we'd decided to part, mature enough to live in the same house – 'not the same beds, of course!' – until the boys moved out permanently. But the reality was Declan had immediately commandeered total freedom to disappear on work trips and weekends away, while I'd remained on call for the boys in their first year at university, their essay crises, their disappointments with job interviews.

But, having come this far, I didn't want to descend into acrimony, so I sent holding messages about 'looking into flights' and 'sorting out the logistics of getting to Portofino'. In reality, Boo and I were exploring the streets of Florence, doing all the major sights – the Uffizi, the Bargello, the Duomo – while Carlo went off to his workshop to finish a commission. The times when Carlo joined us, leading us off to the quieter Bardini Garden or up to San Miniato al Monte to watch the sunset, were my favourite. I found myself longing for the moments when Carlo would challenge my doubts about my ability to do something – 'That's not what I see' – before picking out a quality he did recognise. Shallow it may have been, but Carlo studying my face as though there was more to me than I realised filled me with a confidence that had been missing for years. He had a way of looking at me that made me feel as though I'd swum into a warm spot in a cold sea. If that head tilt and crinkling of those eyes could be bottled as an aphrodisiac, the whole world would be at it like rabbits.

I didn't discuss Carlo with Boo, except in the most general terms, and she reverted to the entertaining irreverent company that had enchanted me on the way to Milan. We went to the central market to stock up on food – the stalls piled high with fat peppers, aubergines, courgettes, squash. None of the uniformity that I was used to in supermarkets but all the misshapen robustness that indicated unforced growth under natural sunshine. That distinctive fragrance of freshly picked tomatoes pervaded the air and Boo leapt upon the trays of porcini mushrooms. 'We have to get some of these.' The closest I'd ever got to porcini mushrooms was rehydrating gritty desiccated specimens when I was making fancy soup.

We spent time combing the clothes market outside – Boo for second-hand military jackets, me for flowing dresses far more in keeping with my bohemian self of old. I celebrated the freedom of floating about in broderie anglaise dresses and flappy trousers.

Unfortunately, ten days after I'd jumped on a plane to Italy, the real world caught up with me. A courier had turned up at home to fetch my work laptop and let the cat out of the bag that I was no longer in gainful employment. Declan had been incandescent. I had hoped to postpone that conversation until I was back in England. My knee-jerk reaction was to rush home to explain myself, but Boo was a great foil for my self-accusatory thinking. 'You'd be better off letting him cool down. I'm sure that fat row will still be available to you in a week or two. And, anyway, you're divorcing him, so...'

I tried to explain that impulsive behaviour wasn't usual for me.

Boo did a derogatory snort. 'But why always be that person? Why always be the sap who's reliable and loyal and basically gets taken for a fool? You won't even be married to him soon.'

I bristled at the assumption that the qualities of reliability and loyalty somehow made me a sap – I didn't want to entertain a world where those traits were a sign of weakness rather than decency.

Before I could discuss it any further, Boo snatched the phone from me and typed, *I'm having some well-deserved time to myself. Normal service as domestic skivvy will be resumed shortly. I'll be in touch.*

She stabbed 'send' before I could grab it back.

'Oh my God, Declan will be furious.' I was horrified and indignant, but also bursting with awe at her daring.

She marched me across Florence to a bar near Santa Croce – 'Come on, let's get away from these touristy crowds.'

The décor was such an arresting combination of colours and fabrics that I had a brief pang of homesickness for my job, the excitement of seeing other people's styles and ideas. A couple of glasses of Prosecco and a platter of cheese and salami distracted me nicely. Until Declan's name flashed up on my phone.

My chest constricted with dread, followed by a flare of annoyance that he was hassling me. I dismissed the call and let out a giggle.

'What?' Boo asked.

'I'm marvelling at the fact that ten days ago I was trudging off to a job I hated and now here I am, chilling in a bar in the middle of Florence with someone I met on a plane.'

Boo raised her glass. 'Here's to discovering there is more to us than we knew ourselves.'

And in that moment, I felt that warm glow of approval, the premium sort that came when it was expressed by someone whose attitude I admired but would never be able to emulate.

Declan clearly had far more interesting things to do over the weekend and, to my relief, left me alone. But early on Monday morning, the buzz of a WhatsApp message woke me. I picked my phone up with a sigh but it was Finn.

Hi Mum. How are you? Are you having a good time? Are you back soon? I can pick you up from the train if you let me know times.

I sensed the bugle call to home in his words. That boy. He hadn't quite found his place in the world. Callum bowled along with insouciance, rarely breaking into a sweat over anything. Finn lacked Callum's hard shell. I'd had to stand by as teachers compared the boys, praising Callum, who was more academic, but barely noticing Finn's ability to turn his hand to anything practical.

Declan bonded with Callum over his natural sporting talent – 'That boy can pick up any bat or racket one day and be giving me the run-around by the next' – but dismissed Finn's interest in woodwork and penchant for scavenging materials from skips. During lockdown, instead of lounging in bed, Finn built a bar in the garden out of old pallets he found in the basement. Declan focused on the fact that when it rained, the water poured off the overhang. 'Bit of a design fault there. Needed a bit of guttering.' I overcompensated by raving about how most eighteen-year-olds would struggle to put an IKEA table together, let alone build a bar. However, as so often in life, the criticism was so much more powerful than the praise. While Finn carried on making things – seats, bird tables and vegetable troughs – he pre-empted any comments with 'It hasn't turned out quite right.'

I was suddenly overwhelmed by the urge to hear Finn's voice. I went out into the piazza, where I FaceTimed him from a bench. He appeared on screen, clearly on his commute to London. 'Sorry, love, I forgot that you'd be on the train.'

He ignored that. 'Mum!' he said and immediately left his seat to squeeze into an emptier area by the door.

'Is Callum with you?'

Finn shook his head 'No, he's working from home.' He looked pale, with dark shadows under his eyes, and I resisted the urge to nag about fish oils and not messing about on his phone until late.

'So, how are things with you both, all calm?' Finn wasn't a person you could demand answers from. Any information had to be teased out as though I was casually remarking on something that carried no weight.

Finn glanced down. 'Yeah, fine. Callum's just earned a big commission for an insurance contract he won last week.'

'That's great.' I had that sense I used to get when Finn was worried about something at school, a heaviness that sat on him, sometimes for weeks, before he told me about it. As lightly as I could, I said, 'And what about you, are you getting on okay at work?'

His eyes flickered away. 'Yeah, it's going all right.'

'You don't sound like you're living the dream?'

He exhaled harshly. 'I'm not sure aircraft component sales is anyone's dream. I've got to go, I'm at London Bridge. Love you, Mum.'

I was unsure whether my 'love you' reached its destination before the screen went blank.

One of the greatest myths about having children was this idea that once they hit eighteen, your job as a parent was done and you could flit about the world, light of heart, leaving them to sink or swim without your brain scanning through a hundred possible solutions to fix them at the first sign of trouble. I didn't love Finn more than Callum, but I felt him more. His brooding reticence, the way he'd always hovered on the sidelines rather than plunging straight in, made me want to stand in front of him and absorb life's blows.

Before I could fully indulge my fretting about Finn, a text

from Declan arrived. I was about to read it when a shadow fell across the bench.

'Good morning. Everything all right?' Carlo asked, looking shower-fresh in a lemon shirt that was most definitely *his* colour.

I forced a smile. I was regretting the tears when I'd first arrived as I could have made use of a free pass right now. 'Yes, fine, just young adult sons who haven't quite found their niche.'

Carlo brandished a bag. 'Come on. I've got the most amazing pastries in here. They'll cheer you up. I'll make you a coffee.'

'Where's Boo?'

'Boo and I stayed up quite late drinking whisky. She'll be sleeping off her hangover. We won't see much of her before midday.'

I felt a little jolt. Boo had definitely made out she was having an early night when we got back from the bar the previous evening. But, there again, I shouldn't begrudge her a bit of time on her own with her friend. But before Carlo got his key in the door, Boo flung it open. 'Where have you two been? Thanks for waiting for me!'

I was always slow to respond to sudden confrontation, especially when it took the form of a teenage tantrum from a sixty-year-old. But Carlo was the master of defusing.

'Back in your box, Boo. I've just been out to fetch breakfast and bumped into Sara in the square. If you don't take that look off your face, I will scoff up your *bombolone*.'

She snatched the bag from him, took a bite of a custard doughnut and, with her mouth all covered in sugar, leant forward and kissed him firmly on the lips. 'Sweetheart you are.'

He wiped his face with his fingers, but he didn't recoil.

After so many years socialising with couples who'd been married for decades, my radar was a little dulled for unexpected intimacies between people who weren't an item. I hesitated, grappling for an excuse to escape. 'I'm not very hungry, so I'll skip breakfast if you don't mind. I need to pop out to buy a couple of souvenirs.'

I darted down the stairs, away from this claustrophobic landing, where unspoken emotions were ricocheting off the ancient walls. I burst out into the September sunshine, striding towards the river, and onto the Ponte Vecchio, where the jewellery shop windows glittered with so many shiny baubles. How anyone homed in on one must-have item, I couldn't begin to imagine.

I stared down at the teams of rowers finessing their strokes on the Arno, powering under the ornate bridges. What a location for training. It certainly knocked the spots off my local leisure centre, with its sweaty rowing machines and showers that screamed verrucas. I continued up Via Por Santa Maria until I reached the market, brimming with stalls selling scarves and leather bags. I stood gazing at the Porcellino wild boar statue Lainey and I had posed by, decades ago, adding our rubbing of its nose to the efforts of everyone who'd shone up its bronze snout. I could even bring to mind our faces in the photo, our 'come on, get on with it' expressions as the young Florentine who'd offered to be photographer kept telling us how to pose, '*Giù, giù, sì, così.*' It was only afterwards that we'd realised that he'd been getting us to lean forward so he could see our cleavages. In the years that followed, Lainey and I had laughed at our naivety and the fact that the spoils would have been minimal for the effort – 'I haven't got much more than a couple of fried eggs even now.'

I continued on my way until I reached Orsanmichele. It had been our favourite church, with its intricately carved niches holding statues of the patron saints of the main workers' guilds. I loved that it had started life as a grain market, surrounded by a vegetable garden in the thirteenth century, before becoming a place of worship. There was something about its grounding in nature and people who worked the land that appealed to me. We'd both adored the ceramic terracotta roundels by Luca della Robbia, the bright blues, greens and yellows a welcome change from the dingy colours I associated with church façades. I walked around the building, ticking off the patron saints for the professions I remembered – St George for the armourers and swordmakers, St Mark for the linen weavers – and googling the ones I'd forgotten. Every now and again, I'd start, as though there was somewhere I should be, something I should be doing.

I headed up towards the Duomo, past the department store of Coin with all the fancy coats in the window, those stylish buttons and collars that elevated Italian winter wear to a dramatic aesthetic display rather than just fabric to withstand the cold. I passed a narrow street to the right, and something about the name, Via del Corso, stirred a distant memory. I turned into it and was immediately rewarded by the sight of an ice cream shop, Festival del Gelato. Its long counter boasted everything from frozen yoghurts to milk-free and vegan ice cream. I was pretty sure that hadn't been a thing in the eighties when Lainey and I were here, but the décor, the green and orange ceramic tiles, the little benches, hadn't changed.

A forgotten image surged up: Lainey and I deciding to skip lunch and eating ourselves to a standstill on ice cream. We both loved 'bacio' – a chocolate hazelnut concoction. That was partly because '*bacio*' meant 'kiss' and we were ever hopeful that some gorgeous Italian boys – who didn't only want a flash of our cleavage – might do the honours. I still recalled how we would wander the streets, eyeing up groups of boys, desperate for a holiday romance to embellish when we returned to our small-town lives at the end of the summer. Except I got more than I bargained for when we arrived in Rome. A chance meeting outside the Colosseum, a harmless flirtation that became so much more. A love affair I simply couldn't forget or leave behind, that came to dominate everything.

I forced my thoughts back to Lainey. In her honour, I ordered a cone of bacio and perched at one of the tables. Remembering the earlier text from Declan, I fished out my mobile and read.

Do you have an ETA for your return home? Walking out as you did shows to me that you are ready to move on and I am too. With that in mind, I wanted to let you know that the estate agent we talked to a couple of years ago rang me because he's identified a couple of cash buyers looking for a house in this location. Seems quite serendipitous, so I've given him the go-ahead to start marketing the house. He's coming round in two days' time to take photos. Declan.

I stared down at the screen. We'd agreed to separate in August 2020, yet, apart from a couple of loose references to how 'it might be a good time to sell' when there were announcements about the housing market hotting up, we'd settled down into our separate, but still family life. Neither of us had proved dynamic about making the final break. And although I knew that this day would come, the fact that Declan had got the ball rolling in my absence, without even discussing it first, winded me.

My first urge was to dash home. An estate agent poking about into every corner without my supervision – Callum's room probably had historic pizza boxes under the bed – tapped into my 'What will people think of me?' paranoia. But experience had trained me to take a beat. So I turned my phone over and watched the young staff darting about with an energy in their limbs that they didn't have to kick-start. Exuberance was still possible for me, but I had to fight harder. I'd felt it when Carlo and I had detailed all the things on our bucket lists as we'd wandered through the cemetery at San Miniato al Monte, his head bent in concentration as though my words were important. And again when the three of us had raced each other down the steps at the Boboli Gardens in a burst of competitive frivolity.

But with the news that our house was going on the market, I knew my time in Italy was over. If the house sold quickly, which it probably would owing to its excellent location between two schools, there was so much to organise. Emptying the loft and the garage. Finding somewhere to live. What about the boys? They would have to share a room again. Suddenly, flouncing out of my job with my skirts held high didn't seem such a glittering triumph.

I hurried back to the apartment, irritated by moped riders who forced themselves past stationary traffic, then emerged unexpectedly at full throttle out of alleyways. My brain chipped away to understand why Declan had chosen now to push the button on selling. The stupidity of never insisting that he put my name on the deeds when we got married, despite paying half the mortgage, meant that I'd left the ability to call the shots in his hands.

When Carlo let me in, all the facts that I'd been mulling over came tumbling out in a torrent of angst. If I'd wanted to impress on Carlo that he'd been harbouring a madwoman in his midst, I was doing a fine job.

He waved me in. 'Coffee is needed.'

I went through to the sitting room. Boo was lying on an orange velvet chaise longue. She looked for all the world like a 1950s movie star, albeit one who'd lived hard and spent more than her fair share of time smoking cigarettes from an elegant holder. She jumped up, totally different to the petulant woman I'd left this morning. 'Are you all right? You look flustered.'

I quickly rehashed what I'd told Carlo and she was all open-mouthed indignation.

'What? Your husband has decided to sell the house from under you? Can he even do that?'

'Apparently so. Long story, but it's only in his name.'

'But he has to give you half in the divorce?'

I nodded.

'So why rush home? What's the point?'

Carlo reappeared with a tray of coffee. We gathered on the terrace outside in the mode of a war cabinet, giving me the sense of an unlikely team of allies, clustering round to talk strategy.

'I can't just let him sell the house without being there. He'll be letting viewers troop round with all the washing-up in the sink and the towels on the floor.'

'And?' Boo was looking at me as though I was making a drama out of nothing.

'I'd feel so ashamed. They won't criticise Declan and think what a slob he is, they'll be talking about how slovenly his wife is.'

Carlo shrugged. 'Why do you care what people you'll never even see say?'

I could name a hundred and one reasons, which distilled down into one – I hated people thinking I hadn't done my best.

We drifted off topic on to Boo's stories about when she was house-hunting and had viewed a doctor's cottage – 'I was expecting everywhere to be pristine and hygienic and it was the filthiest pit ever. There was a pair of her knickers right in the middle of the hallway.'

But whatever they said, I remained determined to return to England. 'You've been so generous putting me up in this lovely apartment and it's time I went before I overstay my welcome.'

Carlo interrupted. 'I've loved having you here. Much as I love the Italians, I still miss that sharp, sarcastic British humour. It's a breath of fresh air.'

I couldn't remember saying one funny thing since I'd been here. 'Thank you, but I'll get a train to Portofino tomorrow.' The realisation was dawning that I would be saying goodbye to

Lainey for the very last time. I gulped back the surge of sadness. 'Once I've...' I didn't know how to articulate the enormity of what scattering her ashes would mean to me. Now the moment had come, I was a coward. I didn't want to cross tomorrow's pain barrier, didn't even know if I could. I swallowed. 'Once I've been to Portofino, I'll make my way to London.'

Boo folded her arms. 'Why are you allowing him to dictate the timeline? If it was my husband, I'd let him get on with it. He hasn't consulted you and is trying to force you to curtail your plans because he can't quite believe that you're not dancing to his tune.'

'I know, but I've got the boys to consider. They've never lived anywhere else. And I'm not sure what Declan has got in mind. I think he's quite keen to get a studio flat as a bolthole in the UK, and use the rest of the money to retire early and do a bit of travelling,' I said.

'But your sons are adults. If they don't want to or can't live with him, they'll have to rent somewhere, won't they? I left home at sixteen and never went back.'

Facts always sounded so simple, especially when they were delivered by people who had no skin in my particular game. Plenty of people moved out much earlier than twenty-one and lived in all sorts of dives and survived to tell the tale. And yes, I was sure it was character building, that you had to have a bit of hardship to appreciate the good times, that this generation wanted everything now, served up on a plate. I'd probably even said those things myself to friends with older children. But the view from your high horse and the view through the prism of a maternal heart were polar opposites.

Of course my boys were old enough to rent somewhere. But the mother in me couldn't quite imagine selling the family home from under them and turfing them out. How quickly could a sale go through if we received an offer straightaway? Callum would probably find a mate to move in with, but Finn didn't have such a wide circle of friends. Callum would simply pack his own clothes, gather up all his designer trainers and tech gear and call an Uber. Any thoughts of bedding, towels and kitchen equipment wouldn't rear themselves until he was sitting on a bare mattress or drying himself on a T-shirt. I couldn't even begin to imagine Finn negotiating a rental contract. He'd probably end up signing a five-year lease for a basement room without a window and washing in a bucket.

Boo obviously didn't think she'd posed a rhetorical question. She was looking at me, waiting for a response.

'They probably will have to rent. Me too, initially, I suppose. Maybe I should fly back first thing tomorrow and deal with Portofino another time.'

Carlo cleared his throat and I braced myself for another unwanted opinion.

'Can I say one thing? Jewellery making is a lot like life. If you are patient, if you don't rush things, you always, always get better results. I've also learnt to start with a strong sense of what I want to do, but then to relax and enjoy the journey, allow myself to drift into other directions along the way.'

Irritation didn't so much bubble as boil within me. All very well for Carlo deviating from the design of a pair of earrings. 'But this is my home, my boys' home. Declan wasn't in favour of them living with us after university anyway. But leaving aside Callum and Finn, I need to sort out a place for myself.'

Maddeningly, neither Boo nor Carlo demonstrated an understanding of my urgency.

My fingers were twitching to start trawling the internet for flights. 'Please excuse me. I need to check out what my options are.'

I disappeared down the corridor to my room, scowling at my phone as it connected to the Wi-Fi at a glacial pace. As I was searching all the usual airlines, Carlo tapped on my door.

'I've just looked. There's a baggage handlers' strike for the rest of the week. All the flights out of Pisa and Florence have been cancelled.'

'Oh there bloody would be.' I pressed my fingers into my eyes. 'I'll get the train to Paris tomorrow and take it from there. I should arrive back by Wednesday or Thursday at the latest.'

Carlo sat on the edge of the bed and reached out for my hand. '*Cara* Sara.' I was slightly ashamed that the way he said my name with an Italian accent momentarily distracted me from my urgent quest to pin down my return journey. He smiled. 'Let me drive you to Portofino tomorrow so you can do...' He paused, as though struck down by the British need to avoid talking directly about death. I wondered if the Italian language also had a whole raft of euphemisms, as if not saying the words 'dead' and 'died' would trick people into forgetting. Carlo resorted to, 'So you can do what you came to do.'

I couldn't think straight. 'That's very kind of you. It does seem a bit stupid to be so close but not go. How far is it by car?'

'About three or so hours.'

'That's quite a drive.'

'I'm okay with it. It's a lovely coast, *proprio bello*. It will do me good to get some fresh air after being cooped up in my workshop.'

I breathed out. A couple of days wouldn't make any difference in the long run. And I owed it to Lainey to do what she'd asked of me. 'Thank you. That's incredibly generous. I'll obviously pay for the petrol and everything.'

Carlo batted me away. 'Don't be silly. My only stipulation is that you come to the music festival at the Forte di Belvedere tonight and have a good time.'

There was no denying that spending the next day in Carlo's company was an entirely appealing prospect.

7

Then

I grew to hate the patronising look on my parents' faces whenever I came home from university. My dad asked endless questions about my economics degree, assuming the responsibility for filling in the gaps in my political knowledge. He rolled his eyes on a regular basis and exclaimed, 'What do they even teach you at this university?'

He still couldn't quite disguise his disappointment that his only child had turned out to be useless at science and stood no chance of following in his oncology consultant footsteps. He'd nearly snorted out his tea when I'd announced that I wanted to read English. Waving his hand dismissively, he'd refused point blank to top up my grant and pay for a 'Mickey Mouse' degree. 'You can read all the books you want in your spare time. Get something decent under your belt that will get you on the career ladder, something you'll always be able to fall back on.'

There was little point in arguing. My father was a man

whose ideas and decisions literally made the difference between life and death, and when he spoke, he expected people to listen. And I'd grown up doing precisely that. In the end, I'd taken the path of least resistance, applied to study economics, the subject in which I'd been predicted an A at A level. I hated every minute of it. I was counting down the terms until university finished, living for the holidays, when I could go to Italy and be with Alessio. I worked in a pub pulling pints to finance my flights, sometimes resorting to the cheaper option of the coach, a journey of over thirty hours. I never moaned, never complained, because I knew it would unleash a sniffy response of 'I hope he's worth it,' followed by a warning about not letting 'all this restaurant work' interfere with my studies. Anything less than a first would be a failure.

Dad never referred to Alessio. He'd simply peer over his newspaper, nod and say, 'Good time?' when I arrived back after a stay in Rome, wrung out from the emotions of the day. Every trip was the same – the relief, the joy of being reunited with Alessio, followed by the sick dread of separation as the days rolled towards the moment when we'd cling to each other in the departure hall. Then the wrench of tearing ourselves away, an immediate chill engulfing me where his warmth had been.

I'd try to tell Dad about what I'd seen in Rome, dropping in cultural references – Bramante's Tempietto, Michelangelo's Pietà, Bernini's Fountain of the Four Rivers – in the hope that he'd understand that there was more to Alessio than an ability to make a cappuccino. Dad would listen in silence, then start filling me in on what had happened at the hospital, the news from our neighbours, my grandparents, his opinion on Maggie Thatcher's latest policies. And the sitting room would pulsate with a frustration, disappointment and obstinacy that we never acknowledged.

My mum simply pulled me into her arms when I walked through the door, my feet dragging, and said, 'Bless you, love. We missed you. So glad you're back.' I'd stand, rigid, wanting to tell her how empty I felt, how I could hardly bear the next few months of snatched phone calls and letters that took forever to arrive. But I couldn't risk her saying again, 'First love always seems so important,' then doing her little laugh: 'You have to kiss a few frogs before you find your prince.'

I overheard Mum telling Dad that Alessio was 'just a phase, she's eighteen for goodness' sake.' Over the years, she repeated the same mantra, adjusting my age – 'She's just nineteen/twenty/twenty-one/twenty-two/twenty-three', but with a little less conviction in her voice. My father's dismissive replies made me determined to prove him wrong. Of course he was a clever man, brilliant in many ways, but that didn't mean he knew everything. However much he was convinced that I'd 'find some professional high-flier and forget all about some boy who works in a bar', that was where my knowledge outshone his.

I didn't. And I wouldn't.

8

At twilight, Boo, Carlo and I slipped into the Costa San Giorgio, a narrow street near the Ponte Vecchio, and headed up the hill. I would never get used to how many treasures lined every ordinary road. I dawdled behind them, admiring a water fountain embossed with the fleur-de-lis symbol of the city. I then stopped to peer at a house with portraits frescoed on the side.

Carlo turned round. 'That's Galileo's house – you know, the astronomer? That's him, in the middle.' It had stopped surprising me how often I stumbled across an important historic place by accident. Carlo dropped back and said, 'It's brilliant you being here. You keep reminding me to appreciate the city all over again.'

And against my will, against everything I knew, and everything I'd learnt, I was allowing myself to hold his gaze, to be sucked into those complicit, secret looks that promised connection.

I broke the moment. 'I'll be very fit with all this walking by the time I get home.' I hurried on, catching up with Boo, refusing to accept that the hammering in my chest wasn't the effort of climbing a steep slope.

We forked right to the Forte di Belvedere and followed a crowd up through a tunnel, emerging into a huge walled expanse filled with rows of chairs and a stage, set against the backdrop of the domes and spires and the distant hills of Fiesole.

Carlo found three seats together and undid the wicker picnic basket he'd been carrying, like something out of *Little Red Riding Hood*. Not for us crisps, peanuts and sausage rolls. This was a feast gourmet-Italian style, with focaccia studded with rosemary and garlic, *finocchiona* – a type of salami with fennel seeds – fat olives, and a salty pecorino cheese. He produced a bottle of Brunello di Montalcino, which even I recognised as a premium wine that I'd seen at the top end of wine lists in fancy restaurants.

'I've been waiting for a good occasion to drink this.'

I resolved to buy him a few bottles as a thank you before I left. There was a little shop around the corner from the apartment, with brick arched ceilings and barrels and wooden crates. The sort of *enoteca* that feels as though it's existed for centuries, handed down by ancestors who trod the grapes with their feet, successive offspring moving the business forward into a modern age, but never losing sight of the original passion in their hearts.

Of course, Carlo had brought proper wine glasses. 'You can't drink Brunello out of plastic. Sacrilege! To fabulous old friends,' he said, raising his drink to Boo and then, turning to me, 'And wonderful new ones.'

We clinked glasses and again, I felt his eyes search mine as though a whole other conversation was happening somewhere else.

Boo took a dramatic sniff. 'Oh my God, smell the sunshine in that,' she said, then proceeded to take a large swig, moaning in delight. Even my uneducated palate recognised that it was a step up from my usual fare.

Carlo pointed to the west of the city. 'This is one of the best places to watch the sunset.'

The sky was a furious explosion of orange and pink, casting its rainbow glow onto the surface of the Arno. I couldn't remember the last time I'd actively looked at a sunset or taken a moment to admire the majesty of nature without a background thrum of wondering whether I had time to hang out the washing before dinner. I felt a rush of regret as the words of W. H. Davies – 'What is this life if full of care, We have no time to stand and stare' – flashed into my brain. I used to read it to the boys at bedtime. I blinked at the image of them in their Thomas the Tank Engine pyjamas, front teeth missing, eyes on me as I read, unswerving faith that I could take their worries downstairs with me and make them go away. If only it were so easy now.

I forced my attention back to the present. From the stage came the sounds of a band tuning up – the throb of a bass guitar and the melancholy notes of a saxophone drifting out into the night air, still oppressively hot. Eventually, the sky turned into a dark blue blanket above us. I tried to impress everything on my memory – the starry sky, the illuminated walls of the fort, the white marble of the churches below gleaming in the moonlight, the animated discussion all around me. The sheer stylishness of the Italians, with their flowing dresses and tailored jackets and jewellery that demanded a share of the spotlight.

A murmur of anticipation rippled through the audience as the compère stood up to announce that the Italian Festival of Street Performers was officially open. A group of young men rushed onto the stage. With their easy smiles and glossy hair, they were the perfect advert for the Italian Tourist Board, all olive oil and Mediterranean mystique. Even their music felt like an anthem to fields of sunflowers and snatched summer kisses. I knew without understanding all the lyrics that they were a homage to love, a tribute to the emotion that breaks down barriers and unites us. I tried to block the thought before it took hold. I never wanted to risk that level of vulnerability again. That daredevil entrusting of yourself to someone else was best confined to youth, when hearts were stronger and didn't constantly anticipate loss.

The next act had a reggae vibe, the type of beat that spoke to every muscle and made your whole body cry out to move. Boo shot to her feet. 'Come on, time to dance.' I was about to prevaricate, to judge whether I could manoeuvre myself into the middle of a group where I could be less conspicuous. Instead, my mind flicked to the period of time after Lainey had discovered she would die. I'd raged about the unfairness of it all, but she'd resolutely stuck to her mantra that if she only had a few months left to live, she wasn't going to waste a single moment weeping into her Weetabix.

One evening, she'd sat there, her face puffy with steroids, her head bound in a scarf, her eyes irritated and red and said, 'Let's watch *Mamma Mia!* and dance.' And we did, right there in her sitting room, singing our hearts out to 'Dancing Queen', awash with good time memories of parties long gone. Eventually, she'd flopped onto the sofa and clinked her glass against mine, 'To living life with music in our souls.' She died six weeks later.

Tonight, I was going to dance and honour Lainey's toast. And the ridiculous thing was that as soon as I followed Boo to the front to join the throngs of limbs moving languidly, I felt joy rush through me. The muscle memory of dancing to Bob Marley and UB40 returned.

Carlo appeared at my side. He had grace and rhythm that meant I didn't have to avert my gaze to avoid being embarrassed on his behalf. He mirrored my movements in a way that felt so sensual that the rest of the crowd faded to the edges of my consciousness. Then the tempo changed to some kind of salsa that definitely wasn't my forte. Boo grabbed Carlo, and with a lightness of movement that surprised me, they held their own among some seriously sexy and accomplished dancers.

I went upstairs to the bar on the next terrace, to buy another bottle of wine and some water, to avoid being a third wheel. I couldn't even work out whether Boo was making a play for Carlo or whether she just didn't want another woman soaking up his attention. Nor could I decide if he was flirtatious with every new woman he came across or simply liked the thrill of the chase.

The barmaid who served me was rushed off her feet and had already adopted an 'I can't understand you' expression before I opened my mouth. I lost my confidence and mumbled, thus turning her expectation into reality. Thankfully, the woman behind me in the queue was English and repeated my order loudly over my shoulder.

'Thank you, that was so kind of you. I haven't spoken Italian for so long, I get very flustered. Where did you learn?'

She laughed. 'Oh goodness, I only know the basics, but I do have an Italian boyfriend, so that helps.' With a little puff of pride, she said, 'He's singing next, I think. He's come up from Rome for a few days and I've flown over to meet him.'

'Is singing his job?' I asked.

Something flitted across her face, a wariness. 'He's a busker in the summer and a ski instructor in the winter,' she said.

'Oh how bloody wonderful,' I replied. I realised I meant it, envious of the freedom from the constraints of bosses and meetings and people half your age telling you what to do. I supposed there had to be some downside – no doubt an unstable income was one of them – but it still sounded infinitely better than slogging up to London on the one train out of five that hadn't been cancelled. And with that, we dived straight into the crux of our life stories in that crazy way that sometimes happens with a complete stranger. I hovered behind her as she ordered her drinks, blurting out that I'd intended to come to Italy for a few days to fulfil Lainey's last wishes but had been derailed to Florence. For good measure, I threw in my current predicament about Declan forcing through the house sale.

While the bartender poured her beer, she filled me in on how she'd ended up in Italy. I took to her straightaway. She looked so normal, yet her marriage imploding had sent her scuttling off to Rome to stay with two elderly women who'd put an advert in a magazine for, as I understood it, a middle-aged Brit who'd lost her mojo.

'That took some guts,' I said.

'Best thing I ever did. Made me realise that my husband didn't love me any more and that I could decide not to mould myself to someone else's view of what I should be. Rico – that's my boyfriend, although I feel a bit stupid saying that at my age – lives in the moment. It's early days for us, but I'm trying to take a leaf out of his book and not worry about where it's all going. Just enjoy the here and now.'

As opposed to my myriad ways of overthinking everything. I wasn't sure I'd ever be able to train myself not to do it.

We were in the middle of bonding over our respective failed marriages when Carlo tapped my arm. 'I wondered where you'd got to.'

I gathered up my bottle of wine and introduced him to my new best friend. She put her hand out. 'Beth. Pleased to meet you.'

'She's here with her partner, Rico. He's singing next,' I said, as they shook hands. 'Shall we go down to watch him?' I glanced round. 'Where's Boo?'

Carlo gestured out into the crowd on the level below. 'She's still dancing, but I was beginning to get too hot. Out of practice.'

I wasn't sure of the next steps of continuing an evening after having a really intense conversation with someone I'd just met.

It seemed a bit weird to simply wave goodbye after swapping potted histories of our lives.

Thankfully, Carlo was adept at sweeping people into his warmth without any of the awkward second-guessing that dogged me. 'Are you here on your own, apart from your man? Do you want to join us while he's on stage?'

Beth accepted gratefully and followed us back to our seats. Boo was sitting down, swaying to the music and, by the looks of things, most of the way through the bottle of wine she had clamped between her feet.

We did all the introductions and Boo filled the conversation with wit and fun in that manner of hers that made her a natural people magnet, a central sunshine whose rays bestowed a warmth when she shone upon you. There was a pause in the music and Boo and Beth were nattering away, exchanging anecdotes about Italy. Boo had a way of making sweeping statements presented as fact – 'Mothers always come first for Italian men. No one is ever good enough for their precious sons.'

Beth said, 'I haven't met Rico's mother yet. We're going down to Rome in a couple of days, so fingers crossed.'

Boo bowled in with her advice. 'Well, if he doesn't take your side at his age, it's better to discover that now. You don't want to be stuck in the proverbial "there were three of us in this marriage" scenario, with his mother dominating everything.'

Imagine having the confidence to tell a total stranger how she needed to perceive events. But, then again, it was that confidence that had won me over in Milan, that aura Boo had of being the person with the key to living life fully, impervious to anyone else's opinions.

I was wondering if I needed to rescue Beth when Carlo pulled his chair round so he was sitting opposite me. 'So, are you enjoying the evening?'

'I'm loving it. How could I not? Great music, lovely

atmosphere and perfect weather. I wish I could spend more time here.'

He leant forwards. 'You could. Don't go back. They're crying out for English teachers at the language schools in Florence. You could easily get a job.'

I laughed at the very idea. Someone had to separate and store my stuff. 'I wish.'

He whispered in my ear, his cheek so close, his stubble brushed my skin, 'I wish it too.'

I couldn't mistake the frisson between us. But before I could react, Boo was shaking my shoulder and the moment was over. 'Beth's man has just come on stage. Drink up!'

She knocked back her wine and hurried us all down to the front, where a tall man was saluting the audience with his guitar and saying first in Italian, then in English, 'What's the most important thing to you?' He cupped his hand around his ear. 'Money?' He pointed to someone else in the crowd. 'Your dog? Yeah, I could almost go with that.' 'Being on holiday in Italy?' He nodded. 'Not a bad answer.' 'Your family? Depends on the family!' His eyes were combing the crowd until he reached us and then his whole face broke into a delighted grin. 'Come on, you're teasing me. We all know that the most important thing in the whole world is love...' And with that, he sang 'All You Need is Love' to a roar of appreciation from the crowd, his gaze roaming over the audience but always returning to Beth for the chorus. Every teenager had kidded themselves that their favourite pop star was singing for them alone, but Beth could properly lay claim to that. Rico was one infatuated man if ever I saw one.

He followed that up with a Van Morrison song, 'Brown Eyed Girl', and I didn't want to jump on the love under Italian skies bandwagon, but I couldn't help feeling that Carlo was really staring into my eyes every time Rico belted out the chorus. He grabbed hold of my hands, intending to twirl me round under his arm, an act I always found excruciating. Feeling the centre of attention automatically made me wooden and graceless, and this was no exception. I turned the wrong way, got in a tangle and ended up with his arms encircling me. I twisted around to wriggle away, but he held me, just for a moment, my heart and stomach acting as though they were switching places. He let me go as the music changed to Ed Sheeran's 'Thinking Out Loud'.

Boo grabbed hold of Carlo and pulled him to her. 'Dance with me. It's our song.' Carlo stepped back and held her at a slight distance. Beth adopted a politely blank face as though the dynamics between us were puzzling but she didn't want to get involved in figuring them out.

As Boo sang loudly about lifelong love, I stood next to Beth and focused on Rico's singing. He owned that stage, with the sort of star quality that draws you in and holds you there. Beth was a woman in love. And I both envied the thrill of the journey and pitied her the possibility of pain.

I tapped her arm. 'He's amazing. He really is talented.'

She beamed. 'He's a lovely man as well. Still can't believe it. About this time last year, my husband had recently told me that I was so boring that he wasn't sure he could stand to be married to me any more.'

'Cheeky sod! Still, it's always brilliant to see that life can take an unexpected turn for the better.'

As I talked, I became aware of a fracas between Carlo and Boo in my peripheral vision. I glanced over to see Boo storming away from the concert area. Carlo was standing blinking, as though he wasn't quite sure what had just happened.

We made eye contact. 'Is everything all right?' I mouthed.

He came over. 'I think she's had too much to drink. Are you okay here with Beth for a minute?' he said as he started to thread his way through the crowd.

I turned to Beth. 'Sorry. Don't feel obliged to stay with me. I'm fine on my own.'

But Beth said, 'Don't be silly. I'm grateful not to be hanging around by myself like some desperate groupie.'

We stood watching Rico for another twenty minutes, with bursts of anxiety intermingling with the real pleasure at hearing some of my favourite songs, oldies that my parents had loved and had stood the test of time. I joined Beth in singing my heart out to John Denver's 'Country Roads', Simon and Garfunkel's 'Bridge Over Troubled Water' and finally, the one that had everyone waving lighters above their heads, Neil Diamond's 'Sweet Caroline'. Rico left the stage to huge applause, pausing to make a heart sign with his fingers and to blow a kiss to Beth.

'There's a man who's leaving no one in any doubt about where his heart belongs. I'll say goodbye. I'd better go and see what's happening with my friends,' I said, feeling uncomfortable that I'd somehow involved Beth in the middle-aged equivalent of a teenage drama.

Just as I said that, Carlo appeared beside me, holding up a tear-stained and worse-for-wear Boo. 'I'm going to take her back to the apartment. What do you want to do?'

'I'll come and help you. Sorry, Beth, it's been lovely to meet you. I've really enjoyed your company.'

At that, Boo swung round. 'That's not the only company you've enjoyed, is it? You doing that little-girl-lost act – boohoo – about to be homeless after your horrible husband sold the house. Didn't take you long to start making moves on Carlo, did it?'

I thought I might melt to the floor with mortification. 'I haven't been making moves on Carlo.'

But Boo wasn't having any of it. 'I invited you here to inject a bit of vitality into you, thought you could ride the wave of rebellion and find some independence, but you're one of those women who absolutely has to have a man, aren't you? Even one that belongs to me!'

My hands flew to my face. Carlo was remonstrating with her, trying to calm her down, but she was muttering and swearing and shaking him off.

In the end, Beth stepped forward. 'We can drop Sara back. We're staying in a hotel near Santo Spirito. You take Boo.'

Carlo looked so relieved, as Boo hung off his arm, telling him she was sorry, in a drunken dramatic way that reminded me of sixth-form discos after a George Michael 'Careless Whisper' finale. 'I think that's probably for the best. Sara, ring me if you want to come home earlier and I'll walk up and meet you.'

Rico and Beth insisted I stayed with them for the rest of the evening, even though I said I'd get a taxi. Boo's accusations had shaken me, so I was happy to give the apartment a wide berth for a few hours. I'd clocked that Boo was territorial about Carlo, but I'd never been accused of stealing someone else's boyfriend. Lainey would have found that hilarious. She'd always teased me about my need to play by the rules.

When the evening finally drew to a close, Rico offered me a lift down the hill in his van. 'You'll have to squash in the back with my guitars because I didn't pack some of the delicate stuff so well and Beth's holding it for me on the other front seat – but it's not very far.'

My rule-following came to bite me on the bottom as I said, 'Are you sure you won't get stopped by the police?'

Rico laughed. 'They are not going to care about one little trip. If we see any police, I will throw my coat over you.'

So, forty minutes later, I was kneeling between speakers and guitars, clinging to their seats while they sang to Eric Clapton's 'Wonderful Tonight'. The van bounced over the cobbles as we careered down the hill and I vacillated between monitoring whether there were any police cars in the vicinity and rejoicing that, at my age, life could still surprise me.

Rico pulled up in Piazza Santo Spirito and helped me down.

Beth climbed out to give me a hug. 'What's your mobile number? Let me text you mine. We're heading off to Rome at some point this week, but if you need anything in the meantime, don't be afraid to ask. Rico has got a few bits of business while he's up here, so I'll be glad of the company.'

'You're so kind. I'm hoping to leave for the UK in the next few days, but if that doesn't work out, I'll give you a shout.' There was something gentle and genuine about Beth, which made me think that I would definitely like to see her again.

Rico glanced over his shoulder. 'Isn't that your guy?'

I turned to look. Carlo was striding towards us, and exchanged friendly words with Rico that led to much backslapping and what I suspected amounted to something along the lines of 'What can you do if all the women fall in love with you? It's a burden to bear.'

Eventually, Beth and Rico drove off, and apart from the sound of shutters clattering down as the last pizzeria closed for the night and a few distant shouts and sirens, the square was silent. So silent, in fact, that our footsteps sounded echoing and loud.

I couldn't bear it any longer and said, 'Is Boo all right?'

He gestured to a bench. 'Let's sit here for a moment.'

I sat down, primly, on one end, like a spinster who'd never been alone with a man without a chaperone. Carlo lay down with the back of his head near my legs and I immediately became ridiculously self-conscious about his unflattering view up my nose.

Carlo stretched. 'Sorry about Boo losing it earlier. We had a thing in the sixth form, but it was one of those funny summer affairs, where we'd end up together after parties but weren't actually boyfriend and girlfriend. That was forty-two years ago.'

'So did she come out here thinking you might rekindle something?'

Carlo swung his legs round and sat up. He gestured to himself, laughing. 'Who wouldn't wait for nearly half a century, hanging onto hope?' He ran his hands over his face. 'I love Boo as a friend, but I don't want to go backwards. If Boo and I were ever going to be a thing, we'd be together by now.'

I frowned. 'I don't understand why she invited me along to gooseberry if she thought this was going to be the start of something?'

Carlo rested his head on my shoulder. I caught a waft of shampoo that reminded me of a scent from my childhood. Silvikrin? Timotei? 'Boo is Boo. She loves being that person who does out-of-the-ordinary things, who invites total strangers on crazy journeys with her. She's almost like a dog that greets you at the door with a sock. You were a kind of trophy for her. "Look at me, can't help myself, met this woman who thought she was just popping over to the Ligurian coast for a couple of days and I've persuaded her to go on a wild adventure!" She also views herself as the champion of downtrodden women.'

I bristled at that. I'd had a successful career in journalism, which wasn't an industry for the faint-hearted, even if I'd got a bit lost between bringing up kids and running a household. Did that make me downtrodden? I loved my boys. I didn't begrudge anything I'd missed out on as far as they were concerned. There was a temptation to counter with, 'Well, at least I'm not stuck in a teenage time warp still mooning after a guy I was at school with.' But I kept quiet.

Carlo leant forwards, elbows on his knees, his fingers buried in his hair. 'Boo is very alpha, the bright butterfly that everyone wants to capture. She's very good at sucking up the oxygen in the room – as long as she's got centre stage, she's not terribly fussed about whether it's for good or bad reasons. At school, she pierced her ear with my compass in the middle of a maths lesson. She was always doing stuff like that, didn't care if it got her into trouble.' He shrugged. 'It's part of her appeal. But it can get wearing.'

I tried not to feel that the implication was, 'Unlike you, who could blend into any crowd, the sort of person you have to be reminded that you've met before.'

'Were you annoyed when she said she was turning up with me?'

Carlo leant back. 'I'm used to a houseful of people coming and going. And since Cesca died, it's been good for me to have distractions. And I like you.'

Next to Boo's kaleidoscope personality, I felt as colourful as a great-grandmother peering grimly out of a sepia print. 'Like' didn't equate to 'you've leapt into the list of the top ten people I'd like to have dinner with'.

'It's probably best if I make my own way to Portofino and head home from there. Boo won't want to get up early and you probably need to sort things out with her tomorrow.' The idea of a road trip with Carlo was very appealing but I didn't want my last ever day with Lainey to be overshadowed by a showdown with Boo.

Carlo shook his head. 'No. I said I'd take you and I will.'

He reached for my hand and brought it to his lips. I kept trying to direct my attention elsewhere, to break the moment, but he didn't release my fingers and every time I looked up again, he was staring at me, as though he had all night for me to decide to stare right back. Every rational fibre in my body was pulling at me to leave right now, to resist the feeling that threatened to obscure reason and lead me in a foolhardy direction. I kept saying to myself, *In one minute, I'm going to get up and walk away.* I reminded myself of that day, that humiliating, heartbreaking day, the one I'd learnt from and never again allowed romantic notions to take precedence over rational thought.

And still it wasn't enough to make me stand up.

I surrendered and held his gaze. And somehow, as though I'd answered him, agreeing to whatever he'd telepathically proposed, he gently lowered my hand into my lap and pulled me to him, his lips searching out mine. And with the Santo Spirito church chiming one o'clock, quarter past and then half past, Carlo and I kissed and laughed.

I had the astonishing realisation that even at fifty-seven, it was possible to feel a dizzying cocktail of emotions – fear of making a fool of myself, delight at someone finding me attractive, my whole being melting into the moment. Unlike the many things I'd forgotten, swirling off into the menopausal abyss – poems, recipes, even names of people I knew quite well – how to kiss someone new appeared not to be among them. I could say, with my hand on my thumping heart, that adapting to gentle new lips was still something safely stored in the memory bank. Not that I'd expected ever to need it again, but it was exhilarating to know that it was there, like a back-up twenty quid you'd didn't expect to use, but oh, the bloody relief that it was there in an emergency.

I tried not to let my thoughts wander to the possibility of Boo deciding to venture outside to see where Carlo had got to. Instead, I lay with my head in his lap, staring up at the sky, which sat like a drape of navy velvet over the square, chiffon strips of cloud passing over the moon, tiny stars glittering like strands of Christmas tinsel. His fingers traced my face and I concentrated on not shying away as I imagined his touch snagging on some spiky little whisker that had evaded my tweezers.

'What?' he asked. 'You're tensing away from me.'

'I'm not used to being under such scrutiny.'

'Why not just relax into the gloriousness of this without sabotaging yourself?'

And by telling myself I'd never see him again after this week, I made those moments on that bench count. Finally, reluctantly, I pulled away from Carlo. 'It's a big day tomorrow. We should probably get some sleep.'

If he'd argued, I might have stayed there till dawn, but he followed my lead and we headed inside. To my relief, Boo's snores rattled through the apartment, but despite the mischievous question in Carlo's eyes, I said a firm goodnight, agreed on a nine-thirty start for Portofino and lay in bed wondering what the rules were for casual flings at my age.

Because this could only be a casual fling.

9

The next morning, I was definitely wearing the late night on my face, grateful for my tinted moisturiser and the magic of mascara. I stepped out of the bathroom and walked straight into Carlo. He put his finger to his lips. 'Boo's still fast asleep. Let's get out of here before she wakes up.' He wafted past, a mix of mint and lemon. He beckoned impatiently. 'Come on. *Amor, tosse e fumo, malamente si nascondono.*'

I frowned.

He did a naughty grin. 'Love, a cough and smoke are hard to hide.'

I darted into my room to grab my bag with Lainey's ashes. This whole snogging on a bench in the early hours was fine under the cover of darkness but beyond mortifying in the bright light of day.

As we clicked the door shut behind us, I said, 'I feel bad about leaving Boo behind.'

He waved his hand. 'Boo doesn't do tough days well. Her modus operandi is to steer clear until the dust has settled, then spring up as the post-trauma entertainment team to "take your mind off it".'

I wasn't entirely convinced but I was also unwilling to involve someone who was seething with resentment towards me in a day that meant a lot and that I wouldn't get a second chance at.

Carlo's mobile rang as we crossed the square. 'I'm having a day off today,' he said, dismissing the call. He led me through the streets, chivalrously stepping into the road whenever we had to squeeze past other people but not holding my hand or making any effort to touch me. I thanked my inner prude for not breaking a lifetime's veto on one-night stands.

A little smile twitched at the corner of my lips as I imagined what Lainey's reaction would have been – Lainey, who'd always been rather more fluid with whatever moral code I'd imposed on myself. 'For goodness' sake! What's the point of being on all that HRT if you're going to do the whole "Not tonight, Josephine"? Who knows how many more offers you're going to get between now and meeting your maker?'

We finally arrived at a lock-up not far from his workshop. Inside stood a red open-topped car, the sort of cliché I associated with middle-aged men having a spectacular midlife crisis. His eyes crinkled under those thick lashes. 'I inherited it, okay. And, for the record, there's no correlation between the car and any body parts.'

I made an attempt to tease him back but didn't commit fully to brazening it out and ended up feeling embarrassed and juvenile.

He took the bag from me. 'Let's stow that safely in the footwell.'

Within minutes, we were tearing along the banks of the River Arno before heading up into the hills and onto the superstrada towards Pisa and the coast. The noise of the wind made conversation virtually impossible, which left a lot of time for me to stress about what Carlo might be thinking, though he was singing along quite happily to Radio Cuore. Now and again, a song would come on and he'd say, 'Bring up the lyrics on your phone and put them into Google Translate. Total masterpiece.'

And I'd see what Carlo called 'the Italian greats' – Antonello Venditti and Claudio Baglioni – had to say about love and loss and broken hearts. I did have to accept that the Italians were the masters of nailing the intricacies of love. The gusto with which Carlo sang *'Questo Piccolo Grande Amore'* – This Little Big Love – made me wonder which thoughts, which memories, sat within those words.

I distracted myself gazing at the Ligurian coast – so many gorgeous villas built into the rocks, with spectacular views. Finally, after what felt like hundreds of twists and turns, we ended up within walking distance of Portofino harbour, where Carlo did that brilliant Italian thing of finding a dubious area to park his car and having total confidence that it would still be there when he returned.

He stretched his arms above his head. 'Crikey, I've seized up. Shall we get a coffee?'

I nodded, resisting my usual insistence of disappearing into the back streets to a little local bar rather than the touristy rip-off hotspot with the glorious outlook. Today was Lainey's last moments with me and we were going to milk that panorama for every eye-watering euro.

As though Carlo had read my thoughts, he said, 'It's one of the few places I think it's actually worth blowing a fortune on a coffee. I love this harbour.'

We took our seats under a shady canopy on a terrace over-looking the sea, surrounded by ochre, red and terracotta houses with the quintessential green shutters. Incongruously, sheets and shirts flapped from washing lines against the frescoed walls. Motorboats, snazzy white James Bond-type vessels and fishing boats bobbed in the sea, while the bunting strung round the square flapped in the breeze. Further out, proper rich-people yachts were moored – enormous floating houses with blacked-out windows that immediately made me think of canapés, caviar and corruption. Palm trees sprouted from rooftop terraces and my heart ached with the desire to tap Lainey on the shoulder and say, 'Look where you ended up. No expense spared!'

In between sips of coffee, I told Carlo about how, when I'd come here with Lainey, she had charmed some twenty-year-old into persuading his cousin to invite us onto the yacht where he was a chef. 'We thought we were so glamorous, lounging on the deck, drinking champagne. It never occurred to me to worry about how drunk they were when they suggested a boat trip to San Fruttuoso or if they even knew what they were doing. We weren't wearing any life jackets or anything. It took them ages to get the motorboat started when it was time to come back and we didn't give a hoot about being stranded, just found it hilarious.'

We laughed about the invincibility of youth and how there was surely a sweet spot between not risking a premature death through your own stupidity when you were young, and the temptation to exaggerate the danger in everything when you got older. I checked myself, worrying that my reminiscing about my time with someone he'd never met was boring. When I voiced as much, Carlo shook his head. 'Not at all. I'm not sure I've ever been to San Fruttuoso. It's just round the headland, I think.'

I frowned, trying to remember. 'As far as I'm aware, you couldn't get to it by car. Only by foot, down loads of steps, or boat, as we did. There was a bronze Jesus statue underwater. You could barely see it was there from the surface. We dived down with our goggles.'

'Christ of the Abyss? I read about that. Wasn't it put there in the fifties or sixties as a tribute to a diver who died there?'

'I don't think I ever knew the history, but Lainey absolutely loved it when we went out there that day. She was always fascinated by things that were a bit hidden – little alleyways, secret passages, priest's holes. I used to tease her that she'd read too much of Enid Blyton's Famous Five when she was a kid.'

My voice caught, as I missed – again – the essential elements that made up Lainey. I studied the harbour, suddenly conscious of the finality of what I was about to do but also wondering how to manage it discreetly without attracting an audience. When I mentioned it to Carlo, he grimaced. 'It's really busy, isn't it? Not conducive to a peaceful and private ceremony.'

The waiter put our bill down before we'd even asked for it.

'Do you think we're making the place look untidy?' Carlo asked.

'Probably.' I reached for it. 'This is definitely on me. Thank you for bringing me.'

Carlo smiled. 'It's my pleasure. I'm not going to argue, but thank you.'

I paid and we stood up to leave.

Carlo pointed to a sign that said 'Portofino boats'. 'What if we rented a motorboat and nipped round to San Fruttuoso? You could scatter her ashes by the statue, if you don't mind me being with you?'

'How far is it?' I asked, meaning absolutely not. 'Do you know how to drive one?' My mind immediately leapt to being smashed onto the rocks or running out of fuel and drifting halfway to Corsica. The last thing I needed was to hit the news headlines back home dangling from the ladder of a rescue heli-copter. Though there was a flicker of a lionheart within me that was drawn to the idea of taking Lainey to a place she'd loved.

'I've actually got a licence. My dad had a friend with a holiday house in Suffolk. We often took a motorboat out there. He taught me.'

Before I could express any more reservations, Carlo was off.

The guy who was hiring out the boats seemed satisfied with Carlo's experience and handed over the keys. Carlo signed something, pulled out his wallet and, before I knew it, we'd walked round to a little jetty and were stashing our shoes and jackets.

Carlo was all bravado and confidence. 'We're not heading out on the high seas, Sara. We won't go very far from the coast at all. I'm keeping everything, including the car keys, with me.'

I still wondered how often the coastguard was called out for tourists who'd overestimated their ability.

However, Carlo manoeuvred through the crowded harbour with aplomb, and as we sailed further out to sea, around the headland and past the lighthouse, I felt like a conquering heroine, taking Lainey on an adventure that also fulfilled her exhortation to challenge myself.

'All right?' Carlo asked.

I leant back, the breeze offsetting the searing glare of the sun on my arms. 'Yes, I'd forgotten how peaceful it is out on the water. I wonder how the people who live in Portofino can stand all the visitors. I know they must be a huge source of income, but even so, it must be irritating when you've got things to do and they're blocking those narrow streets with their queues for ice creams and their iPhones.'

'I know. I think the actual population is only about five hundred people.'

I let Carlo concentrate and sat watching the coast: the grey rock with stepped, inhospitable gardens, the villas with their yellow and ochre stripes, painted to look like marble, the church on the top of the cliff without any windows on the sea-facing side. There was something so soothing about the rhythm of the boat over the waves that I forgot to be afraid that I'd somehow move suddenly and capsize us into the deep, clear water.

We floated past a little rocky inlet where a couple of boats were moored and teenagers were pushing each other off the rocks in a way that made me worry about broken necks. 'Not far now,' Carlo said.

And then, suddenly, a much bigger inlet came into view and there was the magnificent San Fruttuoso abbey, its white stone glistening in the sunshine. I didn't remember the incredible majesty of it, the arches below the monastery that rose straight out of the beach, the domed tower showcased against the green forest backdrop. How I'd forgotten, I wasn't sure. Too busy trying to impress the chef and his cousin or fretting about what I looked like in a bikini. If only I'd celebrated that lithe and capable body, without focusing on some imaginary bit of cellulite or millimetre of fat.

Carlo slowed the engine. The harbour was busy, no longer the undiscovered backwater that I remembered from thirty-odd years ago. 'The statue must be over there on the right-hand side. Where the divers' floats are. I'll get as close as I can.'

'I don't want to feel that people are watching me.' I couldn't bear the idea of anyone gawping while I said this most private of goodbyes.

'We've got all day. We can pick our moment.'

I fought against telling Carlo to forget it, to turn around and that I'd just pop Lainey out into the open sea. But I couldn't quite banish the desire to link my last memory of her to that long-ago day when we couldn't imagine a time when we'd be anything other than full of vibrancy. I wanted to connect today to that image of her leaning over the back of the boat, balancing precariously with her stripy red bikini bottom in the air before diving down and swimming towards the statue's outstretched arms.

We puttered over, gliding the last few metres, pushed by the current. We stared into the water, the Christ indistinct, more like a brown molehill from above, with the faintest outline of a head visible from its depth of seventeen metres.

Carlo tapped my arm gently. 'There's no one down there at the moment. I can try to keep the boat steady if you'd like to do it now.'

I recognised the need to get a move on while there was a gap in people with their underwater cameras, snorkellers and boats. I pulled the urn out. Hesitating before I took the lid off, I tried to block out everything else, to forget about Carlo observing me.

From behind, I heard him say gently, 'I'm going to look away now, but a small word of advice, you might want to empty the ashes out under the water or, at least, tip them to the left of you so the wind doesn't catch them.'

Alongside the tears that were jamming up my chest, I felt an absurd desire to laugh at the idea of Lainey blowing back into my face. 'You had one job and you ended up inhaling me!'

I screwed up my eyes, removed the lid and plunged the urn into the sea, watching the ashes swirl around and disappear far too quickly. I knew that whatever I said would feel totally inadequate when I looked back on it, that I'd wish I'd had some deep and philosophical words lined up. But we weren't those friends. We didn't big ourselves up or pretend to be cleverer than we were. We trusted each other with our hearts, allowing each other to see into the pettiest corners of our souls without fear.

I stared down into the sea where I could see tiny pockets of ashes slowly descending towards the statue we'd dived down to. I imagined the Christ figure welcoming her with his open arms and Lainey exhaling a big sigh about finally being released back into the sea she loved.

'Goodbye, darling,' I whispered. 'See you on the other side. Thank you for being such an amazing friend. I'll never not miss you, but I'll also always be glad I knew you.' The tears started to run down my face, but I had to say it, had to make sure she knew I'd be living life for the two of us. 'Even though I'm nowhere near as brave as you, I'm going to inject a bit of your courage into every single day. I might go really wild so that by the time we meet again, you'll barely recognise me. I'm going now, but remember I love you, always have and always will.

Sleep well, Lainey. *Ti amo tanto.*' I sat back and, after a moment, said, 'I'm ready to go now.'

Carlo put his hand on my shoulder. 'Do you want to go ashore here, or head back to Portofino?'

'Shall we just get going?'

All of a sudden, I wanted to be away from here, with the jaunty sun umbrellas on the beach, the queue of people snaking up to the abbey. I wanted to be alone on the wider sea, without the squeals of children reaching me across the water, without the day trippers shouting from boat to boat and paddleboards passing by.

I loved Carlo for doing what I needed him to in that moment. He started the boat and swivelled it round to face the right way. 'Well done,' he said.

I kept my eyes fixed on the spot where I'd left Lainey until we reached the open water, my stomach churning with all that I'd lost, laced with the responsibility of flying the flag for both of us. She would have done a much better job if it had been the other way round.

We barely spoke until we got within spitting distance of the Portofino lighthouse when Carlo said, 'Do you feel like having dinner along the coast somewhere instead of rushing back to Florence?'

'What about Boo?'

I felt rather than saw him shrug. 'What about her? She's intending to stay in Florence for another few weeks. She can manage for one evening on her own – give her time to get over her hangover.'

'I know you're not hurrying me to leave but I really should set off for England tomorrow. It feels a bit rude to stay out till late on my last evening and eat without her, given that she intro-duced me to you in the first place.'

I couldn't bear the thought that Carlo felt that he had to take me to dinner to reassure me that the previous night wasn't merely too much wine and circumstances and some kind of warped pity. It didn't feel that way, but I'd trusted my instincts before and now I'd learnt not to. I couldn't deny though that his demeanour – decisive but not bulldozing – was very enticing. It was as though he could see right into the bits of me I didn't even acknowledge were there, intent on breaking down every objection I cared to raise. Even at my age. When I'd accepted that I'd never feel anything like that again.

We continued past the lighthouse and around the headland without Carlo responding, beyond a bit of a tutting noise. I didn't know who that was aimed at. As we closed in on Portofino harbour, I was cursing myself for my need to do the right thing, to not upset Boo, to not appear ungrateful, ill-mannered, all the many things that always came before *what I wanted*. Finally, we glided to a halt and the hire owner came down to the water to tie up the boat.

'You made it to San Fruttuoso? Good. Very beautiful.'

We collected our stuff and Carlo led me back to the car.

'There's a village along the coast, Zoagli, about half an hour's drive. It's a place for locals and people with holiday homes down from Milan. But much quieter than here. Shall we get something to eat there?'

A wave of tiredness swept over me. I felt empty and starving, but I couldn't tell if it was a hunger born of a lack of food or the hollow of an emotional void. For once, I allowed myself to take the easy option, pushing away my reservations about leaving out Boo. I murmured my agreement and slid into the passenger seat.

10

Then

Dad relented and gave me a lift to the airport as it was Christmas. We'd barely made it to the M25 when he said, 'Do you know what "the sunk cost fallacy" is?'

I sighed. I'd left university with an excellent degree eighteen months ago and had been on a graduate trainee accountancy programme ever since, yet Dad still persisted in trying to catch me out. 'Yes. Thank you.'

'Explain it to me then.'

I felt guilty about leaving my parents on their own for Christmas yet again, so I was more amenable than usual. 'Being reluctant to abandon the wrong course of action because of how heavily you've invested in it?'

His hands gripped the steering wheel more tightly. 'Exactly that. And I can't help feeling that's what you're doing, persisting in this relationship with Alessio. I mean, where do you actually see all of this going? While you've slogged away at uni for four

years, then worked for nearly two more, what's he been doing?
Serving coffee and croissants? You're not a teenager any more.
You've got big decisions ahead of you.'

'Dad, can we just not?'

I felt tears starting to gather. I'd done everything they
wanted. A degree I hated. Taken a job in accountancy that gave
them bragging rights at their stupid dinner parties. I was making
progress in saving up enough money to rent somewhere in
London. But it all came back to this: my dad didn't like Alessio.
On the rare occasions he'd visited England over the last five
years, Dad had grilled him about his plans for the future as
though interviewing for a new registrar. Alessio hadn't tried to
win him over, offering short, sulky responses to my father's questions about whether he planned to stay in Rome. He'd shrug and
reply, 'I don't think so far ahead. Maybe one day I live in
England.' But Dad wanted definitive answers and, although I
would never ever have admitted it to him, increasingly so did I.

The precious ten days I had in Rome over Christmas 1989
were fraught with more than the familiar tension of making
every minute of my short stay count. This visit I was determined
to pin Alessio down to a timeline of when he'd move to England.
Which made it harder to nod politely when his father, Domenico,
came out with sweeping platitudes about the UK. 'Where in the
world do you eat like in Rome?' he'd ask, brandishing a forkful of
fettucine. 'Not in your country. I could never live there. Such
terrible food. Just fish and chips! And your weather. All that
rain.' Alessio's mother muttered under her breath about my lack
of culinary skills more than usual. Usually I smiled and acqui-
esced and tried to ingratiate myself, but now I burned with the
desire to tell them what I really thought about their parochial
little lives. I couldn't wait to set up home with Alessio far away
from everyone who had an opinion on me, on us.

In between times, Alessio and I walked along the Tiber, stopping to buy chestnuts, our faces cold in the damp December air.

We sat kissing in squares ignoring the chill creeping into our bones, relishing the privacy away from his family. The conversations we needed to have were impossible when we were in their vicinity. Whenever we had five minutes to ourselves, they'd interrupt us, calling him down to help in the bar, to unload crates, to run up the road to the baker's for more panini.

Two days before I came home, his mother had a migraine and Alessio had to work all evening, while I sat watching the football in the bar, my smile at the various comments about 'l'inglese' being back again – 'can't stay away from Rome, eh?' – becoming more and more strained.

The next day, we walked around the lake in the Borghese Gardens, huddling out of the wind on a bench near the Greek-styled Temple of Aesculapius. I watched the couples in rowing boats, leaning over to kiss each other, the boats wobbling precariously, laughing with no thought for tomorrow. We'd been like that once.

The words were out of my mouth before I had time to think. 'Do you still want to be with me? Have you told your parents that you're planning to move to England?'

'Of course I still want to be with you! And my parents, they know. My mother, she just doesn't want to admit it.'

'So if I rent somewhere in London, you'll move over and start looking for a job?'

'Yes. I'll move. We agreed.'

I shuffled round on the seat to look him in the eyes. Something had shifted in me. I was sick of working so hard and saving every penny of my salary, refusing so many nights out with my friends. I never deviated from my goal of providing a base for Alessio so he could settle into London. 'You don't sound very enthusiastic. Tell me now if it's not what you want.' I was starting to cry, my tears turning cold on my cheeks.

'I want it, Sara, I want you. But it's hard to leave, difficult for my family with the bar.'

I nodded. 'But we always agreed that I had a much better chance of making enough money in England to be independent without having to beg my parents to help us out. You'll have better opportunities there too. If you stay here, you'll never get away from the bar. In London, you might start as a waiter, but your English will improve really quickly and before you know it, you'll be able to get going on a proper career.'

He sighed. 'I said I'd come.'

That resigned acquiescence was so far from reflecting everything I'd fought for, every compromise I'd made to keep our relationship strong without letting distance destroy it. All the disapproval I'd withstood distilled into a potent torrent of accusation. The constant sniping from my parents, Lainey's irritation that I never wanted to spend money on going out in the evening, that I was never available to go on holiday with her, all came together in a furious outburst.

'Do you know what? I'm doing this so we can have a future together. I'm working in a job I hate so I can earn enough money to rent somewhere for us. But I really can't be bothered to push the great big elephant up the hill while you sit there looking like you've been condemned to a life in purgatory! You stay in Italy and I'll go back to England.' I leapt to my feet, sobbing with frustration, recognising for the first time that this was how our relationship might end. That I might actually face a future without him.

I stormed off through the park, crying so loudly that people were turning to stare, but I was so devastated at this bewildering turn of events that I didn't care. I marched on, past families, past couples, past women cradling their babies, all these people whose lives were simple and straightforward, who hadn't been stupid enough to delude themselves that wanting something badly enough would make it happen. I ended up by the water clock, leaning on the bridge to get my breath, my mind whirling with the prospect of getting off the plane in London and admitting to *my parents that my relationship was over. I dreaded seeing their concern but, even worse, their relief and ill-concealed delight.*

Within minutes, Alessio was at my side, pulling me into his arms.

'No. I can't do this any more. I can't stay stuck in this limbo.' I pushed him away, but he held onto my wrist.

'I love you. I can't be happy without you. At Easter, I will be in England.' He looked down, paused, then whispered, 'But only if you marry me.'

Two days later, instead of bracing myself for my parents' delight that Alessio and I had finally split up, I braced myself for their horror that I'd got engaged.

11

I barely remembered leaving Portofino and jolted awake as Carlo indicated right off the main road and wound his way down the hill to a car park by some tennis courts. He came round to open my door and help me out. 'Okay? After Cesca died, I was physically tired for months. It's your body's way of recuperating. Let's get you something to eat.'

We walked into a pretty square fringed by pastel-coloured houses with more rows of villas above, right up into the hills. There was a down-to-earth charm about it, with sheets, rugs and shirts hanging from washing lines and the *nonna* army chatting on benches while keeping a collective eye on grandchildren pedalling about on tricycles. Useless warnings: '*non ti bagnare!*' were issued as youngsters squealed and played chicken around the fountain.

To one side of the square were huge railway arches, with the beach beyond. 'There's a beautiful walkway carved into the rocks that leads to a viewing platform. I can pop into the *alimentari* and get a picnic,' Carlo said. And as though he knew precisely what I needed, a few minutes later, he arrived with some cold beer, lasagne, focaccia, olives and salami. 'Come on, let's go and find a spot.'

He held out his hand to me and pulled me along, the first prolonged contact that we'd had since we'd sat kissing like teenagers on the bench in Santo Spirito. I'd convinced myself that Carlo was regretting that particular end to the evening and had only driven me to Portofino out of a sense of duty.

We followed the walkway, beyond the stripey blue and white umbrellas, and continued around the coast, past flat rocks sloping down to the clear turquoise sea, where families had made camp for the day. Nostalgia flared within me as I watched a couple of blonde children poke about with their spades in the rock pools. We came to a set of steps leading up to a raised round platform and settled ourselves onto the benches hewn out of rock. We sat surrounded by cliffs and a castle, the air shimmering with so many things that felt important to voice, yet also too big to address in the time I had left.

Carlo set out the picnic, orderly and aesthetically. I teased him. 'It's my silversmith's eye. I like everything to be attractive.' He looked down for a moment, then straight at me.

I wanted to run away from the confusion that Carlo caused. I'd expected that my sole connection with romance would be a maternal crossing of fingers that Callum didn't get dazzled by beauty and boobs and that the universe would steer Finn in the direction of a sensible and capable woman who could appreciate his gentle and easily wounded heart.

Carlo dug into the lasagne, passing me some plastic cutlery. I hesitated, wondering about the etiquette of double-dipping into shared food but reasoned that he'd kissed me so that probably wouldn't worry him too much.

'So, how do you feel?' he asked.

'I feel relieved mainly. And glad her send-off was original. She would have loved arriving by boat and the Jesus statue welcoming her into the water. She adored anything a bit offbeat.

And I think she'd have been happy that I had someone with me to prevent it from becoming a maudlin experience. She was very keen that I celebrated our friendship, rather than, as she put it, "rolling out the misery manifesto to the nth degree".'

'Is that your speciality?' Carlo asked.

'I don't think so. But Lainey was always good at travelling lightly where emotion was concerned. I used to think it was because she didn't have children, wasn't weighed down by that primeval urge to protect, but, probably, she was just better at navigating life with optimism. I must have driven her mad, always fitting our friendship around what my boys needed. She did sometimes agree with Declan that if I didn't make staying at home so comfortable, they might be keener to move out.'

'So you've raised a couple of *mammoni?*'

I frowned.

Carlo elaborated. 'Mummy's boys.'

Oh how I loved the insinuation that because I'd been so invested in my kids, guiding them through life, that was somehow a personality flaw in me. 'Maybe I have, or maybe one-size parenting doesn't fit all and I did the best I could at all times.' A buzz of irritation combined with the toll of today's mental exertion threatened to open the door on a rant that might not easily be contained in a couple of sentences.

Carlo obviously sensed an incoming tantrum as he held his hands up. 'I was only joking. I'm sure you've done a brilliant job.'

With great effort, I folded myself back into my box. 'If we're judging it on how often I feel really worried about my boys, then mediocre at best. Callum's okay – not earning enough money to live in London, keeps getting ditched by girls because he'd rather play football and go down the pub with his mates – but I don't really worry about him. Finn bothers me more. He's much less confident than Callum and more anxious. Also, we've encouraged him into a corporate world because it feels like the only way he'll ever be able to afford a house, but it's not really him. He prefers being outdoor in nature and working with his hands.' I winced as I remembered Declan's disdain when Finn said he wanted to train as a tree surgeon. I should have encouraged him to follow his instincts, not fallen into the trap of believing a university degree was the be all and end all.

Carlo stared out to sea, his eyes narrowing as though he was puzzling over something. 'But he's only twenty-one, isn't he? I don't remember worrying about buying a house at his age.'

'It's come to a bit of a crisis because it's so hard to find a decent place to rent and so expensive that there's no way they can save up for a deposit at the same time. And now the one place he could count on, the family home, is being sold from underneath him.'

Carlo twisted his long fringe around his index finger. 'Why don't you stay in Italy and get him to come and join you out here?'

I tried to keep the exasperation out of my voice. 'None of them will have the first idea about what needs doing before we all move out: reading the meters, redirecting the post, ordering skips. Plus, I should think all the potential viewers will be tripping over underpants on the floor.'

'But that's not up to you. If they're not ashamed of living like that, why should you be embarrassed for them?'

'It's not only that. I've lived there for twenty-seven years, most of my adult life. I can hardly ask Declan to pack up all my clothes and arrange storage for everything.'

'Why not? He didn't ask you when it was convenient to sell the house.'

This whole devil's advocate stance was beginning to annoy me. 'Okay, let's say for the sake of argument, I decide to astound my whole family by shedding my usual control freakery and refusing to capitulate and help move. What then? I've already overstayed my welcome with you, and the money Lainey left me would soon get swallowed up if I stayed in hotels. What would I even do? My Italian isn't good enough to get a job and I probably can't work here anyway.'

'I'm not sweeping you out of the door,' Carlo said.

I tried not to read anything into that.

He took a swig of beer. 'But, really, what's the worst that could happen? Declan sells the house, gets rid of all your stuff, but you still receive your share of the marital pot. You could start again, clean slate.'

I decided to humour Carlo. 'Wouldn't that be lovely? No keeping clothes I've had for years in case I finally locate a wonder diet and can squeeze into my purple dress again. Never having to look at furniture I hate but is too good to throw out. Was pine a thing in Italy? I've got loads of it. Started painting it in lockdown, but no, still awful. I'd go for one-off pieces, vintage or quirky things that you don't see everywhere.'

And once I got started on what I'd be glad to see the back of, it was both funny and (potentially) liberating: Christmas decorations, cool bags, surplus duvets, waffle maker, garden tools that we'd never used – I still wouldn't have known where to start with a hoe.

'Isn't it Sod's law that any decent wedding present gets smashed in the first five years, but the hideous lamp my mum's next-door neighbour gave me has hung on in there, refusing to bow to the passage of time.'

Carlo wiped the crumbs from his mouth. 'I knew I didn't get married for a reason.'

I did a little gasp, worried that I'd offended him. He laughed. 'I had all the best bits of a marriage without the domestic drudge. I liked having my own home to disappear back to, somewhere where I was in charge. Though, now she's not here, I wonder why I didn't make the most of every moment and live with her.'

'And now you've moved into her old flat? Do you feel you

can make it your own or do you want to keep it as it was to remember her?' I pulled a face. 'Is that rude of me to ask?'

'It's a good question.' Carlo's eyes drifted to the horizon. 'I think it's too soon to answer. But if I were a betting man, I would say that if you come back in a few years, that bathroom might have taken on a more streamlined, masculine look. I mean, I love a bit of pink marble as much as the next person, but...'

And we sat, playing a game called Sara's Sad Stuff in a Skip – Footbath! Welly boot stand! Cake tins! Collection of used giftbags! – until an orange light spread across the sky and Carlo leant over and kissed me and tomorrow started to look very close indeed. Thankfully, I was old enough to know there were no magical endings.

'Don't go back,' he said.

My stupid heart leapt at the little thread of hope: that instead of returning to the UK to battle it out over the one frying pan that hadn't been scratched by everyone ignoring my 'Use a wooden spoon!' instruction, I could install myself in Carlo's flat.

'You can stay at my apartment and take the time to think about who you want to be next.'

'Who I want to be next? I didn't know I had to be someone else.' One day, I might be enough for someone just the way I was.

Carlo pulled me towards him. 'Don't get all prickly. We become different people at certain stages of life. Probably our fundamental selves stay the same but what we believe is important shifts. When I was younger, it wasn't enough to win – I worked as an estate agent when I first left school – I wanted to see everyone else lose. Now I'm all about the good karma.' He pinched his thumbs and forefingers together in a mock-meditative pose. 'Though I still love to see a total tosser get his come-uppance.'

'But did you actually stop and say, "I'm going to be like this or that" or was it something that evolved over time?' He made it sound as though it was so easy to shrug off your old persona and reinvent yourself as someone new.

'I came to Italy because I was getting in with an unsavoury crowd – no off button when it came to all the things that your mother really wouldn't want you doing. I didn't admit to any of my friends that I was coming out to study jewellery making. I told my dad that I was taking a course in the history of architecture, some guff about wanting to understand the origins of building so I could follow him into the trade. He was grumpy enough about that. He wouldn't have understood my passion for jewellery. Not masculine enough. My mum knew.' His face softened. 'She had complete faith that I'd be the best jewellery maker that ever walked the streets of Florence, let alone Croydon.' He cleared his throat. 'She knew I was on a bad path and was grasping at any straw that would keep me out of trouble.'

I wanted to ask more, but he turned the conversation back to me.

'So, if you thought about where you see yourself in five years now you've dispensed with Sara's Sad Stuff in a Skip, what does it look like?' He kissed me gently. 'Does a very handsome Anglo-Italian with a command of acid etching and stone setting feature?' He shot his hand out. 'Actually, don't answer that.'

Carlo then sat there expectantly as though twenty favourable outcomes would trip off my tongue.

I blinked, my mind a total blank. 'That's a big question.'

He laced his fingers through mine and brought my hand to his lips. 'But one you should take a moment to work out the answer to. Do you want to live in the same town? Move to the coast? Relocate abroad? Have the security of owning somewhere or the freedom to move at whim?'

I was already shaking my head at that. 'I don't think I'm cut out for life as a rolling stone. I've always envied people who are, though. I'm a bit too attached to my home comforts.'

'Which home comforts?'

I felt my shoulders rise defensively, as though Carlo was making me out to be a woman who couldn't function without a walk-in wardrobe and climate-controlled handbag storage. 'I like my own bed. I need my reading chair. I get stressed when the dirty laundry piles up and I don't have a full fridge. Can't do without a really hot powerful shower. It puts me in a bad mood if I have to stand under a lukewarm dribble. I don't require great luxury, but I have to have decent pillows and clean sheets.' I didn't add that I also hated silly little towels and rubbish kitchen knives.

Carlo nudged me. 'Now you're talking. Is there anything more luxurious than climbing into a bed with freshly laundered sheets?' He loosened his grip on my hand and stretched his arms out above his head. 'So let's recap. You need a decent bed with clean sheets, a shower and a good reading chair, plenty of food and a washing machine.'

'Well, I'm sure there are other things, but yes, they're the main ones.' There must be quite a lot I'd overlooked, given that you couldn't open a cupboard in my house without a whole ton of stuff cascading out.

'What else brings you joy?' he asked.

It sounded a bit lame to say the greater spotted woodpecker on my bird table and the green woodpecker foraging for insects on my lawn. I dressed it up as loving nature – that sounded slightly less anoraky than birdwatching. I told him how I couldn't wait for spring, how I hated being shut inside over the winter and did a little dance when I saw the first daffodils emerging. 'Weirdly, I've come to love physically demanding chores – clearing the gutters, sweeping up leaves, painting fences, chopping back vegetation. Nothing I like more than being let loose with a pair of shears.'

Every time I finished a declaration about what made me happy, I experienced a rush of bashfulness about how small and simple the things that brought me joy were.

Carlo sat back and tilted his head on one side. 'I'm not sure you need as much as you think.'

I was tempted to respond, 'Says the man who clearly didn't turn down a huge flat in the middle of Florence that he was left in someone's will,' but I didn't want to sound churlish. Instead I said, 'I think human beings like certainty. And one of the things I've found very comforting over the years is knowing that, bar a total disaster on the finance front, no one could take our home away from us.'

'Except your husband.'

Resentment at Declan's behaviour and annoyance with Carlo for pointing it out made me wince. 'On that note, we should probably make a move. I'm supposed to be figuring out my journey back to England tomorrow.'

'Come on, you can stay a couple more days. We won't arrive back in Florence till late. Let's just watch the sun go down. The colours of the sky are spectacular over this coast.' He did that look that he was so good at, big beseeching Italian eyes. I laughed and gave in, forcing myself not to be twitchy, to be in the moment. I barely had anything to pack, and anyway my commitment to leaping on a train in the morning was ebbing away.

He put his hand out to take mine. 'Sorry if I stuck my nose in. I just feel like you're on the cusp of living in a completely different way.'

'But what if I don't want to?'

'You already are. How long had it been since you kissed someone other than your husband?'

I knew exactly how long. That Easter, when I was nearly twenty-four. When I couldn't imagine kissing anyone again. Ever. But I wasn't about to go into all that. 'I don't know. Years.

But...' I wanted to curl into a ball rather than say this out loud, 'it's one thing to kiss someone and quite another to throw your whole life up in the air on a whim.'

Carlo was the complete opposite of me, leaning back, laughing at my embarrassment. 'I'm loving kissing you and totally encourage you to throw your life up in the air on a whim. Why not go and buy one of those one-euro properties in a deserted village in Puglia or Sicily?'

I rolled my eyes. 'I wouldn't know where to begin.'

We fell silent. The waves washed over the rocks below, the surfaces glinting in the fading light. Shouts and car horns from the piazza broke into the quiet now and again. We sat watching the rosy orange glow behind the headland, like a promise of hope in a distant universe. And despite my return to England, the house sale, the financial practicalities sitting like greedy vultures in my peripheral vision, Carlo's hand resting in mine kept claiming my focus.

Eventually, the final fragment of light disappeared, leaving us beneath a dark mantle of sky. We sat, with time ticking away, relentlessly. The minutes were scorching through the possibility of whatever this was, this all-encompassing craving to sit so close that the salty damp of the sea air couldn't squeeze in between us. I wanted to stay forever with my back against those sun-warmed rocks, reminding myself that in amongst the loss of Lainey, the mess of my marriage, the precarious future ahead of me, good times could spring up when I wasn't looking for them.

But as the church bells struck ten, we became grown-ups again. Carlo pulled me to my feet and slung his arm around my shoulders. 'We'd better make our way home.'

We'd just gone past La Spezia and were turning inland when my mobile rang. Finn. I would have been hard-pressed to say which came first – the flash of anxiety that Finn was calling so late or the dart of irritation that even on an emotional day like today, I'd have to rise to the challenge of resolving his issues. For once, I wanted to deal with my own troubles – or luxuriate in my own little frisson of romance – without finding a solution for someone else. Bad and selfish mother.

I corralled my voice into something resembling upbeat. 'Hello, love. Everything all right?' I tried not to feel constrained by what Carlo might be thinking about my interactions with Finn and drawing unfavourable *mammone* conclusions.

Finn's voice was leaden. 'I failed my probation period at work.'

'Oh no! Why?'

'My boss said that he didn't think my heart was in component sales and that it's such a competitive market that only people who had "the killer instinct" could make a career out of it.'

'Was he nice about it at least?' My heart was already revving up for a grudgefest.

'Yes, he said it was better for me to find out now than waste years doing something I hated. He said I was a good lad and that I just hadn't found the right niche yet.'

I clambered off my high horse. 'Did he have any suggestions about what that might be?'

'Not really. Sort of gave me the impression that he didn't think fostering client relationships was my thing. Maybe something more practical.'

'What did Dad say?' I tried not to envy the fact that Declan was in situ and he could talk this through with Finn.

'I haven't really spoken to Dad about it. He's a bit stressed about the house and how much he's got to do.'

'Has he said any more about whether there will be room for you in his new place?'

'The thing is, Mum, I don't want to live with Dad because

he's sort of seeing someone. And that would be weird and awkward.'

I felt the shock land and waited for the concurrent pain but could only muster up something akin to regret that we hadn't lasted the distance. I'd anticipated a twinge of jealousy, a dog in a manger reaction, but, disappointingly, after twenty-six years of marriage, I only registered a relief that it would be up to someone else to look interested in Declan relaying how many hours' sleep his Fitbit had registered every morning. All those things I'd never have to feign interest in again. Marvellous.

Finn didn't seem to have any understanding about the impact that his words might have on me and carried on reporting his day, as though his dad moving on to another woman had all the import of a new kettle appearing in the kitchen. 'One thing my boss did say was that if he had his time again, he wouldn't have gone straight from university into a job. That he would have travelled a bit and maybe learnt another language.'

'That's okay if you've got money, but you've still got to live.'

Carlo's head swivelled round as though he was desperate to be party to the whole conversation. I, on the other hand, was fighting to find the selflessness that usually accompanied any interaction with my boys. Right then, I wanted to lean my head on Carlo's shoulder, and make the most of these last moments, without being plunged prematurely into all the chaos that would be waiting patiently for me when I got back to the UK.

'We'll discuss it when I get home, love. I'll be back in the next couple of days, depending on the train connections, as I don't think there are any flights.' Time to bite the bullet and stop letting Carlo tempt me to linger in Florence.

His voice lightened for the first time. 'Dad gave me the impression you weren't coming back for ages, that you'd dumped him with sorting out the house.'

I couldn't hold in a great snort of annoyance. 'Does that

sound like something I'd do? All I wanted was to come out to Italy for a few days and focus on Lainey's last wishes. Dad was the one who couldn't possibly wait another couple of weeks after waiting three bloody years to put the house on the market.' I had to get off the phone before I said something to Finn about the man who was still his father even if he was soon not to be my husband. 'Listen, I can't wait to see you. We'll talk it all through then. Everyone has a few false starts in their careers, love. There's the right thing just round the corner, I promise.'

'Yeah. All right. Bye then.'

'Trouble at home?' Carlo asked.

I filled him in on Finn's work woes, wondering at what age I would stop feeling responsible for my children's happiness. I'd probably be on my deathbed trying to delay my final breath until they'd had a good night's sleep and time for a hearty breakfast.

As we drew into Florence, he pulled over. 'Don't squander this opportunity to break free. The house is on the market, your husband has already got someone else lined up. What are you going back for?'

I couldn't help but feel mortified and also annoyed that Carlo had managed to overhear that.

Carlo carried on. 'Why not hang out in Italy for a while, bring Finn out here? Show him that there's more to life than fitting into a jelly mould of convention – house, job, marriage?'

He made it sound so easy. It probably was if you chose a bohemian existence, filling your house with friends who could party until the early hours on a weeknight. But nowhere near as easy if you were homeless and relying on the goodwill of someone you'd met through a random stranger in a country where you had no network and rudimentary language skills. And that was before I brought Finn into the equation.

I sighed.

Carlo touched my cheek. 'You can think differently, you know.'

'I'm not brave enough.' Suddenly I felt exhausted. 'Anyway, thank you for taking me today. You must be shattered after all that driving.'

Carlo looked at me, opened his mouth, closed it again and turned the key in the ignition. We drove in silence to his garage, deposited the car and then he walked in front of me on the narrow pavement. We didn't speak again until we emerged onto Piazza Santo Spirito. He reached for my hand, his strong fingers squeezing mine in a way that felt as though he wanted to impart something really important.

'There is so much I got wrong, but I have never curtailed any moments when I was just living joyfully. I rode the wave until it blew itself out. So many people will never understand why Cesca and I never married or shared a home together, never had kids. But I had so much love, so much happiness with her. We lived entirely in the moment up until the last few months, never planning, never overthinking anything. We squeezed every positive out of our relationship. Of course, now she's gone, I occasionally wonder if I should have done it differently, but I can't bring myself to regret it at all.'

I wasn't sure of the point he was trying to make. I regretted tons of stuff. Becoming more entrenched and believing in something more passionately because everyone doubted me. Thinking success depended solely on trying harder, instead of stepping back and looking at the bigger picture. Not allowing for a moment that some of the naysayers might only have had my best interests at heart. And a major one in a long line of regrets: marrying Declan because everyone else thought he was right for me. That regret was more complex, though, because without Declan, there would have been no Finn and Callum. I had to believe that the multiple moments of pleasure with them outweighed the flawed framework that had scaffolded my life.

As we approached Carlo's apartment building, the dismay that this had to be my last evening settled on me. It was a ghostly throwback to the years with Alessio, when I was conscious of every hour that passed, time always running out.

Carlo jingled his keys and held my gaze. 'Be bold, Sara. Be bold.'

There was something monumentally annoying about people implying that you were lily-livered. I'd exhausted my courage reserves by walking out on my job. But instead of speaking my mind, I did one of those funny muffled sounds, as though I was vaguely amused. Not everyone could rely on inheriting a fancy apartment in the middle of Florence. Some of us had to do the plodding graft rather than allowing ourselves to be buffeted about, tempting though it was to see where the music might take me.

He pursed his lips as though he was disappointed that I didn't suddenly grab at a plan for a whole new future, then turned the key in the lock. We made our way up to the top floor, our shoes fitting into the hollows on the steps where centuries of feet had walked before. How many worries, how many hopes, how many triumphs and disasters had made their way up these stairs? How many of them had mattered in the end?

But my introspection was cut short by Boo flinging open the door as soon as we reached the landing. 'Oh, the lovebirds have decided to return then? Thanks a lot for waiting for me. Hope you had a lovely day out without me.'

I could hear the thickness in her voice, the flame of rage that she had probably been teasing into a full-blown fury since she woke up this morning.

I tried to apologise. 'Sorry, but you were asleep and I'm going home tomorrow and I still had the ashes to scatter. You didn't really miss much, it wasn't a particularly fun occasion.'

But Boo wasn't having any of it. 'Well, it would have been

nice to have been invited on a day trip with the friend I introduced you to.'

Carlo tried to put his arm around her shoulders. 'Boo, you
were out of it. There's no way you were going to be bouncing
about at nine o'clock this morning after the booze you put away
last night.'

She shrugged him off. 'I phoned you as soon as I heard the
front door shut. You could have waited for me.'

My mind jumped back to Carlo not answering his mobile.

'You'd have been faffing about for ages and we just needed
to go and get the job done,' Carlo said.

Boo's face screwed up. 'Of course you did. Didn't want me
queering the pitch for you. I know exactly what you're like.'

Carlo's shoulders slumped. 'And what am I like?' His voice
was hard and impatient, the tone of someone for whom this sort
of conversation had been repeated with wearying frequency
over the years.

I was an intruder, an unwelcome bystander observing the
unhappy dynamics between the two of them. Boo was so
mercurial, her ability to switch from generous, funny and kind
to hateful and hurtful exposed the coward in me. I slipped past,
heading for my bedroom, with Boo's voice bouncing off the
ancient walls as she harangued Carlo. 'Never had you down as
someone who'd be happy with a people-pleasing sap.'

I should have marched back to push my face in hers and list
all the ways that I rejected her opinion. But instead I scuttled
into my room, exasperated by my need to placate and smooth. I
shut the door, hearing the calm tones of Carlo's low voice
against Boo's shrill statements. I packed my few belongings into
my rucksack, trying not to notice the extra space now I'd finally
laid Lainey to rest. What a day.

My mind tussled with Boo's unpredictability. Far from
being the woman who didn't need anyone, I was under the
impression that she'd been waiting decades for Carlo to realise

that she was his one true love. Boo had that terrifying determination about her that meant she might indeed be capable of biding her time for so long. Her capacity to wound with her words made me feel exposed and vulnerable. As did Carlo's ability to cut through the layers of indifference that I'd been building up over the years, unaware as time passed that not much hurt me, but not much excited me either.

I lay on the bed to work out what was happening with flights. Every possibility had a warning triangle on the website or the word 'Strike/*Sciopero*' in a rolling banner across the top. I sighed at the thought of the long journey home by train. Such a miserable end to what had been a surprisingly uplifting trip, as long as I didn't dwell on leaving Carlo. I would look back on this in a few months' time and smile at how quickly we'd become close, but there'd be no planning to see each other again, no midnight messages. A glorious interlude. End of.

The noise from the sitting room abated and I was just contemplating a dash to the bathroom when my phone pinged. My friend Lynne. More town crier than friend actually, the sort of person who was great company for her entertaining stories about everyone else, but for whom having your back was not her priority.

You didn't tell me you were moving?! This is your house on Rightmove, isn't it?

I clicked on the link. I hadn't expected the listing to go up quite so soon. I cringed at the toilet plunger visible under the bathroom sink, the two-litre bottle of Coke on the sitting-room table, the mop and bucket in the hallway. Beyond our very closest circle of friends, I hadn't spelt out the fact that Declan and I were splitting up, but if Lynne had seen our house on Rightmove, she'd be canvassing local opinion about why we were selling as efficiently as any politician doing a door-to-door charm offensive.

My tired brain scrabbled around to find the words that wouldn't have Lynne trumpeting the demise of my marriage around the interconnected networks that exist in small towns. Mainly invisible but as active as nocturnal animals on the prowl at the scent of gossip that deflects scrutiny from their own lives. Halfway through typing, I slammed the phone down. Let her think what she wanted. Let them all.

12

The next thing I knew, I'd dropped off, trampled into a deep sleep by the stampede of emotions. It was 6 a.m. and I could hear the rumble of the dust carts and the shouts of the refuse collectors in the square. I shuffled off the bed, trying to remember the last time I'd fallen asleep fully dressed. I creaked open the shutters and peered out, marvelling at the stylish refuse collectors, the women with their hair tied back in glossy ponytails, lipstick in place, sweeping along the kerbs with their witches' brooms.

Departure day had finally arrived. And with Boo in such a fury the previous evening, no good was going to come from hanging around. I mustered my resolve and crept into the bathroom to clean my teeth, dithering over whether to have a shower. The clanking of the old pipes would wake everyone up, so I tiptoed towards the kitchen in search of coffee and a sit on that glorious terrace before I dealt with the complicated goodbyes of today. Carlo's door was slightly ajar and I couldn't resist peeping in. My heart lurched as I glimpsed his thatch of dark hair on the pillow next to Boo's grey and white locks. Humiliation coursed through me at the thought of Carlo reassuring Boo:

'She's a lovely person, nice woman, but not my type at all, far too staid and serious.' I had no place with these odd people who lived and loved in a way that was alien to my narrow view of relationships. But hope had been there. Just briefly, I'd had a willingness to open my heart to something that might have been meant for me, that stirred up sensations that I thought were no longer possible.

I turned on my heel, threw on some clothes, picked up my rucksack and slipped out of the door, pausing on the threshold to make peace with the fact that I was walking out, no goodbye. It was better that way. At a distance of thirty-odd years, I'd allowed myself to be duped again. Tears were stinging my eyes as all doubt, any notion of a last-minute U-turn disappeared. However convoluted the journey, I was going home today. It was time for me to close this final chapter.

I walked past Palazzo Pitti, hating myself for not rejoicing in the relative quiet of the morning. The sky looked moody and purple and there was that indefinable scent of autumn in the air that hadn't been there when I'd arrived a fortnight earlier. I paused at the traffic lights, when the heavens opened in a sudden and torrential downpour. A van drew to a halt right in front of me, its windscreen wipers battling to cope with the deluge.

I heard a shout of 'Sara!' and saw Beth, waving out of the window. 'Here, come on, hop in.'

I was already soaked and worrying about whether my passport was getting ruined in my rucksack, so I climbed in.

Rico was rubbing at the windscreen that had misted over. 'This is British weather, not Italian.'

Beth helped me to remove my rucksack. 'Where are you off to at this time of the morning?'

Without going into detail, I explained my need to get to the train station so I could return to England.

Rico gestured outside. 'We'll take you to the station. We are heading down to Rome, thinking to miss the traffic by leaving so early, but the roads will be terrible in this water, so a few minutes doesn't matter.'

I accepted gratefully.

'Where's Carlo?' Beth asked. I briefly summarised how that territory had become a little tricky. I couldn't bring myself to admit that the man who had made me feel so special had slept with someone else so soon after we'd lost hours to mapping each other's faces with our fingers and talking in that soft, intimate way of people who might become lovers. Beth frowned. 'I'm the last person to feel like I have any idea about relationships—'

At this, Rico did one of those complicit smiles and squeezed her hand. Loneliness wrapped itself around me like mist over a moor.

Beth carried on. 'You were in a relationship with him though, right? He definitely has a thing for you. He did not take his eyes off you when you were dancing at the Forte di Belvedere. That man was smitten.'

I shook my head, making a superhuman effort to smother the wobble in my voice that felt as though it might contain an outburst of tears. 'Oh God no, not a relationship. Or anything, really. It's irrelevant anyway. I've got to get back to England. As you know, my husband – well, soon-to-be ex-husband – is selling our house.'

And in a totally un-English way but what I was learning was very Italian, Rico drilled down into the whys and hows and wherefores until somewhere between Ponte alla Carraia and squeezing past the *motorini* in the narrow confines of Via del Moro, Rico said, 'Why you going back to deal with something the husband has decided to do without consulting? In Italy we say, "*Hai voluto la bicicletta? Adesso pedala!* You wanted the bike? Now you pedal!" You have some bed expression for this in English, I think?'

Beth laughed. 'You've made your own bed, now lie in it?'

'Yes! Completely this.' Rico was smiling as though nothing could be simpler.

I slumped against the van door. Everyone else seemed to find it a doddle to walk out of my life.

Rico pulled up outside Santa Maria Novella. 'What if you just didn't?'

I frowned at him. 'Didn't what?'

'Didn't anything. Didn't go home, didn't help with the house, didn't, I don't know, do what people expect of you.'

I sighed. 'It's very tempting, but I don't know anyone apart from Carlo and Boo in Italy and things aren't exactly plain sailing there.' I tried to make light of it. 'No, I've had my quota of fun, duty is calling my name, loud and clear!' I yanked up my rucksack from the footwell and put my hand on the door handle. 'Anyway, it's been lovely to meet you, thank you so much for the lift.'

Beth's hand shot out. 'Don't go. I've got the perfect opportunity for you.'

Rico's face creased with mischief. 'Ronnie and Marina?'

And they both laughed at the names as though there was a joke that I'd missed.

Rico pulled the van forward past the station and parked with two wheels on the pavement, ignoring the half-hearted protests of the few cab drivers that were already waiting for fares. 'Come on. This is our last-minute try to stop you becoming like one of Florence's marble statues and to make your heart beat again like a true *romano*. But I cannot do emotional resuscitation without coffee. There is a little place at the back here where the station workers have breakfast.'

I disappointed them both by insisting on checking the time of the next direct train to Milan. 'Okay, we've got fifty minutes.' I had no intention of missing it, but the idea of warming up with a strong caffe latte and pastry was far more appealing than loitering in a cold station on my own.

Within a few minutes, Beth – whom I put in the same category as me – a normal woman in her fifties not given to doing mad things – was entrancing me with her story about her experience with two Italo-Anglo septuagenarians who ran some kind of refuge for middle-aged women who'd lost their way in life. From what I could gather, the rather quirky hosts set various challenges that were designed to steer these women into rediscovering joy in the world. In some ways, the idea sounded genius but I was still pushing back, knowing that Rome was a no-go, the city that had been the catalyst for the first mistake that led to all the others.

Somehow, though, Beth's simple question of 'What have you got to lose?' overpowered the many reasons I had for not wanting to set foot in the Eternal City ever again. Before I knew it, I was agreeing to let Beth phone Ronnie to see if they could accommodate me at the palazzo. While she scrolled down for her number, Rico assured me that I could stay with them at his friend's place for a bit if Ronnie and Marina didn't have room for me.

'Normally I live with my parents, but you know, it's a lot, being under the same roof as my mother. She will be putting Beth under the microscope. And my friend, Antonio, is a doctor, he is away working in malaria prevention in Africa, so he leaves me his apartment. He won't mind if you stay.'

The offer was exceedingly generous, but given that Beth had only recently been reunited with Rico, that would have been above and beyond.

Rico brushed away my protests. 'Don't worry. There's plenty of space, and Antonio and me, we grew up together. There is trust. And it is more security for him if there are people in and out. Sometimes his sister, Maria, stays there, but she is used to all different people arriving – she won't worry.'

I smiled gratefully while assuring myself that if I did succumb to the madness of going to Rome, I would definitely be checking into a hotel rather than pitching up at a total stranger's flat. I'd done that once already on this trip and it hadn't been a resounding success.

I tried not to listen to Beth's phone call to Ronnie, the seventy-five-year-old owner of the apartment block where this weird and wonderful 'rejuvenation of women of a certain age' took place. However, within minutes, she'd come up trumps and was hell-bent on persuading me to stay with two old biddies as a guinea pig for their 'restoration' project as though I was a pile of crumbly old columns requiring a community whip-round. Though, actually, that didn't feel so far from the truth.

I made a last-ditch attempt to hang onto some kind of sanity and sense of responsibility. However, Rico finally persuaded me with his simple philosophy of 'When I feel obliged to do something that doesn't bring joy, I wait, sometimes for days, if there is no urgency, like someone dying or a fire burning, until the necessity passes. Often, if you decide not to do anything, the thing disappears on its own. And the less you have – houses, cars, stuff – the easier that is.'

I'd already picked up on the fact that Rico was fairly nomadic, which didn't seem an immediate fit for Beth, who, as far as I could see, was hewn out of a similar motherhood rock to me – a natural worrier, fixer and provider. But she had all the air of living her best life, as though she'd entrusted her lot to the universe and had faith in herself that she'd either get it right or have a monumental amount of fun failing.

Forty-five minutes later, I was texting Declan as Rico swung the van round and made for the motorway.

Decided to stay in Italy for the foreseeable. Will get Finn to set aside a few things for me, so take what you want and either stick the rest in storage or dump it if I'm not back in time. Good luck with it all.

Then I switched my phone off, giddy with recklessness and daring.

13

As we reached the outskirts of Rome, I was struggling to cling onto the wild abandon that I'd experienced three hours earlier. This jaunt was an aberration of judgement and caution I could only put down to grief, lovesickness and lack of sleep as well as a substantial element of 'Up yours', which after so many years of 'Better not' did have a certain cachet. I stared out of the window, steeling myself against an onslaught of memories that were better left buried. Thankfully, though, we were on the opposite side of the river to the one I was so familiar with.

Suddenly, Rico was driving through some huge gates and Beth was shuffling past me, leaping out of the van into the sunshine that had accompanied us as soon as we'd got south of Orvieto. Rico leant over to me and said, 'They are really nice people. Marina is terrifying, but she is like a big barking dog who marks her territory. Throw her a biscuit, and she will rest her head on your knee.'

Beth was flinging her arms around a woman in floaty purple dungarees that matched the bright tips on her grey hair. But this was no purple-rinse granny. This was a woman who'd taken one look at old age and decided to dominate it. A miniature Schnauzer was dancing around, scrabbling at Beth's legs.

Rico and I clambered down from the van and Beth introduced me to Ronnie, who couldn't have been further away from the 'old biddy' I had envisaged. If she was perturbed by my last-minute arrival, she showed no sign of it. Her handshake was firm, and her bright blue eyes were curious and assessing.

Beth said, 'Right, we'll get off. Ronnie, you work your magic on Sara. If you can fix me, you can fix anyone.'

And with that, my lifeline, my anchor, gave Ronnie a hug and hopped back into the van. Rico took Ronnie's hand and kissed it theatrically.

'Go on with you and your flannel. You make sure you look after Beth and don't mess her around,' she said.

Rico clutched his chest. 'The woman has my heart. You too, of course!'

A swift conversation followed in whispered Italian, during which Rico kept glancing at me. I also got the impression that Ronnie was talking about me but had cunningly perfected the art of keeping her gaze directed away from the person she was discussing. And with that, he sauntered away, his cheesy comments managing to sound sincere in a way that only an Italian could pull off.

I bent down to stroke the dog, to give myself a moment before I had to meet Ronnie's eye. Having to voice out loud – as surely I would have to – the reasons a middle-aged mother would throw herself on the mercy of complete strangers in a foreign country made this escapade seem less like courageous spontaneity and more like utter madness. I longed to chase after Rico's van as Beth shouted out of the window that she would call me in a couple of days, waving until they were out of sight.

I immediately turned to Ronnie and apologised for dropping on her at short notice and that if she'd felt bamboozled into having me, it wasn't a problem and I'd go into a hotel before heading back to the UK.

She put her hand up. 'The first thing you need to know about being here is that I, and my friend Marina, who lives on the top floor, have reached a stage of life where we don't do things to meet other people's expectations, only our own. And Strega's,' she said, pointing to the dog. 'But you've made friends with her already. So if I say it's fine for you to be here, it is. And I trust Beth's judgement. There's no way she would dare send me trouble.'

I couldn't see whether she was joking or not as she set off towards steps that led up to the sort of front door that looked as though it had been built to keep out marauding intruders in ancient times. I followed, her words making me feel both intimidated and reassured. I caught a little bit of a south-west country accent as she spoke, which reminded me of summer holidays in Cornwall with the boys. The memory produced a hollow longing in me for those innocent, predictable times.

She beckoned to me. 'Come. Let's get you settled. Then I'll introduce you to Marina and we'll work out a plan for you.' She pointed out her own apartment, then continued along the corridor and unlocked another door. It led into the sort of place that would be top of every Airbnb wish list. I was so flustered by the generosity and luxury of it all that I almost wanted to refuse to stay, struggling to find anything approaching the right words of thanks. 'My daughter was here until recently with my granddaughter, so everything is in working order.'

I pounced upon our common ground as mothers. 'How old are your daughter and granddaughter?'

'My daughter, Nadia, is in her forties, but Flora is just coming up to three months old. Nadia gave birth to Flora here but wanted to bring her up in England.' She did a dismissive wave of the hand, indicating the closure of that topic of conversation. I tucked away the knowledge to tread carefully around what was obviously a sore point. 'Why don't you freshen up and I'll call Marina down when you're ready?'

I hoped 'freshen up' wasn't a euphemism for 'give yourself a good old wash because you stink'. I showered, changed into clothes that were at least dry and knocked on Ronnie's door half an hour later. She came out into the corridor with a huge bell, the sort I remembered the teacher on duty ringing at the end of playtime when I was at school. 'I can't shout up for her any more – I don't know why, age seems to reduce one's volume. And I'm not doing all those stairs unnecessarily, so I've started using the bell. She hates it, but she can't bring herself to ignore me in case she misses out on something – she's such a nosey woman.'

I wondered about the exact nature of the friendship between them. I couldn't work out whether Ronnie was bitching about Marina behind her back in an underhand way or whether they were at that rare point of friendship where they said brutal home truths to each other's faces and no one took offence. I quickly discovered the latter was the case. Marina appeared at the top of the flight of stairs, a haughty vision in a silk blouse and palazzo pants, with her dark hair secured in a loose bun. She waved her walking stick at Ronnie. 'Why are you ringing that stupid bell? You have a phone. Pick that up.'

'I'm economising. It's an era of austerity at Villa Alba,' Ronnie said.

Marina looked outraged. 'Not for me, it isn't. Please don't be telling me that you are cutting back on Prosecco.'

'I'm not economising on essentials.'

Ronnie seemed to magic up a fabulous lunch from nowhere. Her panzanella salad firmly established in my mind that capers weren't odd things that sat in the cupboard for ten years before getting tossed out but essential ingredients in the first and best tomato and stale bread combo I'd ever eaten. The asparagus frittata she knocked up risked making me look greedy.

As we ate, Marina winkled my story out of me. 'Three years and you're still living in the same house as someone you're divorcing?' She said it with such incredulity that I blushed, though goodness knows why she tapped into my shame around it all when close friends of mine had said the same. She clapped her hands when I told her that I'd left Declan to sell and pack up the house on his own and said, 'A pity that he will now discover where the mop, ironing board and washing machine reside just as he leaves. Payback time.' She patted Ronnie on the arm. 'So, we have to make sure that Sara enjoys Rome so much that she isn't tempted to go back and help.' She raised her eyebrows. 'You could be our easiest experiment yet.'

Ronnie tutted. 'Sara's not an experiment. She is a guest whom we are guiding to live her life to the full.'

Marina made a dismissive sound. 'Well, whatever. We've had two successes and I'm not going to allow Sara to spoil our hat-trick.' Her eyes narrowed. 'I think you're a woman who likes stability though. All this not moving out once you've decided to split up. That suggests a certain cautiousness. You'd better not let us down by rushing back to search for a new house. You have to trust that when the time comes, the right place will find you.'

This woman scared the bejesus out of me. I'd only been in her company for an hour and it was as though she could peer into my mind. She'd already identified the fears that were gathering like a gaggle of geese, honking away and distorting my determination to go with the flow.

I must have looked beseechingly at Ronnie, because she handed me a Baci chocolate and said, 'That's easy for Marina to say when she's lived here for twenty years and knows I'll never evict her. But there is a lot of merit in wiping the slate clean. I only brought a suitcase of clothes with me when I first came to Italy. Left everything. And it was frightening but also amazingly liberating. The really important stuff we carry here.' She tapped the side of her head. 'We don't need to clutter ourselves up with mementoes. When I die, I don't want my daughter to weigh herself down thinking she has to keep all these things.' She indicated her beautiful ceramic dishes, the colour of jewels in red and turquoise and sunflower yellow. 'If she loves them, fine. But if she fills her house with them out of guilt for no better reason than "they belonged to my mother", I hope she smashes them into pieces and uses them for drainage at the bottom of her pots.'

I admired the triumph of practicality over sentimentality.

Marina stood up abruptly with an accompanying groan. 'How long are you staying for?'

I wanted to die of embarrassment. 'I'm not sure. Obviously, I don't want to overstay my welcome...' I trailed off in a haze of mortification.

Marina had no truck with my mealy-mouthed mutterings. 'The thing is, Sara, to get the most out of your stay here, you have to give yourself time to change. In your case, I think we are all agreed that means adjusting to living with uncertainty – or, as I prefer to see it, embracing every opportunity that you haven't yet identified.'

Marina's idea of us 'all agreeing' definitely followed the lines of dictatorship, even if it was benign.

Ronnie flapped her hand at her. 'Stop being such a bulldozer.'

'Che bulldozer?' Marina said, doing that Italian hand gesture of 'what are you on about?' that I usually loved when it didn't form part of a discussion about me.

Ronnie's voice took on the tone of someone who had played the intermediary many times before. 'Let me explain, Sara. So, usually, we stipulate a minimum of ten weeks, maybe twelve. But, obviously, our two previous guests, Beth and Annie, had time to plan their decision to come, rather than tipping up on the spur of the moment. So I suggest you commit to two weeks, which will take you up to the beginning of October, with the option of staying for a further two months – or whatever time you are allowed under Brexit?'

I must have looked terrified. A further two months! Anything could have happened by then. The house might be sold. Although I'd loved flirting with the idea of wanging all my stuff in a skip when I was sitting talking figuratively with Carlo, I didn't really believe that I would follow through.

But today, after being on the move so early, I didn't have the energy to debate all that. 'Two weeks would be a great start.' I could just about contemplate the next fourteen days, reassuring myself that a fortnight wouldn't make a significant difference to anything on the house front.

Marina said something in a flurry of disgruntled Italian, leading Ronnie to make a calming motion with her hands. 'Right, first up for your challenges, as it might inspire you to abandon everything you own, is a visit to Basilica di San Lorenzo Fuori Le Mura – St Lawrence's church.'

Marina tapped the tiles with her stick. 'There's a man who never worried about the consequences. He gave away all the church's wealth to the poor and was roasted over an open fire for his troubles.'

Ronnie interrupted. 'Legend has it that when he was dying, he was still defiant and told them to turn him over on the grill, he was done on that side.'

These women seemed to take pleasure in the macabre. It didn't seem like the right time to tell them that when I was home alone, I was such a wuss that I didn't dare watch anything more demanding than *The Durrells* in case there was a creepy scene that kept me awake at night. I hoped these 'challenges' wouldn't mean I had to do anything weird such as hang out in a graveyard after dark.

Ronnie must have seen the dubious look on my face and took pity on me. 'It's actually a beautiful, simple church. You'll love it. I want you to go and visit it and tell me why you think we sent you there.'

I nodded uncertainly. I might as well gather up some great stories to recount. Two more weeks here would make nearly a month away in total. Long enough to make the point to Declan that he no longer called the shots but still time to have a modicum of control over the moving process.

14

I slept astonishingly well, having resisted the temptation to switch on my mobile the day before. I stood on the terrace, forgetting my bizarre circumstances for a moment as I looked at the Vatican. But the need to know what was happening back in the UK was too great. My screen flickered into life and with it, WhatsApp messages clamoured like puppies pawing at their mother.

Declan, Finn, Callum, Beth. I could tell from the first line of Declan's that his words weren't going to enhance my day. I scrolled down to Finn's message, which followed five missed calls.

When are you coming home? Dad is telling Callum and me to start looking for somewhere together because he's renting a studio flat while he works out where he wants to live – says he can't afford anything bigger for the moment because you're taking him to the cleaners so he has to conserve every last penny.

Followed by a shocked face emoji.

I texted a holding reply to Finn along the lines of 'Don't worry, you won't be homeless, will be in touch very soon,' then cut and pasted the same answer to Callum after skimming his complaints about how he couldn't find anything in Clapham within his budget. I ignored Declan's missive and read Beth's message, which delighted me with the suggestion of meeting for coffee that afternoon. I didn't dare disappoint Ronnie and Marina by not soaking up all the wisdom that St Lawrence had to offer, so I asked if we could meet about four. In return, I received an enthusiastic thumbs up and a Google link to a bar in Trastevere.

I hurried off to the Roma San Pietro station, and managed to figure out tickets and trains and get myself to Roma Tiburtina. At Ronnie's suggestion: 'Nothing like seeing all those graves to give you a kick up the backside to make the most of the here and now', I took a detour through the huge Verano cemetery.

Marina had flung her head back. 'Madonna! You and your obsession with cemeteries! We'll be in one ourselves perma-nently soon enough.'

But Ronnie had explained that there was a glorious peace about graveyards that enabled you to ponder what is important. As I wandered through the headstones, enjoying the tranquil-lity after the chaos of the city, I registered the sense of slowing down without dashing on to the next thing. I lingered in front of the walls of inscriptions, dotted with glass-fronted cabinets containing photos of seven or eight members of the same family. There was something so comforting about all the generations being together, watching over each other.

Conscious of my coffee date with Beth, I left behind the family mausoleums and Monteverde's angel sculptures leaning with an air of expectation, as though keeping guard over their charges until someone came to relieve them of their duties. Beyond the cemetery stood the church of San Lorenzo Fuori Le Mura. I crept inside, apologetically, as though anyone watching would recognise me as a fair-weather believer. I was a woman who resorted to prayer in times of emergency, then tapered off into a general 'doing unto others' commitment once the urgency had faded. But no one was taking any notice of me at all.

I smiled at the karma of that, recalling the amount of times I'd tried to reassure Finn with my 'Don't take this the wrong way, love, but everyone is too busy thinking about themselves to give what you said or did any thought.'

I wandered over to the candles and lit one for Callum. 'Please let him find a lovely strong and patient girlfriend who can see through his bluster and tap into his kind heart.' I lit another for Finn. 'Please let him find his place in the world so everything becomes less of a struggle. Help him appreciate all his wonderful qualities – how sensitive he is, how perceptive, how thoughtful. All the things that the school system doesn't measure but that are much more important than exams.' I stopped at that point, deciding that it wasn't fair to subject God to my views on the education system.

I never really knew what to do in churches. It seemed sacrilegious to wander about like a tourist, gawping at tombs and treasures, while people were trying to say their prayers in peace. In the end, I opted for taking a seat in a pew and admiring the mosaics on the floor, and the two storeys of pillars, without distracting anyone.

The silence was conducive to allowing my thoughts to drift. It was so rare to have time to sit without either internet noise – social media shouting about everything, from which politician was responsible for the mess we were in to inciting opinions on how to dunk a digestive biscuit correctly – or actual noise. Despite my best intentions, my mind quickly turned towards problems to solve rather than joys to embrace.

Now I was here, now I'd told Declan to take what he wanted from the house, I was still quite some way from feeling liberated from the responsibility of worldly goods. Instead, although the list of things I wanted to keep was pleasingly small, I had bursts of fretfulness about my photo albums and my scrappy copy of 'Desiderata' that I'd had on my wall throughout university. It meant more to me than any of our non-descript landscape paintings that could have been any old village in the UK.

I'd ask Finn to drop the few things I really wanted round to my friend Cheryl. It was astonishing to me that my brain kept flitting to stupid belongings that I suddenly remembered. The Humpty Dumpty eggcups that the boys loved when they were little. I shouldn't think anyone in our house had had a boiled egg in fifteen years. My huge Le Creuset crockpot, holder of many hearty stews and mother love contained within those patiently chopped vegetables. The cardboard box that contained a lock from the boys' first haircuts, their first teeth, their tiny baby-gros and toddler shoes. This was where I struggled, when I recognised the futility of holding onto stuff that was essentially clutter, yet it felt almost disrespectful to bin it. Who had ever needed a lock of hair or a rotting old baby tooth? Yet on the rare occasion I stumbled across those tokens of the passage of time, maybe once every five years, I stroked and sniffed them like precious access to a time-travelling machine.

I stood up. If good old San Lorenzo could bequeath everything to the poor and needy and still find the chutzpah for a little quip about being roasted alive, I could survive without an eggcup and doll-sized shoes. I blanked the image of Declan chucking it all in a skip without even realising their significance.

I wandered back through the cemetery, this time pausing on a bench as my phone buzzed in my back pocket. The seven WhatsApp messages broke my resolve not to read what Declan had to say. My stomach lurched as I saw that the estate agent had received a cash offer for the house, five thousand less than the asking price but wanting to complete within six weeks.

*So you really NEED to come home, help me sort things out
and stop being so CHILDISH. Rental properties are in short
supply so you'd better start looking sooner rather than later –
I've had to pay a premium just to get a studio flat, and they are
easier to find than a place with two bedrooms, as I assume
you'll be taking Finn with you, given that he's made precious
little effort to find an alternative.*

I focused my eyes on the tops of the cypress trees swaying in
the autumn breeze. Annoyingly, Carlo's voice popped into my
head. 'He's obviously a man who likes to get his own way and
now he's trying to force you into toeing the line. You can always
choose not to.'

In some ways, it *was* childish of me to resist. But that rage
that he'd considered his own needs, then delegated making sure
Finn was okay to me, scorched through me as though I'd acci-
dently eaten a whole Scotch bonnet. I'd had more than two
decades of Declan paying loud and public lip service to the
importance of family, our 'special unit', how no one lay on their
deathbed counting their cash but rather summed up their
success by how loved they were. Yet when it came to it, he
always did what suited him. He absolved himself from exam-
ining whether his behaviour had affected our chances of
survival by repeating a simplistic notion that marriage was a
lottery; sometimes you grew together and sometimes you drifted
apart. However, as much as I fought against it, I also had to
accept the role I had to play: meekly surrendering to everyone
else's view from the get-go that Declan was the man for me.

As I walked towards the exit of the cemetery, I felt certainty
cascade, as though all the cherries had lined up on a slot
machine and released a payload. With a rush of rebellion, I said
out loud – quietly, but still firmly enough to make a commitment to myself – 'I will be available to help when it suits me to
return from Italy and not a moment sooner. I don't care whether

we sell to this cash buyer or not, because I am not in a hurry and do not feel obliged to follow your timeline.'

I did a quick calculation in my head. If I stayed until the very last day that my visa allowed, Declan would have to wait until the beginning of December for any assistance from me. And with that, I took the train to Trastevere, delighted at the prospect of having a friend, even one I barely knew, with whom I could practise this revamped kick-ass version of myself. I hadn't always been a doormat; it was a mantle that had slowly enveloped me over the years. I'd mistakenly believed that the best way to give my boys a stable upbringing was to manage everything myself, rather than to insist that Declan shared the load. But I still wasn't sure it was possible to force someone to take responsibility in a way that made you grow together rather than resentfully driving you apart. Especially if you'd chosen that person to please everyone else in the first place.

As I came into a square, I saw Beth sitting at one of those little wine bars that you dream of stumbling across – bougainvillea climbing up the walls, old oak barrels doubling up as tables, locals gesticulating and laughing and talking over each other, giving new meaning to the word 'vibrant'.

Beth waved and, in that one instant, any lingering doubts darted away. In case the opportunity didn't present itself again, I was going to milk my time here for everything it could offer, gathering up new experiences like autumn apples.

Beth flung her arms around me with an enthusiasm that reminded me of Lainey's exuberance and warmth. 'So, tell me all. Have you had to do a challenge yet?'

15

I told Beth where I'd been and sought her advice on what Ronnie was expecting me to get out of it – 'She just wants you to see the world differently. My guess is that she's hoping you understand that even if you give away everything you own, your value isn't in your worldly goods, it's in the strength of your heart.' She laughed. 'That sounds a bit profound, doesn't it? Rome does that to you.' She told me about her challenges and her frustrations with Marina. 'My goodness, that woman has opinions.' We had a good giggle about how scary she was. 'Kudos to her that she can still rule the roost at her age.'

I leant forward as though I was exchanging confidences with a woman I'd known since childhood rather than someone I'd spent less than twenty-four hours with. It was extraordinary how I felt as though I could say anything to her, without judgement, as though having husbands who'd disappointed us and ending up in Italy meant we could skip several layers of friendship building. There was a sense of diving straight into the deep recesses of our thoughts without having to go through all the 'how do you take your tea?' first.

'Am I mad not to rush back and fight for my share of the

Wedgwood dinner service?' I asked.

Beth shook her head. 'Have you decided what you're going to do in terms of buying somewhere else?'

I shrugged. 'That's part of the problem. Every time I go on Rightmove to see what I might be able to get for my budget, I feel depressed. A modern box in the middle of an industrial estate if I'm lucky. I keep getting distracted with totally impractical places like rambling run-down mansions on the Galician coast, or a Sicilian farmhouse without a roof but with amazing sea views.'

Beth grabbed my arm in enthusiastic solidarity with my impractical daydreaming. 'Oh my life, I know exactly what you mean! We're in the process of selling my marital home at the moment and every time I think, right, I must buy a sensible two-bedroomed flat in Purley with a garden the size of a pinhead, I find myself hankering after a tumbledown barn in Puglia with no running water but a verandah jutting out over the sea.'

We spent a happy half an hour discussing which houses we'd seen and where and guffawing about how ridiculous it would be to buy them. However, we couldn't quite let go of the idea that we might just wake up one day, press the button and find ourselves owning a wreck that no one had lived in for thirty years.

A bit shyly, in case I was overstepping the familiarity boundaries, I asked Beth if she had any plans to move to Italy. She wrinkled up her face. 'It's such early days. I only met Rico five months ago and I wasn't clear that I'd given up on my marriage, so we only really got our act together a couple of days before I was leaving Ronnie's.' But she couldn't disguise that glow that people exude when their hearts are filled up with love and they want to talk about the other person ad nauseam. She glanced down. 'He is lovely though, and whenever I'm in Italy, I get this conviction that I'm doing exactly what I should be doing *now*, that it doesn't matter that I don't have the next steps carved in stone. For the first time in so long, I'm just seeing where it all takes me. I mean, obviously, after being married to a man who works in finance, it's a bit of a culture shock to be hanging out with a guy who sings on the streets.'

I did that whole thing of arranging my face to look like I wouldn't find that a problem, as though worrying about anything as parochial as pensions and savings would be so square and narrow-minded. In reality, I envied her devil-may-care attitude and wondered if I could ever think like her.

Beth finished her coffee. 'It's a bit odd living in his friend's house – it's like being a student, but with better crockery and bed linen. Rico says I have to change my mindset and stop worrying about anything being permanent. It's so alien though. I've spent all my life working to own a house, a car, a right to privacy. It's weird to be getting up in the morning and sharing a kitchen with Antonio's sister, though she's very nice. I guess the alternative would be worse, if we had to stay with his parents. I'm not sure I could face the whole Italian *mamma* experience – can you imagine saying goodnight and feeling awkward about going up to bed with her son at my age? I'm a bit old for all that creeping about.'

We laughed as Beth did an impression of an Italian mother knocking on the door if the sex got noisy.

Then she said, 'On that note, have you heard from Carlo?'

'He's called me several times, but I haven't answered.'

'Why not? I thought you really liked each other.'

I remembered too late that I hadn't told Beth what I'd seen that last morning. But her face was so kind and understanding, I blurted it all out. 'He keeps messaging me, but I'm just deleting them without opening them. I can tell from the first lines, which all say something like "What happened? Why did you run off like that? What have I done?" that it's going to be a whole pile of excuses and I can't let myself get suckered in. I've got enough going on already.'

I still felt winded by how much I'd grown to like Carlo in such a short time. I thought I'd experienced enough shoddy behaviour not to be shocked by anything, but I was so disappointed in him, so taken for a fool. Just revisiting that image of their heads side by side in Carlo's bed produced a fresh flurry of humiliation and hurt.

Beth frowned. 'I never will understand the way men's minds work. When we were at the Forte di Belvedere, he only had eyes for you.'

'I think that was a "for one night only" kind of deal.' I didn't want to sit in her pity or sympathy for a moment longer. 'I'd better get back – now you've told me about Marina's love of fashion and style, I'm feeling that at the very least I need to put some make-up on before I report on my day.'

Beth hugged me. 'Let Rome do its work. It fixed me. Let's meet again in a few days if you're happy to?'

I reminded myself that Boo had seemed like such a great person when I first met her and she'd turned out to have 'hidden depths'. However, there was something so appealing about Beth. She wasn't pretending that she had all the answers – but she possessed a beguiling combination of vulnerability, humour and drive that made me want to spend time in her company. 'I'd love that.'

She pulled a face. 'I'll have met Rico's parents by then, so I'll be able to offer up a full account of whether the matriarch is anywhere near as scary as I'm dreading. Honestly, it's ridiculous to be terrified of someone who's only twelve years older than me. But obviously that's part of the problem – I'm not exactly ideal daughter-in-law material.'

I reassured her that once Rico's mother saw how happy they were, she'd come round, though I wasn't sure I necessarily believed my words. 'Anyone would be delighted to have you as a daughter-in-law.'

Beth sighed. 'I'm probably getting a bit ahead of myself...

Long term for Rico is the next three or four months. I'm trying so hard not to be that woman who says, "But where do you see this all leading?" when the now is so good. But it's like attempting to unlearn a whole lifetime of planning for the future. I was paying into a pension by the time I was twenty-four. Rico has to go out and sing a few more songs so he can take me for dinner on a Friday night.'

I admired her so much for even contemplating such a hand-to-mouth existence. We were similar in so many ways, yet here was Beth resolutely experimenting with an entirely different way of living. I could learn from her.

We parted, promising to catch up later on in the week and I walked to the river, running my hand along the stone wall that bordered it. I wondered how many couples had snuggled up together there or leant over it, watching the lights reflected on the water. How many had felt that indescribable spark of hope that the person next to them was strong enough and good enough and worthy enough to be the one? Not just for this evening, this week, this season, but when summer turned into winter, when the clouds rolled in and they had to batten down the hatches and wait for good times to come again? Love was flimsier than I'd hoped and more disappointing than I'd imagined.

I attempted to estimate how many bridges stood between me and Ponte Regina Margherita, the nearest one to Piazza del Popolo. The place I'd designated a no-go zone in my head. Five, maybe six. I dared not let myself wander north on that side of the river in case temptation to poke the wasp's nest over-whelmed me. I breathed out, loudly, trying to expel all the negativity that had crept in. I didn't want anything to stop me revelling in Rome, or worse, to anchor me in a doom-laden spiral about the years I'd wasted.

Below me, a group of joggers was moving steadily along the banks of the Tiber, with the sure-footedness of knowing their

young bodies would do what was needed. The confidence of
trusting their legs not to buckle or pull for no reason, an out-of-
the-blue injury that would never heal properly, simply
becoming another thing that they would learn to accommodate.

I crossed the Ponte Cestio, arriving at the Isola Tiberina, a
little island in the middle of the river. I carried on past a restaurant where people sat with their aperitivi in the autumn sun,
which still held plenty of heat. What a privilege to leave work
and take for granted the opportunity to sit in the middle of a
river in Rome, surrounded by architectural beauty in all directions. A medieval tower stood to my right, then another bridge,
the Ponte Fabricio. I paused in the middle of it, not quite
managing to resist the temptation to google for information.

A memory popped into my head, a slideshow of family holidays when I'd insisted on taking a guided tour wherever we
were – no crumb of history left unturned in Dublin, Barcelona
or Berlin. Callum and Declan wilted after the first fifteen
minutes, feet dragging, mouths permanently in cavernous
yawns. Finn would be wandering off, transfixed by the dragon
statue in Parc Güell, putting his hand in the gold post box in
Dublin, tugging at my hand to buy him a souvenir of the Berlin
Wall. To compensate, I would become super-engaged, asking
the guide question after question, hoping he wouldn't notice
that the rest of my family had zero interest in the fact that we
were standing in front of the oldest church in the city. It was
hard to believe those days were over.

I glanced down at the facts on my phone and allowed
myself a wry smile. I was standing on a bridge built in 62 BC.
62 BC! My mind boggled at how anyone had been able to build
anything that could withstand over two thousand years of use
without the aid of technology.

At the end of the bridge was a four-headed statue, the stone
pitted and the faces worn away to a suggestion of eye sockets
and nostrils. I traced my fingers over the blank-faced woman,

wondering if that was the lot of all women, eroded over the years until it was easier to fade than to fight.

I frowned at my self-defeating thoughts and headed for home. Time to report back to the two women who definitely had some fight left in them. I doubted that Marina had ever blended into the background; her whole being suggested that no party was properly underway until the main event had arrived. Ronnie had a different sort of presence. Less outwardly ostentatious and flamboyant, but there was a certain steel about her that commanded attention and immediately made me respect her judgement.

I turned into the gateway of Villa Alba marvelling at how fate had landed me in a historic mansion in the middle of Rome – of all the cities – when, less than three weeks ago, I'd been sitting at my desk trapping a sweary synopsis of my thoughts about my boss in my mouth. I still couldn't quite believe I'd walked out. I gave myself a belated cheer of approval, wishing I could tell Lainey exactly how much freedom the money she'd left me had provided. I hoped she was looking down on me, impressed at the rebellion she'd unleashed. I kidded myself that if I concentrated hard enough, I'd be able to hear her applauding my decision to tell Declan to do whatever he wanted with our belongings.

I was just walking up the steps to the front door when my phone rang.

'Finn! How are you, love?'

'I'm all right. How are you?'

I hadn't spent twenty-one years fine-tuning my antennae for problems afoot for nothing. Finn's voice was dull and expressionless. 'You don't sound all right. What's going on?'

'Callum's found a flat with his mates from work, so he's already gone. Dad's being all weird about me staying in his new studio place, says it's too small and I need to stand on my own two feet, keeps telling me to ring the letting agents and see what they've got. I can't afford a flat on my own and I won't have a job soon. I don't know what I'm going to do.'

My temper was rising. Declan had always been hard on Finn, trying to force him into independence rather than encouraging and supporting him, then losing his temper when Finn floundered. 'Callum's managed it and he's exactly the same age as you!' Declan assumed that because they were identical in appearance, they had the same personality make-up.

'All right, love, calm down, we're not going to see you on the streets.'

I felt the tug between my maternal desire to protect and my selfish desire to cling onto my Italian adventure. After so many years of rushing out of work because one of the twins had had an accident at school, or flying out of bed in the middle of the night because one of them had lost their phone, wallet, missed the last train and, on one horrendous occasion, been held up at knifepoint, I felt I'd earned my right to delegate overseeing accommodation for the boys. Payback for all the times Declan had worked or snored on undisturbed.

Maternal desire to protect was a well-trodden neural pathway though, not easily defeated by logic, distance or age. I stopped fighting the inevitable. 'I'll be home next week. That gives us a month before completion. If necessary, we can hang out in a Premier Inn for a week or two. It's not quite Rome, but the beds are comfy.'

Finn sighed with relief. 'Will you definitely come back? I've really missed you.'

'I've missed you too, darling,' I said, mildly ashamed that, much as I adored my sons, I'd been astonished at how much space was freed up when I didn't have the boys to consider. The way he missed me, though, would be totally different from how I missed him. My heart was replenished by his off-the-wall observations about the world, his way of sitting down next to me quietly when he wanted to talk about something important, his outbursts of laughter that were almost childish in their spontaneity. I was certain that if my young adult children noticed my absence, it was mainly for my efficient smoothing of their daily lives rather than my dazzling company.

Ultimately though, Finn was rudderless and Declan wasn't stepping in to help him navigate. We ended the phone call with me offering multiple reassurances that everything would be okay, that the next steps in life would teach us something valuable. I didn't add that it would probably be something we hoped we'd never have to learn, such as how a husband and father could move on astonishingly quickly.

I made my way up the steps, all the grit and determination that I'd gathered over the last few weeks slipping away. It was incredible how much effort it took to build up a new way of thinking, and how easy it was to revert to type. But I couldn't bear the thought of Finn surrounded by boxes and empty cupboards, fearful instead of excited about what the future held for him. The logical conclusion was that I'd spoil my stay by worrying so I might as well go home.

I knocked on Ronnie's door. She ushered me in, clapping her hands. 'You've been out for ages. How did it go?'

Halfway through telling her how much I'd loved San Lorenzo Fuori Le Mura, it occurred to me that she probably sent all of her guests there and was bored stiff with hearing about it.

'Not at all,' she said when I apologised. 'You're actually the first one we've sent there, but Rome saved me at a time when I'd lost my way, so I absolutely love hearing what lifts people up when they're here, what they've seen and what they've learnt about themselves.'

Ronnie had that generosity of spirit about her. She was one of life's encouragers, the sort that restored your belief in yourself with the right combination of 'pull yourself together' and 'I've got faith in you'.

She peered at me over her glasses. 'I'm so impressed that you didn't trot back as soon as your husband put the house on the market. That takes some guts. I wasn't as ballsy at your age. I should have been.'

My heart clenched. I was an imposter. A middle-aged woman who'd briefly masqueraded as a rebel. I could feel my heart thumping at the necessity of saying that I couldn't stay beyond next week. I swallowed, gearing up for her disappointment.

'Ronnie, you've got me all wrong, actually.' I was screwing up one eye in an effort to minimise the full impact of her disdain.

She tilted her head on one side. 'In what way?'

'I do need to go home.' I explained about Finn, how lost he was, pre-empting her disapproval with 'I know I'm mollycoddling him, but I struggle with the idea that there's an arbitrary age when I can cut off all support without assessing whether they need it.'

Unexpectedly, her face softened. 'We're primed to protect. Twenty-one is still young. I thought I knew it all at that age. I won't bore you with the details, but I wish I'd listened to my parents a bit more. I ended up having to move countries to give myself a fresh start.'

I felt myself exhale sharply, astonished that someone as switched on as Ronnie shared similar regrets to me. 'Parents know more than we think,' I said, trying to quash the growing sense I'd had since coming to Rome that the past was catching up with me.

Ronnie pursed her lips. 'What is Finn interested in?'

'That's a good question. We pushed him into an academic degree – economics – for no other reason really than that's what I'd studied and we thought I could help him. Ironic really, because my father forced me into studying that too, and I never liked it either. He's actually quite visual – loves architecture and sculpture but not particularly artistic. He's also practical. Managed to construct a bar in the garden during lockdown, much to everyone's astonishment. I think he'd make a good builder – he's got a real sense of space and possibilities.' I hated distilling the boy who was everything to me down to a selection of traits that the world might deem useful. 'He's much more than that, though.'

Ronnie surprised me with her understanding. 'If I described my daughter to you, I'm not sure I'd even pick out traits that everyone else would recognise as her major characteristics. The way we interact with our children and how other people see them are two very different things.'

At that moment, Marina called out from the hallway and not so much entered into as overwhelmed the kitchen, resplendent in a cerise and orange dress with an embroidered neckline, cinched at the waist with a golden hooped belt. I loved that she wore that as ordinary, around-the-house attire. I'd have thought twice about donning it for a trip to the poshest of restaurants. 'You're back finally,' she said, as though, at fifty-seven, I had some kind of curfew to observe.

I was still feeling my way around Marina, who reminded me of a cat my mum had: elegant, arresting to look at, quite happy to wind in and out of your legs but inexplicably ferocious when you least expected it. I nodded, choosing to ignore the barb if there was one.

'Right, well, I imagine Ronnie can fill me in on what you saw and learnt. At our age, we can't afford to go over the same ground twice because we'll be buried in it soon enough. What's the next challenge for Sara?' she asked, then answered her own question. 'I think she should find five really special free things to do here. So, one, she can cement in her mind that her future might be less affluent but she can still have a brilliant time, and two, she can conserve the money from her friend and still have the adventure that – Lenny? – intended.'

'Lainey.'

Marina obviously wasn't a woman to be corrected, flapping her hand at me as though providing the correct name was bothering her with unnecessary details. She turned to Ronnie. 'How long shall we allow to report back? Ten days?'

I hoped Ronnie was going to help me out here, but she simply raised an eyebrow at me.

'I'm afraid I'm going to have to leave before then to help my son find somewhere to live.'

Marina folded over in an exaggerated manner. 'What is it with these mothers who can't let their kids grow up? Beth was just as bad. She always had one foot in the departure lounge every time that daughter of hers squealed for help.'

Ronnie raised her hand to silence Marina. 'Hold your noise. The person best placed to decide what her son needs is Sara, not you.'

Annoyance was coursing through me at Marina's words, partly because she sounded very much like Declan and partly because I was going home against my wishes in order to be a good mother in Finn's time of need. So being criticised for it on top of my reluctance to miss out on daily discoveries in this most magical of cities for the next couple of months made me want to fling myself on the floor in despair.

I took a few breaths to steady my voice. 'Believe me, I'd rather stay here. I love this city. I feel as though I've been regarding life through such a limited palette of colours. I've suddenly started noticing the different hues of the sky depending on the time of day, the variations in the colours of the buildings – all the white marble, the terracotta tiles, the pinks and yellows of the façades. It's almost as though someone has shaken me awake.' My throat tightened with regret at the years I'd spent surviving in a job where I had to steel myself to go in every day, worrying way too much about what people thought of me, people I didn't even like. For a moment, I was afraid I was going to burst into tears and I was pretty sure Marina wouldn't be a fan of that.

Marina pulled her mouth down at the corners. 'Well, you've still got a few days before you go and martyr yourself on the family pyre. I suggest you take on the challenge anyway. It'll give you a few more memories of Rome to cheer you up when you're trudging around house-hunting.'

Honestly, the smugness of this woman. If I understood correctly, she'd barely worked a day in her life, made a sport out of finding rich husbands and seen at least one of them into an early grave. Then she'd parked herself in her best friend's penthouse apartment to live out her days mainlining Aperol spritz and Prosecco and feeling hard done by if there wasn't a 'chap' around to make her a negroni sbagliato.

Ronnie huffed out a big sigh as though there was no point in contradicting Marina when she was dispensing her brand of wisdom. 'Perhaps you'd like to take some time to think about exactly when you want to leave. No rush from our point of view.'

I flirted briefly with telling Finn that I'd changed my mind, that Declan would have to help. But I knew I was kidding myself. Doormat I might be, but my boys would always be able to count on me, and if I could shield them from that bewildering loneliness of feeling isolated in the world, then I would.

I stood up. 'I'll confirm what I'm doing as soon as possible, Ronnie. Thank you for being so understanding.' I wasn't sure I kept the emphasis off the 'you', but in the circumstances, I was congratulating myself for not being much ruder.

Marina was all wide-eyed innocence. 'See you in two days' time for a rundown of the free things you've discovered so far.'

I let myself out into the hallway before mouthing some very obscene words in her direction.

16

Then

Today I was going to forget about everyone else. My dad driving over to fix the washer on the tap in the flat I'd rented in London and shaking his head in disgust at the old mattress abandoned in the front garden. My mother wincing every time a police car squealed past on the main road outside, then saying, 'I do worry about you walking home in the dark.' Lainey rushing up the stairs doubled over with laughter – 'I've just seen the old man downstairs watching telly wearing a monkey mask and a pair of cat slippers. Bit of a departure from your average Roman neighbour.'

No, today wasn't about them and their disparaging comments. I'd taken Thursday and Friday off work and I'd made the flat as cosy and comfortable as I could. When I'd warned Alessio that the area wasn't that great, he'd said, 'We will be together. All cities have not so nice streets. When I earn money, we can move to better places.'

I arrived at the airport half an hour before his flight landed, even though I knew he'd take ages to collect his luggage. My whole body was humming with anticipation. Finally, we could find a way through together, have time to work things out without glossing over disagreements because we didn't want to leave each other on a bad note. I couldn't wait to be released from running to a timetable of the constant highs of hellos and lows of goodbyes. I craved ordinary evenings when we could cook a simple spaghetti and watch TV, snuggled up on the sofa, my feet in his lap. No one to call him down to work in the bar, no one to raise their eyebrows if we argued – just the space and freedom to find a rhythm and routine that allowed us to explore who we were. And the joy of doing that without having to deal with the barrage of opinions scraping away at our confidence in each other. 'What will he do for a job?' 'Won't you get resentful supporting him?' 'So he's going to do all the housework while you're swanning about at client meetings?' 'It's all right now, but what if you want to start a family?'

I wriggled my way through to pole position at the barrier in the arrivals hall as grandparents ran to scoop up grandchildren, friends slapped each other on the back, mothers flung themselves on sons. I wondered if Alessio's parents had seen him off at the airport. He was his mother's favourite. I might have felt sorry for her if she hadn't spent so many years acting as though it was my responsibility to make sure he never had to sully himself ironing a shirt. Alessio laughed. 'It's the generation. Don't be so serious. My mother loves you.' Which I longed to believe, but the hard evidence was that it didn't matter how educated I was or how much I loved her son, my entire worth resided in my ability to pinpoint when the pasta was al dente.

I was hopping about with excitement when I saw 'baggage in hall' for the Rome flight pop up on the screen. As the silhouettes of young men appeared behind the glass doors, I readied my face to burst into the delight of 'this is what we have been waiting for', only to sag down again when it turned out to be someone else.

An hour passed, then two. He must have been stopped in customs. My adrenaline was fading, the anticipation of throwing my arms around him and welcoming him to England morphing into an irritation that nothing was ever straightforward. I'd imagined him pushing open the doors, his eyes finding mine and having that moment, the one I'd dreamed about recounting years down the line, when we'd be filled with that certainty at long last that nothing could come between us. We'd get on our feet financially, then we'd get married and prove to everyone that because we'd had to pull out all the stops to stay together, it had made us stronger. We'd done the hard yards of more than five years apart. This final stretch wouldn't exactly be a doddle, but it had to be easier.

The flight was no longer showing on the screen. Four hours had elapsed. I tried to find out from the information desk if he'd been caught up in customs, but they couldn't help me. On the cusp of tears, I did what I'd hoped to avoid and rang the bar in Rome, in case he'd left a message for me there. I leant into the booth, ready with my fifty-pence coins, my fingers trembling as I dialled the number.

Alessio's mother answered.

'Non viene,' she said. Then, slowly, in case I hadn't understood, 'He's not coming.'

17

A couple of days later, the buzz of the phone at 7 a.m. woke me. Carlo messaging again. The second person in less than forty-eight hours I wanted to help on their road to hell in such a way they'd enjoy the journey. My finger hovered over the block button, but a little masochistic part of me couldn't quite let go. I googled whether it was possible to turn off the blue ticks on WhatsApp to stop someone seeing whether or not you'd read their message. Feeling as smart as though I'd just gained a first in an information technology degree, I fiddled about until I was sure he wouldn't have the satisfaction of knowing I'd even been tempted to look, then gorged myself on his words, my heart braced and belligerent.

All his messages were a variation on how he couldn't under-stand why I'd left like that, that he hadn't connected with anyone in such a meaningful way since Cesca died, that could I just please explain what he'd done to deserve being ghosted like this. I had a little frisson of triumph that I was so twenty-first century, I'd actually managed to ghost someone. In a previous existence, never speaking to someone again after they'd given you false hope that there might be a proper relationship in the offing was known as 'coming to your senses'.

He obviously hadn't clocked that I'd seen him in bed with Boo. No explanation required. I wasn't going to put myself in a position where he could sweet-talk me round or make me doubt my own sanity. No. If I had to be on my own for the rest of my life, I'd get over that. I'd rather be lonely than lied to.

I busied myself getting ready to banish the infuriating yearning to sit opposite Carlo, lean my forehead against his, and agree final terms for a second chance. I willed myself to chase away the idea of it. Slippery slope and all that. I headed out, armed with an itinerary of free things to tick off. The prospect of being in a capital city and not spending a fortune (except on coffee, which was a necessity rather than an indulgence) felt liberating after Declan turning his nose up at anything that wasn't booked through a tour operator or didn't feature on a top ten best list. I loved a bit of offbeat.

I crossed the river towards one of my favourite squares, Campo de' Fiori, so I could combine coffee with some people-watching – and potentially include it in my list of free things – well, almost free. I wandered down Via del Pellegrino, admiring the shabby chic of a wrecked chair outside an upholsterer's shop – I loved all these little businesses that still survived on the main streets of Rome. I detoured down an alleyway to my right, Vicolo del Bollo, and was rewarded with a huge gilt mirror hanging in the street on the outside wall of a house, its frame gnarled and its mirror pitted, but not graffitied or gratuitously damaged. There was a brightness about my expression, an eagerness, an excited anticipation that acted as a natural facelift. If only I could bottle it. And behind me, the reflection of a woman who was tending to some geraniums in huge urns, snipping away with her secateurs as though she was in a rural garden rather than the middle of a bustling city. It was aston-ishing how the energy of Rome dipped and climbed with every corner, vacillating between chaos and tranquillity in a matter of metres.

In Campo de' Fiori, I took a seat on the sunny side of the square, conscious that by the time I got back to the UK, the clocks would soon be going back and I needed to gather all the vitamin D I could. I tried not to think about all the dark evenings that lay ahead. Every fibre of my being was straining for possible solutions that would allow for more exploring, more finding who I was now I was no longer a wife. I distracted myself by googling the history of Campo de' Fiori while sipping a latte so strong, I had a vision of me running round Rome like a film speeded up for comedic purposes.

As was my wont with Google, I ignored the main results of history about the architecture and clicked on the entry with the title 'Kick-ass women associated with Campo de' Fiori'. Maybe I could learn a trick or two.

I was taken with the history of Giulia Tofana, a seventeenth-century alchemist whose solution to the impossibility of divorce in those days was to peddle poison for eager wannabe widows to kill off their husbands. I had to applaud her ingenuity – she sold her potions of arsenic, lead, antimony and mercuric chloride in perfume bottles embossed with St Nicholas – to be kept on a woman's dressing table without arousing suspicion. A few drops in the abusive husband's food over a week or two and he'd be taught a lesson he'd never forget. Unfortunately for Giulia, one would-be woman eager for freedom got cold feet and confessed to her husband. Her reign of 'liberating' over six hundred abused wives was over and she was hung in the square in 1651. It made walking out of my job and hopping on a plane to Italy look a bit low drama.

I finished my coffee and headed over to the Presidio Nuovo Regina Margherita hospital in Trastevere, where, according to my research, there was a garden where anyone could wander in and sit in the cloisters. It seemed a bit bizarre that a hospital

doubled up as a community park. However, in keeping with
accepting that every country had its own customs, I made my
way over the Ponte Sisto, marvelling again at the ingenuity of
the Romans, with its built-in flood eye – a hole near the top of
the structure to allow water to pass through if river levels rose
too high.

I arrived in Piazza Trilussa and threaded my way through
the narrow streets of Trastevere, soaking up the restaurant
owners shouting across to each other, the efficient cleaning of
the tables in readiness for the long lunchtimes. I crossed the
Piazza di Santa Maria in Trastevere and reached the hospital,
already fighting off an acceptance that it was a wasted journey.
But, to my astonishment, it was as simple as walking through
the main gate. I expected someone to sneer, Marina-like, at my
request and shoo me away, but, in fact, the man at the booth
went to the trouble of pointing out which signs I needed to
follow and wished me '*Buona visita*'.

Within moments, I'd arrived in a sunny cloister and sat on
one of the benches, admiring the palms, the abundant orange
lantana, and a spectacular angel trumpet tree. The noise and
bustle of the *quartiere* dropped to a murmur. I was suddenly
reminded of the 'Desiderata' poem I'd always loved. 'Remember
what peace there may be in silence.' I hoped that Finn had
found my copy and stored it safely for me.

I could live a happy life with less money. I'd have to accept
that I would have to consider more carefully what I was spending, but I knew I'd cope. I did send up a little prayer that I'd be
able to afford something with a tiny garden, or a balcony at least.
I needed a bit of greenery to feel sane.

A cat rubbed around my ankles before doing that feline
thing of dashing off in favour of a more exciting prospect just as
I was becoming invested in the reward of making it purr. I
looked up at the windows above the cloister, the shutters against
the bright yellow and terracotta façades, and wondered how

modern the hospital was inside. I liked the idea that the corridors would have mosaic floors, frescoed ceilings and archways of ancient beauty to distract from the grimness of the malfunctioning bodies within.

In the distance, I heard church bells chime and got to my feet. I wandered through the cloisters, fascinated by the arched ceiling with trumpeting cherubs, the walls embedded with bits of old tombstones, fragments of urns, pillars and frescoes. Further exploration led me to a little chapel with blue plumbago spilling over the steps, and a second courtyard, full of olive trees, with rosemary and thyme bushes diffusing their scent into the air. The splendour of an old monastery contrasting with the modern signs to the diabetes clinic summed up Rome for me. That blend of old and new, the way progress squeezed in alongside history rather than obliterating it, the acceptance that the world evolves but carries with it the beauty of the past.

I finally left the hospital and retraced my steps through Trastevere, stopping to admire the basilica with the gold mosaic and frescoes on the façade. It was so glorious that I was tempted inside, where the gilded ceiling alone made me want to lie on the floor and gaze at it for hours. But the thing that really caught my eye was the statue of a saint, at the entrance to the left-hand nave, holding what I assumed to be a young Jesus. The saint's arms, hands and sleeves were stuffed with notes, scribbled on everything from scrappy bits of paper to elegant notelets. A photo of a young boy was tucked under his chin. A quick search of the internet revealed him to be St Anthony, granter of wishes and patron saint of lost things. Only sheer willpower stopped me unfolding the messages and nosing into the desperate pleas of the faithful.

I sat on the pew and scribbled a note of my own on the back of a restaurant receipt from Florence. I hoped he wouldn't disqualify me for my large consumption of Chianti.

Dear St Anthony, please help me not to panic about the future but instead to have faith that everything will work out for the best. And please keep my boys safe.

Annoyingly, I had a moment of weakness when I considered adding a stupid wish about finding love again. Then a slideshow of quiet, sensuous moments with Carlo rushed into my head and a simple request seemed way too complicated even for a renowned miracle worker to manage. I longed to believe that my whispered conversations with Carlo under the stars weren't purely a cynical strategy to bolster his ego by duping a middle-aged woman into mistaking compliments and caresses for bona fide emotions.

I added my note to the pile of hopes and requests at St Anthony's feet and wandered back out. I threaded my way through the streets of Trastevere, pausing to peer into tiny bookshops, bakeries and bars, with no specific destination in mind. I wondered how property prices here compared with the UK. Suddenly, I hoped that world property prices would be so up the spout that a quirky flat here with a spiral staircase onto a roof terrace and old ladies hanging their bloomers out on the palazzo opposite would cost the same as a two-bedroomed box back home.

I ventured up narrow alleyways into areas that had a cosy neighbourhood feel despite being in the middle of a capital city. Tiny communal gardens with no more than a couple of benches nestled on street corners, clothes airers were jammed between parked cars, rubber plants and fig trees stood in pots by building entrances. There was a sense of community as old men sat outside their front doors nodding quietly, sporadically saying something to each other that sounded more like an observation that required no response. Women were sweeping up leaves and tending to window boxes, occasionally stopping to help up a little kid who'd tripped over or to remonstrate with a teenager sitting on the steps, with that bored but resigned air of waiting for something to happen. The noise of music, conversations, arguments filled the air. Not a place for secrets but not for loneliness either.

I walked back to Villa Alba, quite taken with the idea of living where everyone knew everyone. I'd lived in the same house for twenty-seven years and hadn't spoken to anyone in the road apart from my immediate neighbours. Even then, my main interactions had been to apologise for the boys throwing noisy parties when Declan and I had gone away for the weekend rather than neighbourly swapping of tomato plants or apple chutney.

As I turned into the driveway, I came across Marina in the courtyard, parked on a bench watching the world go by through the wrought-iron gates. 'Afternoon. How are you finding the frugal world?'

'I'm loving it actually. I wish I had more time here before I had to leave. Because of Ronnie's generosity in letting me live here so cheaply, I could spin out the money I inherited for quite a while.'

Marina heaved herself to her feet, leaning on her stick. 'Come. We need to speak to Ronnie.'

I wished that I had mastered that commanding and imperious manner that had grown people obeying my orders. Despite my misgivings about what Marina needed to discuss with such urgency, I followed her up to Ronnie's apartment without a word. I paused on the threshold, feeling awkward that Marina just marched in without knocking, but she waved me in impatiently.

Ronnie was in the kitchen, the smell of garlic and basil wafting through the apartment.

Marina pointed to a chair at the table. 'Sit. We have a proposal for you.'

I felt a polite rebuttal gathering on my lips and chided

myself for my negative thinking. I recognised Declan's influence, that automatic no that always sprang to his lips whenever the boys asked for a lift, a loan, or proposed a day out or where we might go on holiday. He closed down any suggestions as a matter of course without pausing to weigh up the possibilities. With a massive effort, I forced myself to listen with an open mind.

'Ronnie and I think that you need time in Rome to recognise that you have to create a totally different life for yourself, not simply a cheaper, less affluent version of the one you had. Also, you have to make firmer boundaries. If people want your help, they have to do what's convenient for you, not expect you to change your plans every time they decide something on a whim.'

'Do you mean Declan selling the house?' I asked, doing all I could not to roll my eyes at the notion that I could not only magic up a whole new life with half the income but a whole new *different* life.

'Not just the house-selling, but the expectation from your son that you'll rush home because he can't sort himself out.' Marina flared her nostrils. 'Learnt helplessness. All my husbands suffered from it. Perfectly capable in the areas they were interested in, then lying around like beetles on their backs if something was too much effort. So much easier to delegate to me.'

Ronnie caught my eye with a complicit raise of the eyebrows. Somehow, Marina dogsbodying after a husband wasn't an image that automatically sprang to mind.

Ronnie gave the pan a stir, sending a tantalising smell my way. 'So, what Marina and I wanted to suggest is that you tell Finn you will help him, but that he has to come out here.' I opened my mouth to object, but she held up her wooden spoon like a stop sign. 'Hold on a minute, hear us out. So, if you go back to clear out the house, you will do the lion's share of the donkey work. Whatever you think now, I'd bet that organising skips and storage and the cleaning all falls to you. You'll also let Declan take what he likes and end up with all the crud, to keep the peace. But the question is, *why* should you be the one to keep the peace?' She added a scoop of rock salt into the sauce. Clearly blood pressure considerations were not a priority in this household.

'I might not get exactly what I want, but it would be ridiculous not to take any of the basics and have to fork out for them all again when I eventually get my own place. My budget is going to be very tight. I've only got a tiny rucksack of clothes with me – all my winter clothes and boots are still at home.'

Marina was wriggling like an earthworm with the urgency of voicing her opinion. She interrupted Ronnie. 'Right. Make a list of fifteen items of clothing you really like and wear more than twice a year. Send in a friend, relative, someone, to get those for you, or better, make your sons earn their keep and get them to pack them up for you. Then, ten personal items – photos, ornaments, things with sentimental value, maybe a painting or a vase. That's it. Two pieces of furniture. If you've lived in that house for twenty-seven years, your tastes will have changed. Sometimes it's good to start from scratch and make conscious choices. It's a great way to dump all the wedding gifts, hand-me-downs, things you buy but later hate but don't get rid of because they were expensive in the first place.' She ruffled her upper body like a peacock flicking out its feathers. 'So that's the house dealt with. Now your son. Ronnie and I like a female palazzo because we are too old to be told what to do by a man.'

I watched Marina waggling her finger and couldn't imagine any age when she would have been a pushover.

'So this is what we propose. We will be very flexible and allow your son to live here for three weeks. You can stay longer, but three weeks is long enough for him to make a plan and move out.'

A mixture of panic, excitement and optimism gathered pace. Maybe this was what Finn needed, a complete change from everything he'd known. Perhaps it would broaden his horizons and open his mind to the many possibilities available. But what if he didn't find something, what if he relied on me for a solution in a place where I had less understanding of how things worked, fewer connections, no safety net? What if he was homesick and I had to prop him up while keeping my own head above water?

No, I was struggling to be brave enough for myself. I swallowed. 'Ronnie, Marina, you're very very generous, but I don't think Finn would come anyway and it would be such a responsibility for me. We'd probably end up having to slink back home and that would make him feel even more of a failure.'

Marina gave a sharp bark of annoyance. 'For goodness' sake. How about you have faith in him for once and at least offer up the opportunity instead of deciding on his behalf?'

Ronnie waved her chopping knife and wooden spoon at Marina as though quietening down an orchestra. 'Stop shouting.' She put her utensils down. 'Sara, dear. You are a resourceful woman – look how you've found your way to our palazzo without any prior planning. You left your job, your house, your family and met people who've helped you along the way. Every day, I see that your mindset is shifting. You left England, expecting to stay in Italy for just five days and nearly three weeks later, whether you admit it or not, you are buzzing with possibilities, slowly accepting that the old Sara is being shed like an old skin and the new Sara is replacing her. Your son will have inherited some of that courage, but maybe he has to be planted in fertile new ground to grow.'

A bizarre sensation of pride spread through me at Ronnie's words, even if how she phrased it made me feel as though she'd mistaken me for someone far more determined and gutsier than

I was in reality. She smiled, her lovely face crinkling with wisdom and kindness.

Before she could speak again, Marina rapped her cane impatiently. 'Don't think about things too much. Be wild now in case you don't get another opportunity. Show Finn the true meaning of holding your head up and looking the world right in the eye. Go on, for the love of God, ring the boy and then we can all have dinner. I need a negroni sbagliato after all this fussing backwards and forwards.'

With Marina and Ronnie's words propelling me down the corridor to phone my son, I said under my breath, 'Lainey, looks like it wasn't just my freedom you bought.' I hoped with all my heart, she was sitting on a cotton-wool cloud and cackling with delight at this outcome. Merely the small matter of convincing Finn to join me now.

I pushed away the fear that Ronnie and Marina's idea was parenting lunacy. Instead I would fill him with the assurance that taking a chance, being brave enough to deviate from the expected path and not being afraid to fail was the best possible gift I could give him. I just needed to believe it myself.

Many frantic phone calls, WhatsApp messages and just over a week later, I was sitting with Finn and my two hosts on Marina's rooftop terrace, doing that whole mother thing of willing him to speak, act, charm in a way that would reflect brilliantly on my mothering skills. I tried not to wish he'd stop saying 'little' and 'water' with a dropped 't', in some odd attempt to sound street cool rather than Surrey born and bred. I was also having to refrain from pointing out that he could have had a proper shave and chosen something other than baggy tracksuit bottoms with a hole in the knee to make his debut on Italian soil. I was annoyed with myself for getting sucked into worrying about what anyone else thought about these superficial things. He was a good lad, decent and kind-hearted, so who cared if he looked a bit unkempt? Me apparently.

And Marina, who patted his arm after what she must have considered a decent amount of time getting to know him – approximately forty-five minutes – saying, 'So, the quickest way to learn Italian is to find you an Italian girlfriend.'

Finn blushed and looked to me for help. I raised my hands

in surrender. I knew already that Marina was going to have her say. She didn't disappoint.

'You're a good-looking boy. *Bello.*'

For a moment, I was terrified she was going to launch into the 'If I was thirty years younger' speech and poor Finn would melt with embarrassment.

But Marina peered closely at him and said, 'We need to – how shall I put this? – tidy you up a bit. No girl is going to be won over by someone who is too lazy to shave. Curated beard, fine, but random whiskers, no, no, no. And these' – she gestured at his tracksuit bottoms as though Strega had done something unspeakable on the carpet.

Ronnie gripped Finn's upper arm. 'Take no notice of her. She's full of opinions. If you're happy the way you are, then that's all that matters.'

Marina swirled the ice in her glass. 'Ronnie, don't be silly. He needs a decent girlfriend – perhaps that greengrocer's niece? She's a pretty little thing but quite feisty too. And I think she went on some exchange programme to America last year, so she'll be used to foreign men? Anyway, we'll introduce you, but not until we've made a few adjustments.'

I expected Finn to be squirming and sussing out how to exit the conversation as soon as possible, but he was laughing. 'I didn't realise Mum had invited me out here to be fixed up.'

It was fatal to encourage Marina. There was no stopping her now. 'So, tomorrow, we'll go and see Ronnie's hairdresser. He likes a challenge. You've got good cheekbones, so you can take a little bit of facial hair, but it must be neat, and that thick hair of yours needs thinning out. Giorgio will transform you into the neighbourhood heart-throb.'

To my surprise, Finn was leaning back in his chair, looking amused and, if I wasn't mistaken, up for that challenge.

Marina turned to Ronnie and did that very rude thing of speaking in Italian, while obviously discussing my son.

I leant over to him and whispered – also rude, but, in the circumstances, I decided that it wasn't worse than Marina's lack of manners. 'Don't let yourself be bullied by her. You absolutely don't have to do what she says.'

But Finn seemed mesmerised by Marina, as though she was the head of an ancient tribe in possession of the wisdom for his future. It would never cease to amaze me how parents put in all the ground work, offering well-thought-out advice to guide our children, which was mainly nodded at, then ignored completely. Yet a random stranger snatching a judgement out of thin air was immediately viewed as the guru of all that was sage and sane.

Of course, there was always the possibility that I only knew some of what Finn was like, the part that interacted within the well-trodden family dynamics in our household. Perhaps I didn't know him, or all of him, as well as I imagined. But, for the moment, his face had lost that lacklustre expression, the weary demeanour that he was too young to wear at twenty-one. His voice was animated, nothing like the dull, despairing tone that I'd heard so often over the last few weeks. I wanted to cheer with the sheer joy of seeing a spark about him. And I was also quietly proud that Finn being here, me being here, had all stemmed from having the courage to break out from the confines of what everyone expected of me. I still couldn't quite believe I'd told Amber to shove her horrid behaviour right where the Pope wouldn't see it. And now, the Pope, Finn and I were in the same square mile, which was irony at its best. Perhaps I'd send her a little model of the Pope, the solar-powered pontiff that waved its hand, to keep on her desk as a reminder not to be a total cow and risk everyone telling her where to stick her job.

.   .   .

The following day, I knocked on Finn's door, ready to take him exploring with me, all puffed up with the excitement of sharing the places I loved best with one of the two people in the world I loved most. When I told him my plan for the day, he said, 'Marina's already been down. We're going to her hairdresser in half an hour.'

My heart did a little plummet of disappointment that it hadn't occurred to Finn to check with me first. I had been really looking forward to pointing out the treasures that studded the streets of Rome: the ornate lanterns held up by angels, the Madonna shrines tucked behind glass high up on a wall, the fish-mouth fountains on a corner. All the small details that you had to slow down to admire, but that added up to make you feel that there was so much beauty in the world if you only paused to look at it. But as so often in motherhood, the grand plan that I had been salivating over was brushed away with what – insultingly – appeared to be a better offer – a trip to the barber with a septuagenarian.

'Oh. Are you sure you're all right with that? I know we were laughing about it last night, but you mustn't let her bulldoze you.'

'I really like her. I can't believe she's nearly eighty. She's like one of those Italian grannies you see on Insta, who keep the whole family in order.'

And over the next ten days, I vacillated between delight at Finn forging his own relationships within the palazzo – chatting to Ronnie about how she'd managed to carve out a place for herself in Italy, how long it had taken her to learn Italian – and an irritation with Marina at how she assumed Finn was there purely to wait on her: 'Finn, *caro*, just pop up to my apartment and fetch my reading glasses.'

Several times, I'd come back from a continuation of my free

things in Rome challenge that Finn had turned his nose up at –
'Is it another garden thing? Nah. Think I'll go for a wander
later' – to find him up a ladder changing light bulbs, or his head
under the sink fixing a leak.

I tried not to think of the hundreds of times I'd asked Finn
and Callum to give me a hand to move the sofa or to carry the
shopping in and been met with a groan or an 'in a minute' or
some other response that filled me with fury. Despite doing
ninety per cent of everything myself, the tiny ten per cent I
tried to delegate could never be done willingly. And now, Finn
was all 'yes, Marina, anything else I can do for you, Marina.' I
gave myself a talking-to. It would be so much worse if he was
lying around, yawning and unhelpful.

But the downside of him getting his feet under the table was
that, in true Finn style, the precariousness of his existence
seemed to have escaped him. He was assuming his biggest challenge was learning how to mix a negroni sbagliato to Marina's
exacting standards rather than ferreting out somewhere to live
and a means of paying his way. I could easily foresee that he
was going to rock up to the three-week time limit with the
expectation of me stepping in with a solution.

I reminded myself of Rico's words. 'What if you just didn't?'

But when it came to my boys I didn't know how to 'just not'.
Though, selfishly, with eight weeks left before I had to leave
Rome myself to face reality, I didn't want his inaction to become
my problem.

After approaching the topic a couple of times and Finn
doing that nodding thing while clearly zoning out, I lost my
temper. 'I'm not picking up the pieces here. You've got one and
a half weeks before you need to leave here and you need to
think about what you're going to do. I can't afford to bankroll
you.'

'Chill out. Surely they'll let me stay on?'

'No, that's not what we agreed. So, tomorrow, we're going to sit down and make a list of possibilities. You could become a manny.'

'What?' Finn's face was a picture of puzzlement.

'You know, an au-pair, nanny. But it's called a manny because you're a bloke.'

'What, look after babies?'

'Probably not babies, but children.'

'I don't know anything about children.'

Frustration was building in me. 'Well, you might have to learn, love. If it keeps a roof over your head, that's what you'll have to do. Or you could get a job teaching English maybe?'

'Don't you need qualifications for that?'

And so it went on, Finn picking faults in whatever I suggested and subtly, cleverly, putting the onus back on me to resolve the issue.

In the end, I picked up my bag. 'I'll help you, but I'm not doing it for you. You get on the internet and find out what short-term jobs are available for young men, preferably with accommodation, for the next couple of months – or longer, if you decide not to come home with me. You're in the pound seats because you've got an Irish passport, so I don't think there's any problem with you working.' At least Declan had come in useful for something. I carried on, 'Make a list, however unlikely, private English lessons, cleaning, working in a hotel, youth hostel, whatever it is, and pull your finger out.'

And with Finn gawking at this species of mother who didn't cave in to solve his helplessness, I marched out of the palazzo. I headed towards the river and instead of turning right as I usually did towards Trastevere, I turned left, towards the bit of Rome I'd given a wide berth. I told myself that I'd stay on this side of the Tiber, that there was no way that I would allow curiosity to lead me into that one little street that might hold an answer after all these years.

I skirted around the imposing walls of Castel Sant'Angelo,

striding past the people milling about the stalls lining the river-
bank with old maps, comic books, posters, the sort of parapher-
nalia that would have no place in my new home. I felt released
from having to buy something in Rome 'as a souvenir'. The best
souvenirs were the ones I was going to carry in my heart – the
ones that filled my senses – the sounds, the smells, the excitement of being here – so much more than any plaster Colosseum
or arty sunset picture over the Vatican could ever do.

I was so lost in debating whether I could embrace a minimalist future, that I was shocked to realise how far I'd walked. I
recognised the distinctive Somali embassy, with its semi-hexag-
onal tower and red and green carvings over the windows. Piazza
della Libertà. Which meant that Piazza del Popolo was just on
the other side of the bridge, and beyond it, well, that place
where it all began.

I sat in the square, studying the smooth lines of a monu-
ment, a tribute to police who'd lost their lives in the line of duty.
It would make no sense to go poking about in old wounds,
though it did seem silly to be a stone's throw from Villa
Borghese and not savour the view of Rome from the Pincio
Terrace. I stood up. I wasn't going to let events from over three
decades ago dictate what I could enjoy today.

I walked over the Ponte Regina Margherita, elegant in its
simplicity. How many times had I – had we – crossed that
bridge? My heart was starting to beat harder, but I forced
myself to lean on the balustrade to look at a two-storey house-
boat moored a little further up. In my mind, living on a house-
boat was one up from camping, but having to have a specific
place for everything and no space for clutter to languish was
beginning to appeal. I could appreciate the peace that
descended in the evening, when the traffic and tourists faded
away. How glorious to sit on a candlelit deck, surrounded by
terracotta urns brimming with geraniums, the glow from Rome's
skyline reflecting off the water. Lainey would have killed herself

laughing if she could have seen me getting carried away. For now, I'd stick to ditching the inflatable Christmas reindeer and foot spa without a second glance. One step at a time.

I carried on to Piazza del Popolo, a huge square dominated by an obelisk and the twin churches of Santa Maria in Montesanto and Santa Maria dei Miracoli, the fountains with Neptune, his tritons and dolphins, and the she-wolf feeding Romulus and Remus. I steadied myself, feeling the spectre of a long-ago life dragging me back to the past at the very moment I'd committed to focusing on the future.

Forcing my attention onto the activity around me, I sat on a stone bench and watched men with toddlers on their shoulders. Couples pressing their cheeks together for selfies in front of the stone lions. Siblings in baseball caps play-fighting next to their parents. My heart registered a pang that my family unit had failed, that as a foursome we'd never be in an Italian square discussing which direction to take and whether we needed to reapply our sunscreen. Banal moments that nonetheless signified belonging. Was that why I'd been so afraid to make the final move to get the house on the market? That desire to stay in an accepted cocoon, however unhappy we were?

A little boy having a meltdown after he'd dropped his ice cream on the floor snagged my interest. He was screaming and stamping up and down, his mother crouching trying to console him. His father looked on the verge of his own tantrum, repeating an aggressive 'Stop it! Stop it!' with absolutely no effect before walking off and shouting, 'I can't handle this' over his shoulder.

To my left, a woman in her twenties with the sort of waterfall hair that suggested a good half an hour with the straighteners was pouting away in front of the Neptune fountain. She was instructing her boyfriend to zoom in, to step back a bit, to make sure he wasn't pointing directly into the sun. Suddenly, he marched over, thrust the phone at her and said, 'I'm not spending every day pratting about for the perfect picture for Instagram,' to which she replied that if he loved her, he'd want the perfect picture of her.

It was tempting to steam over, grab her by the shoulder and chip in my own little rant about how love wasn't about photos or making everyone think that you had the perfect relationship playing out on the perfect holiday. I wanted to tell her that love was about finding each other interesting long after you'd heard your other half's best stories umpteen times. That it was not about comparing yourself to other couples, not chasing some jewellery-filled, present-laden, anniversary-celebrating life but about showing up when the clouds rolled in. About taking it in turns to hold the umbrella over one another until the sun came out again. I wanted to take her hands in mine and tell her, 'Forget the photos. That's not love. Make sure you have each other's backs, that you're each other's priorities. Don't spend so much energy on convincing everyone how happy you are that you wake up one morning and realise how deeply, desperately sad you are.'

She stormed past, not even looking around to see if her boyfriend was following. I tucked away the lesson in not assuming that people in a 'traditional' family or a couple were happier than I was bumbling about the world in my newly single state. At least I wasn't having to be disappointed when someone else failed to deliver. I batted away the memory of Carlo quietly offering to look away while I scattered Lainey's ashes, his instinctive knowledge of what I needed. Instead I marched up the steep stone staircase to the Pincio Terrace with quite a schadenfreude spring in my step.

As I reached the top, the heavens opened, sending everyone who'd never holidayed on a rainswept British beach on a bank holiday scuttling for cover. I leant on the wall and watched the clouds close in, the rods of rain batter the cobbles. Down below in the square, people ran in all directions, bags clamped to their heads as inadequate shelter. I turned my face to the sky, letting the water pour over me, revelling in the sensation of not trying to control anything but simply standing there in one of the most beautiful cities in the world with no idea what my future held. I was soon soaked right through to my underwear and my commitment to a bohemian bonding with the weather waned disappointingly quickly.

The rain tapered off and the sky turned dramatic, with tiny fronds of sunshine burning magnesium bright behind the dark smudges of cloud. St Peter's dominated the panorama, but in every direction, pillars, domes and spires proliferated. I shivered and gave the view one last long glance. I wouldn't come back over this way again. Too many blurred memories were swirling around me like ghosts. How many evenings had I walked through these very gardens, countering every objection with a solution, convinced that any pitfall was no match for the intensity of our feelings? And I'd been in danger of falling into the same trap in Florence, relaxing the barriers I'd constructed. I'd trusted when I shouldn't have trusted, and been too feeble to confront Carlo for pretending to have feelings for me.

This last thought, that sense of being taken for an idiot for a second time, unleashed a rage that I'd never allowed myself to embrace. It might be thirty-three years late, but fury propelled me back down to the square, past the busker who was wasting his amazing voice on a stupid song that actually included *spaghetti al dente* in the lyrics. I stomped down the steps, drops of water flinging off my hair. My feet were mapping out a route that was still familiar, automatic so many years later when everything and nothing had changed. I strode between the twin churches, down Via del Corso, my anger directing itself at the people ambling in and out of the posh shops, spending outrageous sums of money on a new dress or suit that they hoped would make them feel better about their miserable lives.

I turned left, never faltering, never pausing to double-check where I was until finally I arrived in the narrow street that I'd known so well. As with so many places in Rome, it was like stepping back in time, into a totally different world, away from the tourists and into a micro-community. I caught a glimpse of a man in a tiny workshop, painstakingly repairing a wicker chair, all manner of furniture in varying states of decay hanging from the ceiling. Impossible to believe that this business had survived in an economy that had changed so dramatically since I was last here. The original owner, who'd seemed ancient to me then, must be dead by now. Perhaps that was one of his sons. Next door, in a glass-fronted room barely bigger than a shed, an elderly woman was bent over a gold picture frame, touching it up with careful brushstrokes. She glanced up as I walked past and I increased my speed. No one would recognise me, but I didn't want to take any chances; I wanted to do this in my own time and on my own terms.

I hung back, my heart hammering as I realised that the bar I'd been looking for was indeed still there. A more modern sign, but the same name. Bar Conti. Didn't mean the family still owned it though. I pulled my hair forwards to cover my face and walked past. Still the same cramped space with locals standing at the counter, sucking back an espresso, no doubt complaining about taxes, the government or football results. Still a TV showing the sport in the corner.

My whole body tensed as I caught sight of the back of a grey head. Too much hair to be his dad, who'd been quite bald already. By my reckoning, his parents would be in their eighties if they were still alive. I didn't want to wish ill on anyone, but I wasn't in a hurry to make his mother's reacquaintance. I understood her better now, though, her fear of a future that might take her son away from her, to a different life that she wouldn't be part of.

A couple of middle-aged men came out of the bar, shouting their goodbyes, and I scuttled up the street, leaning against the wall on the other side, pretending to look at my mobile while I gathered my courage.

I ruffled my hair and used my phone screen to check my appearance. A bedraggled mess wasn't the 'look what you could have had' version of myself I'd hoped to present, but I couldn't guarantee I'd ever be here again. At least not with the same amount of adrenaline pumping through me.

My need to know, my desire for answers, outweighed my vanity. I squared my shoulders. I would have my say. As I pushed the door open, I paused on the threshold, feeling reason edge in alongside my rage. Goodness knows what I hoped to achieve.

Too late. The man behind the bar had turned, lifted his head and greeted me.

19

Then

It was ironic that the nineteenth was the only Saturday in April with a free slot for Declan and me to marry in our local church. No one else appreciated the irony of it. Seven years to that awful day, when I'd realised that nothing would ever be the same again.

I couldn't turn the date down. It was the last one until November and my mum was adamant. 'You don't want everyone to be standing around in a bitter cold wind. And, anyway, spring is such a hopeful season.' She'd patted my hand, as if to reassure herself that those bad times were firmly in the past, now I'd snagged a husband. And not just any old husband, but one who had a great job in pharmaceutical sales, which gave him some common ground with my father.

Dad had bestowed the highest seal of approval on Declan by supporting his application to join his golf club. The prodigal daughter had finally redeemed herself, especially as Declan also owned his own house. 'In a nice street, as well. You've really landed on your feet.' He'd cleared his throat. 'Well done, love.'

My mother was acting as though unless I whisked Declan up the aisle quick sticks, he might get cold feet and I'd be back on my dusty old shelf for the foreseeable. She was impervious to my protests that we'd been together for less than two years. 'When you know, you know.' But I wasn't sure I did know that he was 'the one', although that didn't seem to matter to my parents. They were wheezing sighs of relief that someone 'normal' had materialised, mirage-like, on a bleak horizon to rescue me. Like a mantra, my mother repeated, 'At your age, you want to settle down and get on with it.' 'Getting on with it' meant elevating myself from living with Lainey in a rented flat – 'It's all right when you're young, but you're thirty now' – and submitting to the stultifying responsibilities of adulthood. In short, less dancing till dawn and more drudging until dusk. Especially since I'd 'lost my mind' and jacked in a lucrative career in accountancy for one in journalism paying peanuts. But the real driver for my mother, if not for me, was to crack on with providing a grandchild to spoil.

I hadn't thought I'd ever be able to love again. But everyone loved Declan – 'such a charmer, gorgeous manners, I can see what you see in him, adore that Irish accent' – which eventually persuaded me I loved him too. I convinced myself that my reservations about getting married were a good thing, linked to maturity, to weighing up the pros and cons without being consumed by that fevered, all-encompassing energy that propelled me towards Alessio.

So with no viable reason to reject the April date, I dismissed my reservations and clambered aboard my mother's gravy train of flowers, place settings and sugared almond wedding favours. I refused to believe in superstition, that the date could possibly be a bad omen.

My mother bought the biggest hat and blubbed all the way

through the ceremony. My dad kept giving me the thumbs-up as though I'd galloped over the finishing line first in the Grand National. I never told anyone, not even Lainey, that straight after the photos of us gazing into each other's eyes when Declan lifted me off my feet and twirled me round, I shut myself in the loo and cried, holding toilet paper along the edge of my bottom lashes so that my mascara wouldn't run.

20

'*Buongiorno, signora.*' A perfunctory greeting, distant, the sort reserved for strangers to the neighbourhood.

A burst of disappointment registered. I'd expected something more than this, imagined a throwing up of hands, an exclamation, even a flurry of swear words. But as I stepped towards the counter, I wasn't sure it was Alessio. Or even his brother. I'd expected to *know*, but now I was here, I wasn't sure. He was about the right height. He looked older than fifty-seven, but that might have been the grey, almost white, hair. Nothing like the lithe young man who used to flit around making drinks, while I sat patiently, waiting for the moment that his dad would grudgingly nod towards me and then to the door. The moment that we'd scoot off on Alessio's *motorino*, away from his parents' disapproval and into precious hours where all we needed was each other. I struggled to match my memory of the young man who used to lean over me, his fringe flopping over his eyes, with this rotund man in front of me. His eyes disappeared into his rounded cheeks, his shirt was straining over his stomach. Though to be fair, I'd also fast-forwarded thirty odd years and no longer possessed the smooth skin and nipped-in waist of my early twenties.

I ordered a cappuccino on the grounds that drinking the wrong sort of coffee at the wrong time of day was the least of my worries. I watched him moving about, dredging my mind for tell-tale mannerisms. Shock was coursing through me, the disbelief that I didn't instinctively know whether this was even him, the man I'd dreamed about, longed for, held responsible for defining so much of my life.

After her initial sympathetic outrage – 'What guy spends five years promising to move to England, lets you bankrupt yourself renting a flat in London for both of you and then just doesn't turn up?' – Lainey had become more and more exasperated with me. 'It happened when you were twenty-three. You've had a whole lifetime since then. A husband. Kids. It's not like you've never had another relationship.'

And she'd been right, of course. But I'd never trusted again with my heart. Only my head. Taking the easy option when I met Declan. A safe, sensible option – a man with a house and job and the added bonus that he spoke English in a way my parents didn't have to make allowances for. Exactly the sort of man they wanted for me. I wasn't sure I'd ever loved him for who he was. Or maybe I had, in my own way. In a measured, careful, one-foot-on-the-floor, ready-to-be-disappointed sort of way.

I glanced over to the far corner of the bar, subconsciously looking for the phone that used to hang by the door that led through to their apartment. It had been a public service back in the day. People had queued for their turn, with Alessio's dad charging them for the units they'd used at the end of the call. There was a mirror there now. I'd become quite unpopular for hogging the payphone in my university hall of residence. I'd rung every few days when I returned to England after that first summer, his mother shrieking up the back stairs for Alessio as I fed my fifty-pence pieces into the slot. Despite Alessio stretching the cord through the door as far as it could go, I'd often had to strain to hear him over the noise from the bar. I wondered how different our lives would have been if we'd had email and mobiles.

Alessio/maybe not Alessio pushed the coffee towards me, a wedding ring embedded in the flesh on his left hand. The sight caused a stir of emotion, even though I wasn't totally convinced it was him.

I picked my coffee up and started to move to the table in the corner. The two other women got up to leave, and as the door swished shut behind them, I knew I had to seize the moment while the bar was empty.

'*Signore?*' I said.

The bartender raised his eyebrows in a disinterested way, making me falter.

'*Questo bar appartiene alla famiglia Conti?*' I asked.

He gestured towards the sign, as though the answer was obvious, a veneer of distrust clouding his face. I remembered Alessio as being quick to smile, always ready to laugh. This couldn't be him. A family member possibly. He had an older sister and a much younger brother. A cousin? All the men in his family had had a pronounced, slightly hooked nose.

There was nothing about him that encouraged further conversation, but I couldn't pass up the opportunity to do what I'd come to do. My Italian was hesitant as I announced that I had a strange question to ask. He didn't understand me the first time, screwing up his face. Suddenly I saw it, in that gesture, in the way his face moved, the shadow of that young man, the one who'd taken me to the seaside on Sundays, kissed me until our lips were bruised, made me promises that he couldn't keep.

'Alessio?' I said, braced for the man to frown, to shake his head, puzzled. But he peered at me, as though he was focusing for the first time, instead of my face blurring in front of him as another forgettable tourist. His mouth dropped open slightly, his eyes twitching as though he was making sure that he was actually seeing what his mind was telling him.

'Sara?'

I nodded.

'*Cazzarola!*' He came out from behind the counter. 'It's really you. What are you doing here?'

He looked like he might throw his arms around me. But having dreamt of our reunion for so long, the torch I'd carried for him reigniting like the trick candles on the twins' birthday cakes, I found I didn't want to be hugged by this person who'd done so much damage to me. In fact, I didn't want to be hugged by this person that I didn't know any more.

I shrugged and stepped back. 'I was in Rome. I've been in Italy for a few weeks – Milan, Florence, Liguria,' I said, wanting to make the point that the purpose of my trip had not been to track him down.

'I don't know what to say. I can't believe it's you. How long you here for?'

'I'm living in Rome at the moment. With my son.'

The blink of surprise that met the announcement I had a son gave me a burst of satisfaction. I didn't want him thinking that I'd spent the last three decades wistfully pulling out my trousseau from under the bed and spending my evenings embroidering samplers like a Victorian spinster. Nevertheless, now he was making no effort to disguise the fact that he was looking me up and down, I was wishing that I'd dolled myself up rather than making an off-the-cuff appearance after a good drenching in torrential rain.

'Stop, stop a minute. So you have a son?'

'I have two sons. Twins.'

He pressed his fingers against his forehead as though this was almost impossible news.

'Wait, wait. There is so much to know. I call my daughter.

She can look after the bar. We go somewhere to speak. Not here because... my wife...' He gestured with his hands to show that she would give him hell. 'Two minutes.'

He went back behind the counter, opened the door to his home and yelled up the stairs. I had the strongest sense of déjà vu. I registered with annoyance that his daughter was called Sofia. We'd discussed that as a name for *our* future daughter. I wondered if he even remembered. I bet his wife wouldn't be happy that she hadn't had the monopoly on that. A disgruntled shout echoed back down. I was always astonished by how the simplest of Italian communications sounded as though a great big row was erupting.

A young woman in her late twenties emerged, asking how long Alessio was going to be. She barely bothered to glance in my direction, which made me feel as though I was so faded and old that I couldn't constitute a threat to her mother. I didn't want to be, of course, but it would have been nice not to be dismissed as so past it that the possibility couldn't exist.

Alessio muttered something along the lines of 'As long as it takes' and ushered me out.

I followed him along the street, battling between irritation that he'd taken it for granted that I'd just go with him and my desire to find out how his life had turned out without me.

He pushed open the door to a cocktail bar, nearly deserted at three in the afternoon, and led me to a booth at the back. 'What you drink?'

'Hot chocolate, please. And some sparkling water.'

'This is a celebration. Prosecco, at least.'

I almost slid into the role that he would have expected of me. That I would go along with what he said, because this was where he lived, where he was in charge. But afternoon drinking did me in. And. And. I wasn't that person any more. I needed a clear head for this. It would most likely be my only chance to understand an event that I'd never made peace with.

'No thank you,' I said, a bit primly. My perspective was that this was more of an opportunity for an unreserved apology rather than an occasion for popping corks.

He stuck out his bottom lip and shrugged. 'Okay. Hot chocolate and water.'

I leant back in my seat, my mind alive with memories of us throwing coins into the Trevi Fountain. Talking into the early hours in piazzas all over the city, oblivious to anyone else around us. Searching out the quiet corners in quiet gardens where we could do everything we couldn't do when his parents were buzzing about.

I stared, trying to dredge up that feeling, or the memory of that feeling, when the only thing I wanted in the world was him. When the focus of my day was writing a letter, receiving a letter, waiting to phone him, counting down the days when we'd be closer to seeing each other than to the last time we'd said goodbye.

I let him talk, about how his parents had died within six months of each other five years ago, how he had one daughter – 'more didn't come' – how she'd got divorced and moved back home. He didn't appear to see the irony of his comment that 'young people give up so easily'.

Before I could stop myself, I said, 'You gave up easily.' And for the first time since we'd been chatting, my emotions rose in a bitter surge.

Alessio looked affronted, as though he'd really believed that this was a social visit, a friend dropping by after all these years, to see what had changed, what had stayed the same, but not someone who *needed answers*. He flicked his hands out in a gesture of surrender. 'We were young and *innocenti*. How were we going to live in London together with no money? If I was working all the nights as waiter, what life we'd have? We never see each other.'

'But when did you decide that? I'd seen you at Christmas.

We'd discussed splitting up then, but you asked me to marry you instead. That was only four months earlier.'

He looked down at his hands. 'The night before I was coming, I walked around the streets, all the places I know – the bars, the houses of my friends, the bakery where we buy our bread, the butcher who always save the best *trippa* – tripe – for my grandmother. It's a lot to leave where you know.'

'But we'd talked about that. Endlessly. We'd agreed that London offered the best opportunities. That I'd carry on with accountancy instead of taking my dream job at the advertising agency so it would be easier to get a mortgage.' I sipped my hot chocolate. 'But that's not the point anyway. The point is that you didn't come, you didn't let me know and you left me standing at the airport waiting for you.'

'I was going to come, but my mother was crying, telling me how she would have grandchildren who never speak her language. Then my dad was shouting that he needed help in the bar and my brother was too young and, I don't know, I couldn't. I couldn't leave. I can't remember really, I'm old now.' He smiled apologetically, and despite the wrinkles, the eyes more hooded than they were, there was a spark of recognition, a familiarity that made me feel as though I was peering into the past. Looking back at the times when he'd race up to meet me, late, because he'd had to look after his brother, carry the shopping for his grandmother. But the humiliation, the anger of believing in a future that never came to pass after years of defending Alessio stopped me reaching across the table to pat his hand with understanding. He was angling for forgiveness, for me to say, 'It was such a long time ago. And we've both had other lives. And we have our children, so it turned out all right.'

Instead I said, 'You broke my heart. You wouldn't take my calls. Your mother kept making excuses for you, that you were out, that you were fetching milk, that you were looking after Nonna Chiara. I was expecting to marry you and you didn't even explain. I wrote to you, letter after letter, and after weeks, you managed one short note saying you were sorry but it was better that we finished.'

'I didn't know what to say to make it right. I was sad too.'

In that moment, I realised that everything I'd invested in wholeheartedly – the saving every penny to come to Italy in the holidays or to pay for Alessio to visit me at university, sacrificing what I wanted for the all-encompassing goal of being together – had only ever been one of several options for Alessio. I'd made the fatal mistake of believing that the strength of my love could paper over any hairline cracks in his. My wanting to make it work with all my heart had effectively swept Alessio up, tornado-like, whirling him along with my solutions and my determination. I'd refused to accept from anyone, least of all him, that anything could compete with the magnitude of what we felt for each other. When he was backed into a corner and finally had to break it off with me, he was 'sad'. Whereas I was shattered into bits. In a way that, because I was young, no one took seriously. Not even Alessio apparently.

After that day at the airport, I'd dragged myself to work, then collapsed into a heap in the evenings. I sat all summer in that grotty little flat, listening to other people's parties, the smell of cheap fatty sausages on a barbecue wafting in through the window. Lainey had been angry on my behalf, then frustrated with my listlessness, then worried enough to ring my parents, who packed up my flat, dealt with the admin and forced me to come home.

I'd quietly suffered all the circular conversations about 'plenty more fish in the sea' and 'lucky escape' and the dazzling good fortune of not having had children with him. Little by little, in increments that were so tiny as to be imperceptible, I emerged into life again. Yet that experience, that giving myself to someone one hundred and ten per cent only to discover that all that hope and planning could smash into a dead end overnight, had shaped me.

I pushed my cup away. 'You must have known you weren't going to come. You must have considered the possibility at least, long before you were supposed to arrive.'

He frowned. 'I cannot remember exactly.'

'But you must have guessed how terrible it would have been for me? You could have phoned my parents – they would have got a message to me somehow. You could have sent a telegram.' All the things I'd been saving up to say came pouring out, Alessio shifting in his seat and looking for all the world as though he was appreciating what a near miss he'd had.

He circled his fingertips on the table. 'You've had a good life without me.'

We argued backwards and forwards, with him deliberately misunderstanding my points and stopping short of the one hundred per cent apology that I had come in search of. Finally, I couldn't stand it any longer and told him I needed to head off.

And as he gestured for the bill, I'd expected to feel the distant echo of love, a remnant of desire, some ember that with the right care might even be resurrected. Yet all I could think was I should have come back ages ago and seen Alessio for what he was. Just an ordinary man who'd been in my life for a season, who had lacked the courage to move countries and hadn't been as in love with me as I was with him. Plus he'd been too cowardly to admit the truth and instead had humiliated me by hiding behind his mother in Italy while I had to respond to everyone's incredulity – 'Alessio isn't here?' 'When's he coming – did he miss the plane?' 'He didn't turn up?' People's faces had taken on a whole repertoire of expressions, ranging from the eyebrow lift of 'That doesn't surprise me' to genuine shock.

But what I realised now, that I hadn't been able to accept at the time, was that there were so many elements that made relationships succeed or fail. Love didn't exist in a vacuum. It relied on timing, environment, circumstances, other people's support and acceptance. Even finance. Much easier to remain blissfully in love if you weren't cold and hungry. But, most of all, love relied on both of you being prepared to fight equally hard to stay together. There was no room for one person to sunbathe, only lumbering to their feet with an umbrella on rare occasions, while the other person was running round deploying sandbags and nailing down loose debris. I'd been the sandbagger and Alessio had been the sunbather. Inevitably doomed to failure.

I said goodbye and gave him a brief hug, still struggling with the weird knowledge that I'd once known every inch of his body. I wondered if the fact that we'd seen each other naked had drifted into his mind during this conversation as it had into mine. And just as I was dealing with that rather uncomfortable thought, he said, 'Come and see me next time you're in Rome.'

'No.' And for once in my people-pleasing existence, I didn't feel the need to explain why.

21

I walked back to Villa Alba in relentless rain. I was shivering with cold but also glowing, as though I'd shed a weight that I'd carried through my whole life, that sense of not being good enough, of deserving what had happened, of not meriting anything other than second best.

Marina was leaving Ronnie's apartment as I came into the entrance hall. '*Madonna*! You are soaked, quick, come in, you will get a *colpo d'aria*.'

Ronnie appeared at the door. 'Don't worry, all Italians think you will get a chill or a cold or earache, neckache or some other dreadful malady if you have wet hair.' In a theatrical whisper, she said, 'You can imagine how successful a British barbecue would be over here. All the Brits in T-shirts and shorts standing under golf umbrellas and singing in the rain, with the Italians barricading themselves inside under mohair blankets.'

Marina flapped her hand at me. 'This is ridiculous. How can this be good for your health? You want to spend the rest of your time here in bed with the *febbre*?'

'I'll go and have a hot shower. Have you seen Finn?'

'He's been amazing,' Ronnie said. 'Before it started

chucking it down, he did a brilliant job cutting back all the roses in my garden. They were all flopping off the wall and everywhere looked so untidy. I don't dare climb up the ladder any more. Well, only when Marina isn't watching.'

I struggled to compute that Marina, Ronnie and Finn had been doing mundane chores while I'd been gearing up to confront my past, to discover that Alessio was neither evil nor extraordinary. He was basically your average Joe, quite small town in his own way. He hadn't intended to hurt me, but in the end, blood had been thicker than water and our love hadn't been able to compete. But that wasn't a failing in me.

For so long, I'd been sick with envy whenever I met anyone with a foreign husband, studying them to understand what special qualities they had that meant their husband had been prepared to move countries, to sacrifice family ties. Maybe it came down to an adventurous spirit, bravery, independence, self-reliance, even optimism. Perhaps it wasn't even the people who loved each other the most who survived, just the ones who were prepared to give it their best shot.

Ronnie invited me in for coffee and I ended up telling her all about my afternoon. 'See! There was a reason you ended up back in Rome.' She clapped her hands in delight and winked. 'Now you've got rid of the tickbox husband and finally snuffed out the torch you've been carrying for the one that got away, you'll be able to have an affair of the heart.'

I nipped that conversation in the bud straightaway. I'd almost gone there with Carlo and that had been a disaster. 'No, no. That ship has sailed for me. Though there is something both disappointing and comforting about a guy I'd put on a pedestal turning out to be your run-of-the-mill, overweight, middle-aged man rather than the demigod I remembered. Should have come out and confronted him ages ago.'

Ronnie laughed. 'Always better late than never. You're just getting started on life.'

'Hardly. I'm fifty-seven.'

Ronnie fixed me with one of her stares. 'As I say, just getting started on life. It takes decades to stop worrying about things, people, events that don't matter. Gobble up every opportunity, say yes to things that excite but scare you and give people who whine about their lot a wide berth. With any luck, the next thirty years will be the best you've ever had.'

I made my way to Finn's apartment, frowning and smiling, feeling as though I'd been catapulted into an alternate reality populated with wise women. I half-expected to turn the corner and find Marina sitting on the steps offering to read my Tarot cards or realign my chakras.

Much of my annoyance with Finn from this morning had dissipated. Perhaps I'd been living with Declan too long and expected too much from my son. It had to be good for his confidence to have Marina and Ronnie singing his praises. But a bit of rose pruning wasn't the answer to how he was going to support himself out here. However, for the time being, it was at least rendering him welcome where he was.

I knocked on his door after I'd showered and warmed up. 'Hello, love. Gather you've been busy.'

He was all smiley as he filled me in, aglow with the satisfaction of doing a job that the other two struggled with. I managed not to voice my opinion that a bit less time gawking at his phone and more getting out in the fresh air and getting some exercise – whether that was gardening or walking – was obviously making him feel better.

'I could stay here forever,' he said.

And just like that I was snapped back to reality. 'But you can't, love. That's the whole point. I'm going home in less than two months and if you're not coming with me, you need a plan.'

His face clouded. 'I know. You tell me every time you see me.'

'Finn, don't be like that. I honestly want nothing more than for you to be able to discover the city and have a bit of a breather to work out what you want to do.'

Finn's face bore so many emotions – defiance, uncertainty, denial – but the most prominent was his desire to halt this conversation. If ever a conversation got tricky, Finn would default to escape rather than have it out. Callum was just the opposite, never backing down from an argument, quick to anger but quick to forgive. I wondered if Callum was furious because I hadn't been around to help him move. If he was, I hoped he'd transitioned into the forgiveness phase by now. He'd sent me a couple of photos of a reasonable bedroom and a kitchen that looked as though a steam mop wouldn't go amiss, but he seemed happy enough. I considered texting Declan to suggest he gave my steam mop to Callum, then reminded myself that the chances of it ever being used were nil and I shouldn't be getting rid of my clutter on my boys.

My phone buzzed. I did what I hated Finn doing during a difficult conversation and looked at it. A WhatsApp from Beth.

> How's it going? I've finally had the grand invitation to Rico's parents' house in two days' time and they want to do a proper welcome and gather friends and family to meet me. Can you imagine?! Rico wants me to invite you, Finn, Ronnie and Marina to provide a safe shelter for me if all the neighbours and friends get too much... Please say you'll come! I could do with some back-up. Address and time to follow.

I smiled. Rico might not be thinking wedding bells, but it sounded to me as though his mother was desperate to get him married off. But what was even funnier was that Rico, a forty-two-year-old man, was going along with it. Callum and Finn would point-blank refuse.

> I'll definitely be there with Finn.

He might not want to come, but he'd have to. If Ronnie and Marina didn't want to go, I'd need my own back-up.

As expected, Finn sagged in the middle at the thought of making small talk with a load of people he didn't know. 'I can't even speak Italian.'

'It doesn't matter, Beth is my friend and we're going to support her. We only have to show our faces and you never know who might be there.'

'Oh my God, you'd better not be introducing me to people and asking them whether they've got any work for me.'

'I wouldn't show you up like that, don't be silly,' I said, thinking that I would absolutely be meerkating round the room for possible job opportunities.

He sighed. 'How long will we have to stay?'

I could feel my irritation rise. 'I don't know, love. There's always a chance it might be the best evening we've had in ages and it will only be a few hours out of the rest of your life.' I didn't articulate the words, 'So suck it up,' but Finn got the gist because he shrugged and said, 'Fine'.

I had noticed that when I felt a bit apprehensive about doing something, I was irrationally annoyed when the people around me showed anything other than unbridled enthusiasm. I softened my tone and said, 'We won't have to stay long. It'll be great for people-watching anyway.' I walked over and gave him a hug, which he accepted. 'Let's go with a glad heart.'

He surprised me then. 'I love Rome.' And in that one short sentence, I switched from exasperation to feeling proud that my boy had pushed himself out of his comfort zone in the first place.

22

I'd half-expected Ronnie and Marina to decline the invitation. Marina was always so dismissive of most social interactions – 'Such a dreary woman. To think I might only have one year left to live and I've wasted one of my three-hundred and sixty-five evenings with her' or 'It's hard enough to stay alive without him boring me half to death.' But they both leapt at the chance to get out on the town.

Ronnie said, 'I do feel a certain sense of responsibility to check out Rico's background because we did rather push Beth into his arms.'

Marina, on the other hand, was far less altruistic. 'If there's free food and wine, count me in.'

Ronnie rolled her eyes. 'She's pretending it's all about the catering, but she never could resist an invitation to someone else's house. Criticising their design choices will keep her in conversation for the next month.'

So our unlikely band hopped into a cab a couple of days later, and all the way there, I kept thinking about how quickly I'd gone from plodding along in the UK to being jobless and homeless but undeniably more alive. It was surreal to be zipping along the banks of the Tiber with my son and two eccentric women who – truth be known – I aspired to be like. Especially – I conceded grudgingly – Marina, who was wearing a black and red silk dress, diamanté earrings as big as Christmas tree decorations and a feather boa. 'Well, Beth said party attire and this is what I wear to parties.'

Ronnie raised her eyebrows and said, 'Very Sophia Loren.'

Marina's chin jutted out. She pointed at Ronnie's wide-legged palazzo pants and floaty handkerchief top. 'At least I'm not coming as a spare tablecloth.'

Finn and I gave each other a 'look', our code for 'How exactly do these two women stay friends?' before turning away to hide our giggles. But there was no denying I'd had more adventures, more food for thought, more stories to recount in the last month than in the last decade. Not to mention finally making peace with Alessio, or the spectre of him, anyway, because I no longer had any real knowledge of who he was. All I knew was that now whenever I remembered standing in the airport long after the very last passenger had exited, the indignation, hurt and shame no longer electrified me. It was as though my central nervous system had finally disconnected, failing to trigger a reaction. I sent up a thankful little salute to Lainey.

It was ironic that it had taken a shock of such magnitude – her death – to kick-start my determination to live rather than simply exist. There was some synergy in there, but even now, if I could have her back, I'd resign myself to sleepwalking through my days. To which she would retort, 'Then it's a bloody good job I pegged it, isn't it?'

The taxi raced through the confined streets of Trastevere at a speed that had tourists diving into doorways and tucking their toes in. Eventually, the roads opened out again on the outskirts and the cab came to a halt in front of some intricate steel gates, inset with shells and butterflies. Behind them was a short path lined with candles to one of those imposing porches I associated with English country hotels – pillars and sturdy benches and pot plants.

Ronnie squinted about, puzzled. 'Is this it?'

I pulled out my phone, my heart dropping with the dread of messing up the directions and finding that we were half an hour away from where we needed to be. I checked the number. 'Yes, this is right. Unless there's another road with the same name.'

'Well then,' Marina said, stabbing the intercom, while Ronnie and I were too polite to voice our surprise that a busker's parents lived in a great big villa with a dolphin fountain in the front garden.

The gate clicked open and we trailed behind Marina as she marched up the path. Finn was markedly more energetic in his stride at the prospect of spending the evening in a Roman mansion rather than a cramped flat.

Beth appeared at the door, looking lovely in a long turquoise dress. She hugged me, whispering in my ear, 'I had no idea he lived somewhere like this. I feel like the understairs staff in *Downton Abbey*!'

She greeted everyone else and beckoned us through an entrance hall that was all huge oak beams and a staircase flanked by life-size stone statues with lions' bodies and women's heads. Everywhere I looked, there was a bust or nymph or a head, brass, glass and marble, glinting and sparkling.

I hung back and said to Finn under my breath: 'Wasn't quite expecting this. I thought we'd be standing round eating pineapple and cheese on sticks with Great Zia Giuseppina in her widow's black.'

Finn's hand twitched towards his back pocket. I pre-empted it. 'No. You can't walk into someone's private house and start taking photos.'

'I just want to show Callum.'

I shook my head. 'You can't. That would be really rude,' I said, absolutely itching with the desire to do a full panoramic video, never mind a few hastily snapped pictures. I brought my mouth close to his ear. 'We might be able to get a sneaky pic later on.'

We followed Beth down a long hallway. I practically cricked my neck craning round any doors left ajar to catch glimpses of majestic sitting rooms and morning rooms and snugs. They were crammed not with the heavy wooden furniture I associated with this calibre and age of home, but with jewel-coloured sofas – crimson, neon pink, burnt orange. I could quite picture myself stretching out with a book, snuggling down into their velvety cosiness. Though I wouldn't have been averse to skidding about in my socks on the shiny parquet floors either.

Finally, we arrived in a glass atrium hung with fairy lights and a huge olive tree growing up through the roof. Finn's attention was immediately drawn to how it had been constructed to keep it watertight. I, on the other hand, was admiring the décor, which managed to be luxurious but also eclectic and welcoming. Candles flickered on every windowsill and huge potted ferns lent a tropical vibe to the setting. A long table at the side of the room was brimming with charcuterie, cheese, piles of artisan bread, salads in ceramic bowls the colours of the sea and sunshine, with seating for about thirty people.

I glanced down at my black trousers and plain white shirt and felt distinctly underdressed – I wouldn't blame anyone for mistaking me for staff and asking me whether I could fetch them another glass or if there was any butter.

Finn's eyes lit up at the sight of the table. 'Wow. That looks good.' I wondered if Rico's mother would think I never fed him when she saw his ability to pile a plate sky-high and still remain slim.

Rico hurried over to us, wearing a lime green shirt that took a certain presence to carry off and, to my relief, jeans. He was a welcome sight in the midst of all these people milling about in their jackets and backless dresses and tiny dainty feet arching into strappy stilettos. He threw his arms open. 'Sara! Thank you for coming.' I was so glad he didn't say 'to my humble abode' because that would have made me like him a bit less. I could feel his eyes scanning my face for a reaction to seeing where he lived, but I wasn't sure what he was hoping for.

I introduced Finn, who was a bit shy in the presence of someone so cool and bohemian, but, as was becoming obvious, wealthier than we had first supposed. I didn't think I was alone in making some assumptions about him, given that I'd taken the penniless busker persona at face value. Beth had definitely commented on how she had had to adjust to the idea of being with someone who didn't have his own home or a steady and reliable income. I was dying to have a debrief with her. As far as I understood it, they'd been staying in a friend's apartment and sharing with his mate's sister? I didn't think a house like this would be missing the odd guest bedroom or two.

Before I could attempt to hazard guesses about why they'd be staying elsewhere, Rico was greeting Marina in a theatrical way that involved much bowing, hand kissing and extravagant compliments. Very few men could have delivered the words without sounding ridiculously insincere and very few women would have had the ego to accept without feeling forced into a self-deprecating comment. Marina was waving her walking stick at him. 'I only look seventy because I live a good life, and I do not waste my time worrying about other people's opinions.'

That didn't bode well for me. If that was the secret, at Marina's age, I'd look like an accordion.

Rico stepped around Marina to enfold Ronnie in a bear hug. I loved the warmth and welcome of this man. He put his arm around Beth and shepherded us over to a curly-haired woman in a halter-neck dress of rainbow striped silk. She had that grace and elegance about her, the sort of woman who swished and flowed, all long swan neck and hollows in her collarbones. In her wake, I would immediately feel heavy-footed and clunky, however lightly I tried to tread.

She put her soft hand in mine, her bright orange nails contrasting against my unmanicured paw. 'I'm Costanza. *Piacere*, welcome. This is my husband, Arturo,' she said, introducing us to a quietly-spoken man, so like Rico that it was like looking at an age-enhanced police photofit.

There was no question of who ruled the roost as Costanza despatched him to fetch more champagne flutes.

She gestured expansively. 'Make yourselves at home. Please take whatever you would like to drink. Thank you for coming. I'm always happy to know my son has lovely friends.'

Rico threw his head back in mock despair, the universal son to mother reproach of 'You are so embarrassing!'

Once I'd clocked the house, I'd fallen into the trap of expecting her to be aloof, superior in her manner and status, but she had Rico's same down-to-earth charm.

Marina took Costanza at her word and installed herself like a Roman empress on a bright pink velvet throne with legs that ended in gilded hooves. 'Bring me some Prosecco, Finn, darling.'

He hesitated, awkward about marching over to the table and helping himself.

Rico gestured to Finn. 'Come with me to sort out the drinks.'

It didn't take much to win me over. Anyone who took an interest in Finn and eased him into this new chapter, however transitory it might turn out to be, was guaranteed a bucket of goodwill from me.

Beth pulled up a small striped armchair for Ronnie and a couple of pouffes for us.

Marina leant forward immediately. 'I thought that *fidanzato* of yours was nice but not money material. I was worried that we might not have done you any favours, condemning you to an impecunious life.' She clapped her hands. 'I am *thrilled* to see this is not the case. Maybe you should marry him.'

I actively had to think about closing my mouth at Marina's rudeness. I barely dared look at Beth, but her months at Villa Alba had obviously provided some kind of immunity to offence. She was laughing. 'That's why he hasn't let me come here before. Why he made us stay in his friend's place. He wanted to know if I loved him.' Beth coloured up as though she hadn't expected to say that out loud. 'He wanted us to get to know each other without the money thing getting in the way.'

Marina frowned. 'Well, that's all very honourable, but, honestly, what a silly man. What if you'd decided that you couldn't be doing with someone singing songs in a park and collecting money in a hat? He'd have missed out on one of life's true treasures.'

I could quite see how Marina had managed to keep people on side, delivering insults and barbs with a charm that almost made you feel singled out and special. Ronnie was quietly shaking her head.

Marina blundered on. 'You must have felt lied to, tricked?'

Ronnie scratched at the arm of her chair. 'Keep your foghorn down, Marina. We are guests after all and I'd quite like a bit of that asparagus frittata before we get thrown out.'

Beth smiled at Ronnie. 'It's okay. I did feel a bit odd about it, to be honest, as though I'd entered into a relationship without knowing all the facts. We only came here last night. It's been a bit overwhelming – I was expecting to be ushered into a bare little single room with an old-fashioned eiderdown and a crucifix hanging over the bed and, instead, Rico has his own apartment.'

I cleared my throat to warn her as Rico and Arturo came into view behind them, carrying a tray of champagne flutes and some bottles, with Finn holding an ice bucket.

But Beth was in full flow. 'I thought I'd fallen for an overgrown student and I'd just got comfortable with that. It was like he'd put me to the test without me knowing.'

I was trying to signal to Beth to stop talking, but it was too late. Rico was right behind her.

He placed everything on a table beside us, then gently put his hand on Beth's shoulder and said, 'I didn't lie. I wanted to strip everything back to basics. I hoped to get to know you when you were focused on me, the person I am, in my heart, without slotting me into some imaginary idea of who I might be, because I grew up here, in this place.'

Beth didn't apologise, didn't gasp at being caught talking about him, even in front of Rico's father, and I admired her for that. 'I do find it a bit insulting that you didn't trust me to see beyond all of this,' she said, waving her hand around the room.

I wished I'd been brave enough to say it how I saw it in front of Alessio's parents all those years ago. At the very least, I might have understood that I couldn't compete with the pull of family here in Rome and cut my losses much earlier. There was so much to applaud about the confidence that came with getting older. Beth had nailed the laying out her cards on the table and not caring who saw them.

While Rico nodded and considered his reply, Marina tapped her long pink nail against the rim of one of the champagne flutes. 'If we have to get dragged into your relationship shenanigans, I need a drink.'

Rico's dad laughed – thankfully – and uncorked a bottle with practised ease. He poured everyone a glass.

Rico raised his to Beth. 'Money changes how people see you. Before I gave away my heart in a manner that meant it would be difficult to get back, I wanted to know that you would love me, whatever was in my wallet.' He stepped forward and stroked her face. 'Am I forgiven? My intentions were good.'

I glanced at Finn, who looked like he wanted to crawl under the big banqueting table and stay there until all this love stuff was done and dusted. I, on the other hand, wanted to give a big cheer for their openness, for not succumbing to the pressure to pretend that everything was endlessly rosy in the garden, even the moonlit, floodlit, statue-studded one I could see beyond these windows. Maybe if everyone stopped putting on a perfect façade, we'd all find it easier to admit when things were difficult. So much better to let off steam and get help before the terminal stage that Declan and I had arrived at – tipping over from relative contentment to marching about the house compiling a mental list of wrongs. And once that point had been reached, once I'd allowed myself the luxury of accepting I might be more out than in, the list had grown at a frightening speed. Everything from not shaking out shirt sleeves before hanging them up to dry to leaving the milk out of the fridge joined the inventory of laments.

Arturo had obviously decided that Beth was 'the one' because his whole face wore an earnest expression of 'please forgive my son, it all came from a good place'. I was reminded of my mother's desperation, bigging me up to Declan the first time I introduced him to her. We'd joked about it in the car on the way home, with Declan doing a brilliant impersonation of my mother: 'Sara always wins at Trivial Pursuit, knows everything, especially the nature questions,' as though knowing the scientific name for a rabbit's tail would be the key to eliciting a marriage proposal.

I was practically swooning on Beth's behalf at Rico's declaration of love. It took me all my restraint not to stand up and start chanting 'Forgive him!'

Marina swigged back her champagne and said, 'Of course she forgives you. You had to make sure that she wasn't a gold-digger.'

And with that, Beth said, 'We'll talk about this later,' but her eyes had that glittery look that people get when they're filled with hope and love and optimism.

Rico pulled her to her feet and there was a little beat when their gazes locked. Something about the intention and promise in that exchange reminded me of Carlo and I had to look away. I didn't want my expression to betray that odd emotion for which I'd never found the correct name: when you are delighted that it's all come good for people you like and don't want to take anything away from them but, at the same time, their happiness underlines the complete dog's dinner of your own life.

Rico whispered something to Beth, turned to the rest of us and said, 'Excuse us for a moment,' and led her away.

At the same time, Costanza clapped her hands. '*A tavola!*' The whole room moved towards the long table, a crowd of gorgeousness, like a Christmas advert flogging a perfume that deluded us into thinking we too could be that sultry and sexy.

Costanza directed people to their places with grace and finesse, an experienced hostess, for whom this gathering of twenty-five plus people of diverse nationalities presented no more challenge than knocking up a quick plate of pasta for one unexpected extra guest. I longed to be like her. I used to be when I was younger. Before I got sucked into the idea that having friends over for dinner was a display of cookery skills rather than a chance to push light into dark spaces and refill our hearts with fun and joy. I made a promise that I'd never faff about with anything that involved a vegetable spiraliser, a blow-torch, an icing bag ever again. Then I smiled as I realised that even if I wanted to, I doubted that Declan would consider them items worthy of storage and they were probably headed for a skip right now. And instead of that making me feel panicky, I felt free. I'd never do a starter again, a souffle, a jus. No. From now on, my friends would eat hearty casseroles and cheese and biscuits and ice cream. I would sit at the table and enjoy their company instead of spending all day cooking, then being on edge about timings so I never relaxed into the conversation.

Rico sat opposite me with Beth, which felt like an honour I

didn't deserve, an empty seat next to her, that Marina was keen to move into, but that he politely reserved. 'I've actually saved that seat for a friend of mine who doesn't know anyone else.'

Marina started to complain that if friends wanted a prime position then they should have had the manners to arrive on time. Rico switched into Italian, delivering what must have been the killer argument, as Marina ruffled her shoulders and twitched her glass back into a space a bit further along.

Costanza was moving up and down the table, filling glasses with water. She tapped Finn on the shoulder. 'Could you help me serve some wine, please?'

Finn got to his feet and I felt obliged to hiss, 'The red goes in the biggest glass, the white in the smaller one.'

He hissed back, 'I know.' I had to stop thinking he was twelve.

I watched him doing the rounds of the table, more charming and confident than I expected. What if I just didn't, with Finn, too? What if I didn't try to foresee what might happen and had faith that if he made a mistake, he'd pick himself up? After so many years of being primed to protect, to stop him getting run over, burning himself on the oven, wrapping his car round a tree, it was as though my highly developed early-warning system was stuck in constant alarm mode. I'd have to work out how to switch it off.

In the meantime, though, I took a large swig of red wine and relaxed into the chatter around me. Dishes of panzanella, platters of seafood and glorious bowls of the greenest rocket with salty parmesan were passed along. The colours popped with freshness; the scents of garlic and thyme swirled around.

There was something fidgety about Beth and Rico. My eyes flew open with sudden understanding. Perhaps he was going to propose to her. Surely it was too soon? And in front of everyone? My stomach knotted with dread. What if she said no? I looked over at Costanza. Had she been waiting all these years for a daughter-in-law? Praying that this woman, no, perhaps that woman, would be the one? How would she feel about Beth, from a totally different background, country, too old now to bear her grandchildren? Would it be enough for her that Rico was happy? Maybe, over the years, she'd loosened her expectations, understood that there were many ways to find fulfilment, not just the narrow and accepted pathways we expected our children – and ourselves – to follow. If she was anything other than happy for them, she was hiding it well.

I was so lost in these thoughts and Marina's constant requests to pass the salt, the oil, the lemon wedges that I didn't pay any attention to Rico leaping to his feet and leaving the table. I was picking up my napkin from the floor when I became aware of a slight lull in the conversation, a drop in the hubbub of noise. When I straightened up, Carlo was standing behind the chair next to Beth, diagonally opposite me. I forgot to be that neutral woman and heard my intake of breath, a gasp of surprise. Hope flared, ferocious and steely, against the counterweight of resistance, forcing me to stay rooted to my seat.

Carlo raised his hand in a greeting, drawing my eye like the one bright detail in an otherwise black and white painting, everyone else fading into a blur around the edges. 'Hello, Sara.'

'Hello.' My chest felt thick with feelings, feelings I couldn't yet tame.

'Good to see you again,' he said.

There was that sensation building in me, not dissimilar to the day I walked out of my job, that this was simply too much, that I wouldn't, and couldn't, and wasn't going to. I glanced towards the door, my desire to start shouting about the sheer gall of him turning up here, all 'Good to see you again', narrowly constrained by how ill-mannered it would be to make a scene in someone else's house, at someone else's party.

I looked down at my plate. 'You too,' I said quietly. And as the shock of seeing him subsided, my heart was flaming, little fires lifting me from that placid acceptance that love was something for young people to experiment with. Instead, a greedy urge to fling myself into the fray once more was surging through me, to risk again, against all the evidence that Carlo was not someone to trust.

Marina's head was swivelling around like an owl. Finn thankfully created a small diversion by sitting down, his sommelier duties complete. I introduced Carlo to everyone and explained that he'd been kind enough to offer me somewhere to stay when I was in Florence.

Ronnie threw me a lifeline by asking Carlo how he'd ended up moving from England to Italy while my heart stopped thumping. Rico was grinning away as though he'd successfully pulled off a sleight of hand, though Beth was sending me looks of solidarity or sympathy, I wasn't sure which.

My stomach had closed over, the array of salami and fat prawns suddenly an insurmountable mound in front of me. I slipped them onto Finn's plate, who looked at me sideways but troughed on without a word. I excused myself and headed off to the loo.

In a move that felt like I'd been transported back to sixth-form parties, Beth knocked on the door. 'Sara? Are you okay?'

I came out and we stood whispering in front of the marble sink about how Carlo had found Rico's busking videos on Instagram and asked him if he knew where I was. 'He didn't tell him straightaway,' Beth said, defensively.

'Did you tell Rico that Carlo had slept with Boo?' I asked, half-expecting to be joined by a posse of teenage girls with hennaed hair, crying as though their worlds had ended after too much Pernod and black, before making a miraculous recovery when Wham! came on.

Beth pulled a face. 'I sort of suggested that his behaviour hadn't been exemplary.' There was absolutely no mistaking what nationality Beth was.

Whether it was the British understatement, the wine or a release of everything that had been building and bubbling since I left England, I didn't know, but within minutes, we were doubled over with laughter. Every time I said that we should go back in, I'd think about the 'not exemplary behaviour' and we'd become hysterical again. Beth did manage to say, 'I think you should hear Carlo's side of the story. But don't hate us for telling him where you were.'

'Did you invite him?'

'Rico did. He's a big believer in taking chances where love's involved.'

'I won't hate you,' I said, as we walked back into the atrium, where the multilingual conversations had resumed several decibels louder. Finn was up again pouring wine, and Carlo was talking to Marina and Ronnie, his gestures vibrantly Italian. His eyes straightaway searched out mine, as if he'd been waiting for me to reappear. I felt the energy of him land, creating a twist in my stomach that I wanted to ward off, push back to a place where life wouldn't become problematic, yet I was still propelled towards him.

Thankfully, Rico stood up. 'It's getting warm in here, so if anyone wants to take a *digestivo* outside, you're more than welcome.'

Without looking at Carlo, I headed towards the door. Marina had commandeered Finn to help her out into the garden. 'I'm perfectly capable but you need to carry my wine.'

Ronnie hung behind. 'Is that your young man?'

'No. He's just someone I met when I was travelling. He took me to Portofino to scatter Lainey's ashes.'

She raised her eyebrows in a move that made her resemble Marina. 'He's only here for one reason and it's not the *torta della nonna*, good though that is.'

'It's complicated.'

Ronnie batted at the air as though I was splitting hairs.

'Love is complicated, but it brings joy. But not loving when you have the chance is also complicated and doesn't bring joy.' And with that, she walked on, leaving me sifting through her words.

As I reached the threshold to the garden, Carlo caught up with me. 'Hey.' His hand cupped my elbow and his touch made me lurch with longing. He steered me away from the floodlit fountain dominating the courtyard, where people were sitting trailing their hands in the water. We ended up in a dark area in the corner with a huge rubber plant hung with tiny bulbs. We stood, the lights reflecting in his eyes. He put his hands up in surrender. 'Hear me out.'

'Give me one reason why I should.'

'I didn't do anything with Boo. She was drunk and hysterical and I was worried about her choking in her sleep. I know what it looked like. And of course, what she said, and obviously you're aware there's history. But it's really, really old history. Forty years old.'

He'd moved a step closer, and briefly, I felt the hairs on his arms graze against mine. My fickle heart folded around the memory of us watching the strands of sunlight bouncing off the sea in Liguria, kissing until the last shreds of pink disappeared and I'd remembered what it felt like to be invincible.

'But Boo doesn't realise it's history. She's still holding out for you and you haven't done enough to quash her expectations. I've been in a marriage long past its expiry date and I'm happy on my own. Plus, you're here, I'm there.' As the words left my mouth, a sizeable part of my soul was hoping he would come up with all the reasons why this stupid and difficult thing was still an excellent idea.

Carlo moved back slightly. 'Boo's gone. I couldn't have been clearer with her about where I stand on the matter. She's a friend. That is all it can and will ever be now. Does that make a difference?'

'What are you doing here, Carlo? I mean, is this some odd

"didn't quite get me into bed, let's finish what we started" thing?' I blushed as I realised how arrogant that sounded. As though I'd been some femme fatale playing hard to get, rather than a woman who had the beginnings of a bunion and boobs that juddered to a halt when she took her bra off.

'Is that what you think? That I'd track down Rico, spend days persuading him and Beth to let me know where you are, just to have sex with you?'

The contrariness of my mind decided to read that as an insult rather than proof of effort.

Noise from the party drifted over as we stood in silence. Shouts, laughter, water splashing.

'I should go. Finn is on his own.'

He put his hand on my arm. 'Finn can manage for five minutes. Please just listen to what I have to say.'

'What's the point?' I asked.

'The point is this, Sara. I didn't know I could feel again. I thought my heart was so broken, so shattered after Cesca died that it would forever be a dried-up husk barely capable of pumping blood round my body. I have not stopped thinking about you since that day at the Forte di Belvedere. Before that, probably. But here's what I know. There's a million reasons to talk yourself out of things, to project forward what might or might not happen, what could go wrong. But what if we thought about what could go right? What if we threw ourselves in at the deep end and worked out whether we could swim, rather than assuming we'd drown? Why not wring the most out of what's in front of us rather than waiting for guarantees of future happiness?'

Something in his words echoed Lainey. Something she'd said one day when she knew she was dying. Among all the things that made her furious – not taking her whole holiday entitlement every year, forcing herself to go to the gym when she was worn out – she raged about the fact she'd cooked a blackberry crumble with less butter and sugar than the recipe suggested in order to be healthy. She'd ended up chucking it out because it wasn't very nice. 'Look where that got me. Always projecting forwards instead of having the best possible time right now.'

I knew what she would do if she was in my shoes at this moment.

Carlo stepped forward and leant his forehead on mine. 'Give me a chance. Give yourself a chance.'

I breathed in the scent of spicy aftershave. And with a quick glance over my shoulder to check that we were out of sight, we kissed with an intensity that my teenage self would have applauded.

23

In a pathetic attempt to pretend that I hadn't been hiding around a corner kissing, I left Carlo and tried to slip into the melee around the fountain. I cast about for Finn, feeling ashamed of abandoning him. The laughing and the noisy chatter seemed so loud after the temporary cocoon with Carlo where the world had fallen away. I scanned the crowd, looking for his blonde hair among all the dark heads. As I drew closer, I realised that there were people actually in the fountain – Rico, Finn, a couple of other lads, all sitting there in their boxer shorts, holding themselves up by hooking their arms over carved fish and dolphins.

Finn waved at me. 'Hi, Mum, cooling down Roman-style!'

My immediate reaction was one of horror, that I'd brought my son to a posh dinner and he'd leapt into their fountain in his underpants like some New Year reveller in Trafalgar Square.

Rico must have seen my face because he said, 'Don't worry. My family have always used this to cool down. Even my mum and dad take a dip, though it's rare we are still able to do it in October. This year has been crazy hot.'

Life in Rome was full of surprises.

Carlo nudged my shoulder. 'That puts a new twist on must-have items for summer. A seventeenth-century fountain that doubles up as a swimming pool. Like their style!' His hand rested in the small of my back like a promise of good times to come.

I felt something in me give. My need to do the right thing, to control everything I could in order to avoid people thinking badly of me or my family suddenly seemed so futile. No one was paying any attention to Rico and Finn, sitting side by side, chatting between pouty fish mouths and a nymph cascading water. If nothing else, Finn's memories of Rome would stretch beyond the well-worn trail of the Colosseum and the Spanish Steps.

I watched him, my heart lifting as he engaged in earnest conversation with Rico, his hand occasionally shooting out to make a point, sending drops of water scattering. This boy who used to have to be persuaded to take off his T-shirt on a family holiday, self-conscious about how skinny he was, now sitting quite happily in a clam shell, half-naked and as broad-shouldered as the rest of the men. I would store that sight in the mental archives labelled 'Most surreal moments with my kids' but also, 'Happiest moments with my kids'.

Ronnie came up to me and did a knowing little smile as she clocked Carlo's hand on my waist. Her eyes darted about with merriment. 'Isn't Rome magical? Lovely seeing your boy having fun.'

'I wish he'd come out to Italy sooner. I knew he wasn't happy in his job, but I never know whether to say, "Oh poor you, jack it all in and do something you really like" or to tell him to get a grip, work isn't supposed to be one long party and the sooner you grasp that, the better. I mean, it's not that I think going to work should be unmitigated misery, but in the end, most of us would rather be on holiday than drudging off to an office with people we don't particularly like.'

Ronnie tilted her head on one side. 'How would you feel if he stayed here after you have to go home?'

'What? At the apartment? I thought you didn't want any men there.'

'We don't.'

I blinked, trying to get my head around how Finn might be able to remain in Rome.

Ronnie did that grin she did when she had a plan up her sleeve. 'I just need to know if you're wedded to him leaving with you?'

I glanced over at Finn, animated and intent on his conversation. 'Not at all. I'd be thrilled for him to stay, but he's a long way from sorting out all the practicalities – job, accommodation, income.'

Ronnie beckoned to me, raising an apologetic hand to Carlo. 'Back in a moment.'

She led me over to Marina, who'd found a swing seat and was rocking happily backwards and forwards with a full glass of wine that looked perilously close to slopping all over her dress.

'Put your glass down for a minute. It won't run away,' Ronnie said. 'Tell Sara your stroke of genius.'

Marina took a large swig of wine and flapped away Ronnie's efforts to take it from her. 'I don't know whether Ronnie said, but I own a villa on the coast, at Santa Marinella, about half an hour away on the train. It's been standing empty since the pandemic and needs some attention. Nothing structural, but the rooms could do with a lick of paint and the terrace needs a new canopy, some of the shutters are hanging loose. That sort of thing. It's been on my mind for a while. It's crying out for someone young and strong. The guy who's been looking after it is getting on a bit.' She shrugged. 'He's younger than me, but he can't do all the ladders and heavy lifting any more.'

I suppressed a smile. Marina said it as though, given the right equipment, she'd be up on the roof fixing tiles, when everything about her suggested that there was no way anything she deemed 'man's work' was getting pushed onto her plate.

'Anyway, he can order in all the supplies and whatever is required, talk Finn through the basics – and he can *talk*, I will be glad not to listen – then Finn could spend a couple of months sorting it out. If he's really up for it, he can tackle the garden. I'd pay him and he can live there for however long he wants.'

'Wow, Marina. That's a very generous offer, thank you so much. But it's not up to me what he does. He's an adult. I'm sure he'd love the opportunity, but I'll let you ask him.' I felt the liberation of stepping back from the mediator role, of accepting that the next stage for Finn had to be forging his own relation-ships. As well as managing his own successes and sucking up his own disappointments.

Alongside that, I had a pang of envy for the glorious oppor-tunity that had dropped into his lap. I wished she'd offered me the chance. I could wield a paint roller as well as the next person and I couldn't think of anywhere I'd like to be doing it more than in a villa right on the Tyrrhenian Sea.

Marina tucked her chin in as though I'd said something astonishing. 'Look at you, slashing away at the apron strings. I was expecting you to grill me about – what do they call it? All those fussy rules?' She slapped her hand on her thigh. 'Health and safety.'

For the hundredth time since I'd been in Rome, I reminded myself that Marina was just being Marina, rather than deliberately offensive, though the dividing line was admittedly quite fine. 'As long as the roof isn't about to cave in on his head, then I will consider him a very lucky boy, thank you.'

'Well, go and get him. Tell him to come and talk to me.'

Ronnie tutted at her. 'Stop being so immediate. You can wait until tomorrow.'

But at that moment, Finn was climbing over the side of the fountain. Beth handed him and the others a towel. Marina waved her walking stick in the air like a tour leader trying to gather her group and shouted, 'Finn! Finn!'

I walked back over to where Carlo was standing, passing Finn on the way. 'Marina's got a proposal for you.' With great self-control, I didn't go with him, despite the temptation to stand right next to him making encouraging noises because, frankly, I wasn't sure what other options might exist for Finn in Italy. I felt a stab of guilt at my enthusiasm for this as a solution, not least because Finn settled doing something he enjoyed would free up a huge amount of my headspace.

Discreetly, Carlo took my hand. 'What was all that about?'

I filled him in.

'Nice work if you can get it. Good for Finn,' he said.

The words spilled out before I could harness my new persona as the mother who could withstand seeing her fledglings flop to the ground a few times without squawking over to see if they were all right. 'I hope he'll be okay. He's hardly lived on his own at all because he did most of university from home during the pandemic.'

Carlo squeezed my hand. 'One, Florence is only an hour and a half away from Rome by train and I can help out if there is an emergency. Two, I'm hoping that you will come back here on a regular basis. Three, well, can I say this? As far as I can see, you've been a great mum, but being a great mum doesn't mean you have to fix everything for him. He won't keel over if he's a bit homesick or lonely for a few days.'

I glanced over my shoulder. Marina was hugging Finn, then he was jumping about, twirling Ronnie around, everyone shrieking with laughter.

'I think he's said yes,' Carlo said.

He came running over to me, the towel round his neck, excitement pouring out of him as he relayed the conversation with Marina. 'I told her that if she doesn't want to use the villa herself, I could run it as an Airbnb. I'll take one room and rent out the rest for her. She was quite keen on the idea, said it would pay for her to have a lift installed at Villa Alba when her knees give up the ghost.'

I choked down the words, 'I'd better show you how to clean a bathroom properly then,' along with the warning that was straining to fly out of my mouth, 'Let's not get carried away, don't run before you can walk.' Why shouldn't he gallop gloriously, learning as he went? Who dictated that you had to have all the answers before you started? Wasn't part of living life to the full gathering information and adapting to circumstances as they arose, rather than standing paralysed at the starting line because of what could happen?

I hugged him. 'That would be amazing. Do you think you could rent a room out to your old mum now and again?'

'And Callum.' He ran his fingers through his hair. 'And Dad.'

'Of course, Dad as well. He'd love to come and see what you're doing out here.' Even Declan couldn't fail to be impressed if Finn established himself abroad.

Finn rubbed the towel over his hair. 'I'd better go and put some clothes on.' He turned to go. 'Mum, thank you. Thank you for making this happen.'

'I didn't make it happen. You did.'

And briefly, I buried my face in his neck. He might fail and fall or soar and succeed. I sent up a wish into the universe that it would be gentle with him.

He stepped back. 'Do you think I'll be all right?' he asked.

'Yes. Yes. I really do. It will be a brilliant experience for you. I'm the one who needs to get my act together and find a job now.'

'You'll work it out. You always do.'

And we hugged again, filling each other's hearts with confidence to take the next leap into the unknown. A half-tick in the happiness checklist on the stability front, which I would count as a win.

EPILOGUE

I returned to England at the beginning of December. Unsurprisingly, the house sale had taken longer than Declan's speedy six-week prediction and I actually arrived home three days before everything was finalised. As I walked through my old front door, I felt as though I'd come to say goodbye to my former self, to the person who'd been prepared to settle for the mundane and the unrewarding. The woman whose zest for life had routinely flickered along on the lowest heat setting, with occasional jets of flame for my sons. But the weeks I'd spent in Italy, dividing my time between Rome and Florence, had proved that the real me had been hibernating for several decades. When I stepped into my old hallway, I had the sensation that my heart was fuller than it had been in years, bubbling over with experiences and emotions.

In the kitchen, I scratched at the remains of the sticky tape that had held our family planner on the fridge. A true end of an era, yet it didn't seem as difficult as I'd envisaged to accept. Callum had gathered up the few small mementoes I'd specified for safekeeping. Declan had taken the pick of our furniture, grudgingly sticking some basics in storage for me; a clearance company had collected the rest. As I roamed the bare rooms, I was bemused by my lack of nostalgia for what Declan and I had created in the good times. The house had the familiarity of someone I once knew and liked but had grown apart from without any hard feelings. Someone I wished well with a residual fondness but without any desire to reacquaint myself with them. I had a little cry when I did the last tour of my garden, where the images of my boys – playing football, making dens, having water fights – were the most powerful. By that evening, however, I felt the lightness and relief of having survived the hardest part.

I couldn't, however, avoid the obvious: meeting Carlo had smoothed the transition. Despite dedicating considerable effort to fighting the idea that such a thing might be possible again, a feeling a lot like love kept catching me off guard. I found myself smiling at a memory of Carlo tucking his scarf around my neck as the mild autumn gave way to a Florentine winter, with blue skies and a crisp chill. If I ate out with my friends, I'd automatically look to see if scallops were on the menu, Carlo's favourite dish. And I couldn't escape the flare of joy every time his name popped up on my mobile.

December passed in a flurry of precious evenings with Callum, who was living it up in London and squeezed me in on a Tuesday if I was lucky. Finn FaceTimed me far more regularly to download all his worries about whether he was doing a good job at Marina's villa. I then lay awake worrying about the various plumbing and painting issues, fretting about him being out of his depth. When I enquired about whether he'd managed to resolve them the next time we spoke, Finn would frown and say, 'Oh yeah, it was fine,' and be annoyingly reluctant to expand further.

To my great delight, Carlo had travelled to Rome to take

Finn out for lunch one weekend and was very reassuring: 'You don't need to worry about him. He's got a great social circle there. A good-looking young lad like him with his cute British accent is quite the honeypot. The handyman's granddaughter seems to have taken it upon herself to introduce him to everyone in the area.'

'Did he seem happy?'

'One hundred per cent. He was full of plans to expand his property services to wealthy holiday homeowners. You might have to get used to the idea that he won't come back to the UK in the near future.'

Although I missed Finn, I was selfishly relieved only to have myself to worry about as my own living arrangements veered between unpleasantly chaotic and enchantingly nomadic. There was a certain student charm about living in my friends' worlds, unairbrushed, alongside them, proper shared experiences rather than snatched dinners when there was always so much more to say. But, by January, I was becoming less of a novelty and more of a bad smell, with husbands starting to whisper, 'How long is she staying for?' At which point, I found my niche as a serial house-sitter, mastering everything from the idiosyncrasies of greyhounds with sensitive stomachs to temperamental electric gates. I went through the motions of finding somewhere to rent, struggling to be anything other than lacklustre in my effort.

On one of my nightly calls with Carlo, when I was ranting about the lack of places within my budget, he simply said, 'Why not wait until you can return to Italy in six weeks' time and come and live with me? You can pay me in cappuccinos. Florence is glorious in the spring. You could visit Finn in Rome as well.'

I hesitated. 'Is that a "you'd like me to come out" or a pity offer of temporary accommodation because you don't want to see me homeless?'

'Come on. Don't make me plead.' His voice went quiet. 'I miss you.'

I bit my lip. 'That feels like quite a big step, coming to Italy to stay with you.'

'We managed to spend a lot of time together here last year without killing each other. I mean, sometimes you even appeared to quite like being with me.'

The days I'd stayed with Carlo in Florence had been little oases of bliss, light-hearted but intense bursts of hedonism when every day had felt like a gift, insulated from the rest of the world. He'd walked me up to the Forte di Belvedere and down through the Boboli Gardens, pointing out his favourite features: the monkeys spouting water in a fountain, the *putti* playfighting in a grotto in the Palazzo Pitti courtyard. We'd strolled hand-in-hand through his neighbourhood where he showed me the wine windows built into the walls of some of the palazzi. 'The nobles used to sell wine from their vineyards through these little hatches – that way they didn't have to open a shop and pay taxes. They also came in handy when there was a plague in the seventeenth century; they didn't have to mix with the hoi polloi.'

The evenings were my favourite when I'd watch his face, serious with concentration, as he chopped herbs and diced onions for a sauce. Or when I'd pretend not to hear the waiters at Dante's teasing him about being in love while the core of me would blaze with hope and longing.

But I didn't know whether I was brave enough to put my feelings to a proper test, outside the previous parameters. There'd always been a fairytale element to our relationship – the knowledge that we didn't have to deal with anything too uncomfortable or inconvenient as I would be leaving for England in a few weeks anyway.

In the end, I opted for a brave truth. 'I loved being in

Florence with you.' Although a braver truth would have been 'I loved being with you.' Anywhere.

'So why not give it a go? Apart from a bit of furniture storage, what's it going to cost you? Why not enjoy Florence with me and then, who knows?'

I floundered, caught between wanting to throw caution to the wind and the difficulty of letting go of how I'd assumed my life would pan out, with a definite plan and a stable base. 'I don't think I've ever really gone with the flow before. I'm a bit more of a planner.'

He'd laughed and said, 'Well, give it a try. You might love it.' But his words didn't feel critical, as though I had to change to please him. He presented it in a way that felt as though he was inviting me to step into a world that I might find invigorating and inspiring.

So, at the beginning of March, when Finn suggested a reunion for his twenty-second birthday in Santa Marinella, I accepted the challenge. Time to see whether the 'you hang up first' that dogged the end of every conversation could translate into something bigger.

Which is how Carlo and I, Ronnie, Marina, Callum and, yes, Declan and his new girlfriend, Hillary, found ourselves all having lunch together in the newly painted dining room in Marina's villa. Finn had assumed without consulting me that Declan and I were grown up enough to deal with each other's partners. After Declan had jumped at the chance of a free weekend in Italy with 'Hills', I'd had no choice but to put my best face on.

Carlo had shrugged. 'I'm not bothered. Always good to check out the competition.' He'd covered himself in glory by being charming and funny and – as far as I could gather – Marina and Ronnie's favourite.

I'd overheard Marina say to Finn when he was showing her round the latest improvements – her roof terrace jet-washed and a new canopy for the summer – that she was delighted he'd invited us all out. I was about to credit her with a generosity of spirit I hadn't hitherto recognised when she'd added, 'Nothing as entertaining as watching ex-husbands square up against the incoming replacement.'

Finn had looked puzzled, as though the thought hadn't even occurred to him. He still had a lot to learn, though there was something endearing about his naïve belief that 'grown-ups' would always behave in an adult manner.

I spent the weekend silently gnashing my teeth while Hills giggled and patted Declan's knee as though he'd missed a career in comedy every time he spoke. I watched her as she went to the buffet first, bringing a plate back for him as though he'd lost the use of his legs and double-checking that she'd brought enough bread. She was kind to Finn though, praising everything he'd done in the house and, to my ear, genuinely enthusiastic when she was looking at his before and after photos. If she wanted to dogsbody after Declan, that was none of my business.

Ronnie kept sending me little smiles of solidarity every time Declan piped up about how he'd always encouraged the boys to consider living abroad for a spell – 'mind-broadening'. He then went on to pontificate about how he and Hills were considering 'overwintering' in Thailand next year, as though they were some exotic birds requiring warmer climes rather than two people from the outskirts of London considering a fortnight's holiday in Phuket. It reminded me that Declan always felt that anyone else's achievements somehow diminished him, even his own sons'.

I watched Carlo asking Callum all about his job and nodding approvingly, 'Fair play to you knowing what you want to do at twenty-two.' I felt quietly smug. Or rather loudly, earsplittingly smug that I'd upgraded to a man who didn't have to compete and establish himself as 'the one who had' to feel comfortable in his own skin.

Marina dinged her knife on her glass. 'As the elder stateswoman here, I feel obliged to say a few words. Happy birthday to these two delightful young men and huge thanks to Finn for bringing my villa back to life.' She looked down, as though a memory had crept in, unbidden. 'I've always felt a little ambiguous about this place. My husband – the third one, Alfredo – loved it and after I stopped loving him, I decided to hate everything he loved.' She said it as though it made perfect sense and that we would all follow her seamless logic. 'But now, with all these beautiful rooms in their very majestic colours – have you seen that sitting room in navy? – I feel that I have reclaimed the house and the ghost of Alfredo has been banished.'

I didn't dare catch Callum's eye in case we got the giggles. He hadn't had the benefit of several months to become immune to Marina's theatrical declarations.

'So, we must all raise a glass to Finn, who is now in charge of running the house as an Airbnb. We're going "live" next week. Which has to be better than being dead. Well done, Sara, for raising such a wonderful son.'

Declan's eyebrows shot up expectantly, waiting for his moment of acknowledgement. He didn't yet know that Marina shared the spotlight very sparingly and that was as much as she could manage for one day. His mouth dropped open with indignation at being excluded from the praise.

Callum tipped his glass to Finn. 'Well done, mate. Proud of you.'

Finn grinned and said, 'Cheers,' and bore little resemblance to the boy who'd been bumbling along aimlessly a few months earlier. My boys were actually more sorted than their mother – a fact that didn't escape Finn's notice.

I wished he hadn't chosen that moment to say, 'So, that's me settled for the foreseeable. What's next for you, Mum?'

I'd mooted the idea to Callum that I might stay out in

Florence for a few months. His reaction had been typically self-interested – 'Oh great. Can me and the boys come out for a holiday?' – but I hadn't yet had the opportunity to enlighten Finn about my plans. It was a conversation I'd hoped to have discreetly and certainly not with my ex-husband listening in.

'If you don't need me to help you here... I might spend a bit of time in Florence,' I mumbled. Carlo shuffled in his seat until our thighs were touching under the table. Despite my awkwardness, I registered that there was someone in my corner, who had my best interests at heart.

Finn knitted his eyebrows together. 'No, I don't need help. I'm okay, thanks,' he said, nonplussed. 'Marina and I have got it all planned out. And one of the first guests is Ronnie's daughter, Nadia, with her baby and husband, so that should be pretty straightforward.'

Marina muttered, 'If you can keep Nadia happy, everyone else will be a doddle.'

Ronnie swiped at her and then said, 'Rude, but probably fair.'

'So, you're confident you know what you're doing?' I asked Finn.

'Mum, I'm fine,' he said, sounding impatient. 'I'll figure it out.'

Marina glanced at Finn. 'And the handyman's granddaughter, Mirabella, is going to help you with the beds and laundry, isn't she, Finn?' she said, with a lot of emphasis on 'help' and 'beds'.

Finn blushed.

I smiled. No, there was a boy who definitely didn't need his mother hanging around. I expected to feel a stab of sadness at my definitive redundancy, but instead I felt a settling, a sense that it was no longer up to me to create, fix and protect. Of course, I would always be a safety net, but I had adventures of my own ahead that I was going to hurtle towards. I'd finally managed to convince myself that it was exciting to be unburdened by all the things that had given structure to my life to date – belongings, houses and jobs. At some point, I'd have to work again, but for the moment I would live uninhibited by 'should' and 'ought to'.

I reached for Carlo's hand. 'So. Looks like I'm going on an escapade to Florence.'

He kissed my cheek. 'Lainey would be thrilled.' There was a pause while everything that we didn't say, everything we didn't yet dare to say, surged through our palms, burning through our fingertips. 'I am, too,' he said, his face a mixture of hope, excitement and if I was reading him correctly, a touch of vulnerability.

I might do Lainey proud after all.

A LETTER FROM KERRY

Dear Reader,

I want to say a huge thank you for choosing to read *Escape to the Rome Apartment*. If you did enjoy it, and want to keep up to date with all my latest releases, just sign up at the following link. Your email address will never be shared and you can unsubscribe at any time.

www.bookouture.com/kerry-fisher

If you've read the first two books in the *Italian Escape* series, then you might already be aware that I lived in Florence and Tuscany for five years in my twenties. In this book, I wanted to share some of the treasures of Florence, as well as my love for Rome. It's been so gratifying to see readers enjoying my descriptions of Italy and I'm thrilled that some people have booked holidays there so they can walk in my characters' footsteps.

Alongside the location, which is very prominent in this series, there are always many other influences that inform my writing. In this book, I was drawn to exploring that tricky transitional period when young adults have their own lives but haven't quite flown the nest. Despite them being totally independent in some ways, the maternal urge to protect and smooth their passage in life still remains so strong. It's very hard to stand by and watch children make decisions that – with the benefit of more experience – a parent can foresee are likely to make their lives much more difficult. It's such a fine line between advising, and entrenching everyone in opposing camps as Sara's dad managed to do. The years have taught me that my mum and dad were right about many things and I've been lucky that they've lived long enough for me to realise that while they are still here! From my observations, it appears to be much harder than parents anticipate to accept that adult children must make their own mistakes, in spite of simultaneously acknowledging that there is much useful learning to be gained from failure!

On the other side of the coin, I wanted to examine Sara's sense that the hard years of child-rearing should – at some point – come to an end and that it's not unreasonable to want to reclaim some space for yourself.

During the writing of this book, I became taken with the Swedish idea of death cleaning – reducing the amount of items you own well before you die to make life easier for the people who have to sort out your affairs later on. There's a constant battle in my house between hoarding and banishing 'stuff'. I like everything to have a use and a place. There's a real appeal in not having to make decisions about every last item in the house and I envied Sara for her ability to leave the majority of her things behind and travel lightly into the future, embracing the uncertainty of not having a fixed place to live.

Lastly, despite being highly unromantic myself, I'm finding that in the books I read, I am always rooting for characters to find love. So having initially set out to allow Sara a bohemian and transitory fling, I couldn't resist making it something more. I hope it works out for her!

If you enjoyed *Escape to the Rome Apartment*, I would be very grateful if you could write a review. I'd love to know what you think, and it makes a real difference in helping new readers to discover one of my books for the first time.

I love hearing from my readers – you can get in touch with

me on social media or through my website. Whenever I hear from readers, I am reminded why I love my job – your messages never fail to brighten my day.

Thank you so much for reading,

Kerry Fisher

www.kerryfisherauthor.com

 facebook.com/kerryfisherauthor
x.com/KerryFSwayne

ACKNOWLEDGEMENTS

'Thank you' seems a rather underwhelming expression for the gratitude I feel for the support of my editor, Jenny Geras. Her vision always plays a significant role in transforming my scrappy, half-baked ideas into fully-formed stories – a feat she pulls off with grace and patience.

Huge thanks to the Bookouture production team working their magic to make the finished product the best it can possibly be, plus the wonderful publicity team – Kim, Noelle, Sarah and Jess – who do a great job of connecting our books with the right readership.

Thank you to the brilliant Clare Wallace, my agent at Darley Anderson – I've been so lucky to have you championing my books over the last ten years.

I couldn't finish my acknowledgements without saying a massive thank you to all my readers – you are the best cheer-leaders – I love the conversations and interactions I have with you on my author Facebook page. Your enthusiasm for my books really gives me a lift when the going gets tough. Thanks to everyone who helped with my plant pictures in the cloisters of the hospital in Trastevere – you were far more accurate than Google in identifying a lantana and a plumbago. Also to the many people who added their view to my questions about which outside influences can kill off a relationship... some of the answers felt like very hard-won knowledge and it was generous of you to share.

Finally, to my husband, Steve, for patiently reading his Kindle in myriad Italian cafés while I race around double-checking all the details of places I've written about. In the words of the great romantic that I am, 'You've turned out all right.'

PUBLISHING TEAM

Turning a manuscript into a book requires the efforts of many people. The publishing team at Bookouture would like to acknowledge everyone who contributed to this publication.

Commercial
Lauren Morrissette
Jil Thielen
Imogen Allport

Contracts
Peta Nightingale

Cover design
Jo Thomson

Data and analysis
Mark Alder
Mohamed Bussuri

Editorial
Jenny Geras
Lizzie Brien

Copyeditor
Jade Craddock